LEGEND OF THE LEOPARD
An Ellora's Cave Publication, May 2004

Ellora's Cave Publishing, Inc.
PO Box 787
Hudson, OH 44236-0787

ISBN #1843609436

ISBN MS Reader (LIT) ISBN # 1-84360-845-6
Other available formats (no ISBNs are assigned):
Adobe (PDF), Rocketbook (RB), Mobipocket (PRC) & HTML

Edited by *Briana St. James*
Cover art by *Syneca*.

LEGEND OF THE LEOPARD

Melani Blazer

Dedication

For the real 'Julia': you're more than a hero. There's no way to thank you enough.

And to Briana, my editor, because not only does she make dreams come true, she turns them into miracles.

Special thanks to my husband, for without him my belief in true love would not motivate me enough to write about it.

Chapter 1

The silence was a dreadful thing. Of course, the sputtering of the engine had taken any fight out of her. The first half of the flight, the small commuter plane had rocked ever so slightly and the hum of the motors nearly lulled her to sleep. Then it lurched, and the engine coughed — as if it was choking on the hot African air. When it died, and there was nothing but silence, she'd all but accepted her fate, slipped her hand into her sister's and whispered she loved her.

They were going to die.

Outside the window, the night was a pure black hole, like a mouth, ready to swallow them up. And it would, she was certain. The waiting was the hard part.

Her sister prayed ceaselessly. She knew her brother-in-law, seated behind her, was doing the same. Their calm whispers in the otherwise silent night comforted her. She didn't want to look over and see her sister gripping the arm of her seat with white fingers. It was enough to see the lines of worry on all the other passengers' faces in the pale emergency lighting system. This was it. She offered up her own plea for mercy as the belly of the plane made its first contact with the wild African turf.

* * * * *

Four passengers, including herself, huddled around a fire. In the light cast off by the barely wavering flames, foreign pieces of metal and debris seemed like a separator wall. And none of them knew what lay beyond.

Julia Haverstock crouched, warming her fingers, staring beyond the flames. The tears in her eyes blurred everything. The pain in her left arm dulled her senses. Her sister and brother-in-law were gone. No one could find the pilot. The other three were passengers, like her. She didn't know them, they didn't know her. They could barely communicate.

No one knew if a beacon had gone out. No one knew what to look for in the shattered remains of the cockpit to send one. Where were they? Africa was all she knew. They'd been scheduled to land at a missionary camp in Ethiopia. The airport in Cairo was far behind them.

They were supposed to have been at their destination hours ago. Safe and sound before any hint of dusk. But customs issues had delayed things. She didn't even know the details, just that they spent nearly five hours in the hot terminal waiting for a thumbs up.

And now this. She shivered and moved closer to the fire. She'd never officially agreed to come along. Her sister, Chelly, had bought the ticket and promised her she could leave in two weeks if she didn't like it. Julia, a basic science professor at a small community college in Albany, New York, had balked every step of the way.

She didn't like to fly. Never had. Her preference ran to curling up with a book or on the sofa to watch Discovery channel, not to exploring a wild country in person. Which is why, she had told Chelly, she *taught* science, not practiced it.

Didn't matter. Her sister was dead. Science would do nothing to get that plane back up in the air and them onto their destination.

Chelly was dead. Julia's chin dropped to her chest and she let the sobs take over. She was numb with shock, but it didn't stop the intense grip of pain in her chest. Why did it have to be Chelly, the gentle woman who gave and asked nothing in return? She rocked on her heels and let her emotions take over.

What if it had been her? What would Chelly have done? Wiping her eyes, she took a deep breath and stared into the flames. Her sister would comfort the others, take inventory of supplies and try to prepare some kind of shelter for them. She'd become a den mother, despite her grief.

Which had made Chelly a hell of a lot stronger woman than Julia was.

She turned away from the fire. It took a moment for her eyes to adjust. Best thing she could do was find something to lie down on and get through the night. Things would be better in the daylight—the sun would chase the hopelessness away. Search parties could find them. Tomorrow she could deal with her loss and bury her sister.

A deep-throated growl broke the stillness. One of the men

screamed. She whirled and let out her own scream. They were surely dead now. Cats, big spotted cats, circled the edge of the firelight. Bile rose in her throat as she saw two of them fight over the fallen man.

Julia ran. Blindly tripping over pieces of debris and uneven savannah she ran. Any one of these steps could be her last. Her lungs screamed, her body throbbed, but she pushed onward, amazed she hadn't been knocked down and mauled. It was inevitable; she was going to die—the knowledge thundered in her veins as she waited for that giant leap.

But it never came.

Her feet hit water. She stopped. Over her own ragged breathing and pounding heart, she struggled to hear. Were they behind her, crouched low to the ground and ready to pounce? Or were there other dangers? She knew very little about the workings of Africa's habitat. What were the dangers this water offered? She'd heard that hippos were deadly, but what of lions, hyenas, snakes, crocs, and others?

The darkness never ended. Behind her she saw no sign of the fire, ahead of her—nothing. Other than to keep the water to her right, she had no way of knowing what direction she was going.

Terrified wasn't the word. She walked, keeping the water just to her side. She trekked south. At least it felt like south. Her mind rolled over and over: visions of herself and her sister throughout as many of her twenty-six years that she could remember. Then thoughts turned to the god-awful memory of the leopard's white fangs ripping through her travel-mate's prone body, the stench of airplane fuel, burnt oil and blood still stung her nostrils.

She stumbled. The ground rose up to meet her hands. A knife-like pain sliced through her left arm, all the way to her head. She cringed against the white-hot streaks that blinded her. But they faded.

* * * * *

What radio station did she have on? And why did she hurt so bad? Damn, what had happened to her arm? She couldn't even move it.

A hand touched her. She screamed.

The light, a primitive looking torch, blinded her momentarily. She

9

stared up into a nightmare. Four men, only whites of the eyes visible on pitch-colored faces, looked down on her. They rattled off something in a tongue she didn't understand, pointed to her arm, then babbled some more.

Her head throbbed, but not as bad as her arm. Lord, look at it. In the faint orange light she could see the discoloration, the huge swelling. Broken. Her fingers barely moved, despite her attempt to make a fist. Very broken.

Through the pain, she remembered the flight, the crash, her escape. She watched the men, were they hallucinations? She'd expected men in normal — western — clothes, but these seemed...tribal. Where *had* they landed?

One word caught her ears as the man holding the torch proclaimed something and pointed to the bank of the stream. She struggled to sit and see what they were doing.

Snow? She knew that's what he'd said. Probably meant something completely different in whatever his language was.

But then she saw what he pointed to. With the torch right above it, it was unmistakable. A footprint, hers, clearly, from the running shoe pattern and small size. But beside it, half again as big and twice as wide was another print. Feline. *Leopard?*

The light faded again. She slept.

When she opened her eyes again, a wrinkled brown woman stood above her, cooing. Her arm had been stabilized and wrapped in something that smelled like rotten garbage. But it didn't hurt. And she was beyond being scared. She didn't trust herself to think. This might be a dream. What had really happened to her? Bolts of pain streaked behind her eyes at the effort it took to remember.

"Where am I?" she asked the woman. Her voice broke. Everything hurt, including her throat.

Her answer was unintelligible. Didn't anyone, *anyone*, speak English here?

Julia sighed. She needed to get home. Have her arm looked at by a real doctor, arrange for her sister's burial. And her brother-in-law's. His family would need to be notified as well. It was too much to fathom doing right now. Tears came then, first an unchecked pair, then a flood. Hopelessness.

If anyone did track the plane, they'd assume she, too, had fallen prey to the giant cats. She'd be left behind.

The old woman pressed a canteen-like sack up to her lips. She drank. Bitter, vile, but wet. She prayed it would stop the frantic thoughts and leave her in peace, just for a little longer.

The sun hung high in the sky when she forced her bruised body from the mat on the floor of this tiny, cluttered hut. Her dream had been vivid — she'd been frozen, prone, able only to watch as a giant white cat leapt at her, its mouth open, its teeth blood-stained.

A white leopard? She could faintly recall water and strange men and even stranger paw prints. Something about snow.

The village — a series of huts that wasn't far from the primitive, nomadic lifestyle she'd envisioned — could fit inside the college campus where she taught. The stream branched into a small trickle of muddy looking water, which bisected the thatched houses and snaked further south.

She could feel, more than remember, that north was the direction she'd find the wreckage.

Her arm throbbed with every step. Muscles protested the fast pace. Behind her, she heard shouts, but didn't turn back. She couldn't stay there, desolate and alone, where no one could understand her. That was almost a fate worse than death.

This part of Africa was different than what she expected. Somehow she'd had a stereotypical vision of endless deserts or lush jungles. But of course there was a middle ground, an area that saw both extremes. It was a good month or two before rainy season. Her sister had explained that away from the Nile and the main tributaries, everything would be dead and brown by now. But the grasses of the savannah here were tall and thick, and the sparse trees still green. Behind that line of trees, a snow-white leopard followed her.

Her heart pounded, as did her temples. She reached up with her good hand to pinch between her eyes. She couldn't pass out now. But the pain and panic seemed to be taking over. She continued, afraid to stop.

As she ran, he followed. He slowed and even waited when she paused to splash cool water on her face. She had to stop, despite her instinct to run as fast as she could back to the village. She couldn't go much farther. The horizon dipped, her stomach revolted from the pureness of the pain that tore through her heart and body.

The sun was hot, almost blinding. Unforgiving. But she dared not leave the edge of the river for the comfort of the trees. She turned to look at the cat, wondering why he hadn't pounced. Toying with her? Waiting for her to tire? Leading her to cubs or a mate? What the hell was he waiting for? She was so tired, hurt so badly that she didn't care. Death might give her the peace she craved. Finally.

Or so she thought.

The leopard's lips curled back, exposing glistening white teeth that gleamed like the moon. He growled.

Julia ran then, fast as she could, letting adrenaline mute her body's complaints. She ran for life, for death, praying all the while she could find someplace to hide, somewhere that his fangs couldn't reach.

Once she looked behind her. He was coming, hard and fast, eating up the yards between them. There would be no making it to the distant pile of what she knew had to be their plane. Black spots obscured her vision. It was so hard to breathe. She'd be lucky to make three more steps.

He struck. Her body shook with the impact as he pinned her to the ground. She could swear her ribs gave under the immense weight. His teeth sunk into her left shoulder. She waited for death.

Then he growled, his white muzzle and gaping jaws stained with blood. Her blood.

She fainted.

* * * * *

Julia woke up in a village. Not one that belonged in National Geographic as the first she'd been in. This one was more modern, almost like a rural city. She heard the whistle of a train. Streets were hard-packed, buildings were permanent. Pack animals walked past her, barely missing her outstretched legs.

How'd she get here? How had she come to be propped in a sitting position against a dusty building with her feet nearly in the street?

"English?" she asked of everyone who walked near her. She got to her feet, no small task considering her strength reserves had been used up long ago. All she received were puzzled looks and shakes of head.

But she wouldn't give up. She was hurt, afraid and alone.

Desperation was required for survival. Hearing many voices behind her, she pushed open the door to a train house. "English?" she continued to ask, to no avail.

"English?" she heard, finally. A young man, one who looked as out of place as she imagined she must, walked up to the doorway. She'd guess he was Mediterranean. Greek or something. But to hear the word, even just repeated, was like food to the dying.

She followed his crooked finger out of the train house. She'd hold on to any thread of hope she could find.

"Tio talk English," he finally said as he grabbed her hand briefly to pull her toward his car.

The touch alerted something inside her. Why could she feel? Why was she still alive? Hadn't she been attacked, and bitten by a wild leopard? What grace of God had led her to be alive and feeling?

Not one to question luck, however, she stumbled to keep up with the fast moving boy. He waited, despite the fact that he got to his dusty old Land Rover well before her. Still, she hesitated. He couldn't be more than sixteen years old. How could he help? He wasn't a native, he was an outsider, like her. But he was her only link to the civilization she knew. And if she'd guessed right, he had an uncle who could help her even more.

Her chances weren't good if she stayed. So she got in the SUV.

As they drove away, Julia mourned. She had no clue where she was, or where the plane crash was, but she felt as if she were leaving them behind. What if someone came to investigate?

She couldn't leave. Not permanently, without erecting some memorial to her sister. Even if it meant facing that white leopard again, she'd return. As soon as she could, she'd go back. Then she'd go home.

She straightened her shoulders, wincing against the pain that ebbed back up her arm and spider-webbed from her shoulder. Almost as if a painkiller was wearing off. Bizarre. It didn't stop her resolve, however. She had survived, against odds she didn't care to figure. She wasn't going to give in now. Chelly would be proud of her.

She choked a sob back.

The boy stared at her.

"What?" she asked.

He shook his head, color staining his cheeks and returned his focus to the barely visible path through the dusty grassland. Here the foliage was more sparse, the sand more prominent. But then they turned a corner around an uprising of rock. She gasped.

The house was enormous. Completely out of place. It belonged on a mountainside in Greece or Italy and not in the plains of Africa. They drove through automatic gates—high, wrought iron gates with giant panthers, like gargoyles, guarding them atop brick posts. More questions. She had thousands of questions to ask whoever this boy's uncle was. Obviously someone rich. Maybe one of those game hunters who lead tours. He probably owned the town and the railroad. Hopefully he'd have mercy on her and help her arrange for a trip home.

The boy tugged her by her good arm through the house. She felt as if she'd stepped into a time warp. They passed a couple of other people in the yard and in the house, but she guessed they were natives, not European like this boy. Chances were, they didn't speak English either.

She was dying to hear someone say something in her language.

"Salvatore!" the boy called, letting her arm free and breaking into a run when he saw a man in a white coat.

The one called Salvatore straightened from his microscope. "Paolo." He clapped the boy on the shoulder and started questioning him in what Julia could only assume was Italian or Greek. One look at Salvatore and she knew he wasn't African any more than his nephew.

Damn. Heat seeped immediately through her bones and liquefied her joints. Men weren't allowed to look so good. So serious and mischievous all at once. She already hated the way he smiled when he looked up at her. Like she was some bounty or something. And they were discussing her! She gritted her teeth. It was only obvious they would. But that didn't make her feel any less helpless standing there, waiting on someone to decide her fate.

Paolo's excited voice quickly settled with his uncle's soothing. Salvatore certainly was a charmer, despite his white lab coat and wire-rim glasses. They did nothing to hide his appeal. Snake charmer. She was mesmerized already, with just one look.

No, this one wasn't nerdy or boring or...anything she'd imagined when picturing this "Tio". This one was sexy and pure male. And he was looking at her in a way that had her wondering why she couldn't have met him under different circumstances. She closed her eyes tightly but couldn't so easily erase the image of his tanned face and sparkling black eyes. She shouldn't notice that. Thoughts of him as anything but a way home shouldn't enter her mind. Her way home.

She nearly took a step back as he dismissed Paolo and walked toward her. Such strong, purposeful strides. Intimidating. "I'm Sal," he offered a hand. "You are?"

"Julia. Julia Haverstock. I'm American."

"My nephew says you have problems. You were in the plane crash?"

His voice was purely musical. How could she concentrate on the words with that melodic tone reverberating through her body? She swore her skin hummed where his thumb grazed her wrist.

Stop. Plane crash. Pain. Any minute now her brain would explode. Why was she reacting to him like that? This was about a ride home, about people who died out there on the savannah, not about the awakening of her libido. "I need to go out there, to the site. To see if anyone —"

"No one else survived." His voice was short, clipped. No music at all.

"They didn't?" A fist hit her full force in the chest. How? When? How did he know? She could only guess. "The panthers, cheetahs, whatever they were?"

"Leopards. *Panthera Pardus*. There is a large group that live very near the crash site."

"Oh," she answered. Her arm tingled. "The white one attacked me."

"Tio!" the boy cried from the doorway. Salvatore cut him off with a quick look that included a narrowed eye frown. The boy left and closed the door behind him.

"There are so many stories of the white cat. You wouldn't have heard them. Some call him a ghost. Others insist he lives, wild among them. I'm most interested in your story. Tell me, what happened when he attacked and why aren't you dead?"

She started with the night of the crash. "I didn't see a white leopard that night. But I saw two cats fighting over the body of a man who shared the plane with us." Saying it out loud was almost like reliving it again. The dancing silhouettes and spraying blood. The growls and roars of hungry animals.

"I ran." Julia shook her head and babbled on, "I remember stepping into the stream, then following it for a while. It was so dark, I couldn't see anything. I must have fallen, or fainted. When I woke up, locals were standing over me with a torch. They said 'snow'. I saw where they were pointing. A cat's paw print right next to my own footprints."

The corner of Sal's mouth drew up. She looked away. So much for noticing how attractive he was. He was patronizing her. Laughing at her story. Probably thinking she made it up. But God, what if she had, how *did* she know what was dream and what was real? Hadn't she lost time, space? How had she gotten from place to place with no memory of it?

"This is all?" Sal spread his hands wide. "You say you were attacked."

"I was." She drew in a breath and tried to remember. "I woke up in a village where some old woman took care of me. I know I slept and when I woke up it was day again. That's when I tried to make it back to the plane."

"And?"

She didn't even want to finish. Felt like she was talking to air. "It followed me."

"What did?"

"The white leopard. I saw it through the grasses. It followed me almost there, and then attacked. It bit me on the shoulder. I remember seeing its teeth over me, all bloody. I must have fainted." Or died. Boy, she did sound crazy. Maybe she couldn't blame this guy for being amused. He was a scientist after all, at least his equipment indicated so. He needed facts, not unexplainable things like she was telling him.

"How did you come to be in Juba'i?"

He had spread his hands, so she could only imagine he spoke the name of the town or area they were in now. This was the part she hated to admit. "I don't know."

He nodded. His eyes gave him away. She could see clearly that he didn't believe her. It was almost mocking. "Show me," Sal said. "Show me your wounds and then I will believe."

Julia looked down at her shirt. The sleeve was torn and blood stained. She pushed it aside. Her shoulder felt fine. There were no palpable holes where the leopard's teeth had sunk in. They had, she was sure of it. What in the world was going on? She remembered the breath of the beast, the yellow eyes, the blood-stained muzzle. She had felt the teeth break the skin, the searing hot pain. How could she have dreamed that? Yet, by the look of her shoulder, she had. She glanced up at Sal, saw his grin, and closed her eyes. "I have none."

"I see."

Things stalled. Well, conversation stalled. Julia couldn't help staring at the tall man before her. Never had she imagined she'd come face to face with someone that would leave her trembling. And it wasn't just his looks—she'd seen plenty of beautiful men. Rugged men. Handsome men. This one? He was simply a sexy man.

"What do you want from me?" he asked, chuckling. "You stare like you have a dozen questions, yet you don't ask. You look as if you haven't seen a man before."

She felt the blush burn her cheeks. Not one like him, she hadn't. "I'm so confused. I need some answers." She took a deep breath. "And ultimately the means to arrange a trip home." It took everything she had not to throw herself in his arms and make him promise not to send her back to that dusty town where no one could understand her. He *had* to help her. Had to.

"First the questions. Would you like some lunch? I intended to take a break soon anyway. Sokhra should have something prepared. She or one of the servants can set an extra place without problem."

Servants, formal talk, an in-house laboratory. Was *this* the dream? Was she floating between life and death after being mauled by the leopard? The hunger, however, seemed real enough.

"Yes, a meal would be wonderful."

"*Un momento,*" Sal said. He turned and walked quickly through the door at the back of his laboratory. He knew Paolo'd be there, in the kitchen with his ear to the door, straining to hear more and struggling to decipher it.

The boy was curious, way too curious. Paolo knew the lab was off limits. Yet he'd caught him in there several times just this week.

He'd already arranged for his nephew to go back to Sicily when he returned to Florence to report his lab findings to the university. It was pretty clear he'd have yet another traveling companion.

Julia. He'd berated himself even now for saving her the night of the wreck. But there was little he could do when she tried to return.

And now he was bound to her. And his body was already realizing that it wasn't such a bad idea. Her blue eyes were clouded with distrust, and those full, pouty lips tight with fear. Despite that, she was beautiful. The long muscles of her body were taut and strong. She was fit. And she'd fit him perfectly.

He was hoping to leave by the end of the week. But he couldn't have her talking about the white leopard and the wound that healed itself. Even if he did convince her she had dreamt it, she'd talk. He had to prevent her from sharing this story, crazy as it sounded. What if he convinced her to stay?

Sal reached up, removed his glasses and slid a hand down his face. He'd been warned, he'd have to say that. And to a point, he'd heeded that warning. Never had he brought a woman into his home for companionship. He'd hired local women to work for him, and very rarely invited a fellow researcher to substantiate some of his work.

Pleasure was saved for his jaunts home. For women he knew. Safe, sex-only women.

He'd already exposed Julia, and in turn, been infected with her. She was in his blood, his soul. It'd never be just sex with her.

But...he smiled wryly and slid his glasses back on. That might be the glue he needed.

Chapter 2

Sal would need to work fast if he was going to make it happen. He pushed into his private office and latched the door behind him. First things first. He punched up his email program. Then cursed. Better to do this live. But the details wouldn't be safe over that open line.

Fingers flew over the keys, then he lifted the receiver.

He spoke in his native Italian. "Add a ticket to flight itinerary. Open date, same as mine." He paced, not wanting to say too much now. Partly because he didn't trust the phone line integrity. The price he paid for such a remote location.

"No," he sighed in response. Time to change the subject before too much was said. "Paolo's doing well, though I know he's bored. What I'm working on in the lab right now is rather important, and I don't have the time I'd like to teach him the ropes."

All he wanted to do was hang up and return to his lab. Where he'd left a virtual stranger. Heaven help him if she could read Italian. His notes, including information about *her* lay open on his desk.

"Listen, Antonio, read your damn email, okay? The details you'll need are in there… Got it? Now don't say a word over this line."

His brother could be a pain in the ass. Always asking questions. But he'd invited his own trouble this time, and her name was Julia Haverstock.

A nagging voice in the back of his head reminded him that he could have killed her, easily. Then these complications wouldn't have surfaced.

"Ah, hell," he swore after hanging up. He didn't kill for sport. And there was no way he could have considered it anything else but. So she lived, burden or not.

He rubbed his eyes and pushed his hair back off his forehead. This would be a science experiment unlike any other. And it would start as soon as he could get back out there.

"My apologies," he said, sweeping up Julia's hand and planting a kiss on the back of it. "I've already been able to set the wheels in motion for your return. Shall we discuss that over dinner?"

He poured it on, the charm, the smile, everything he needed to gain her trust and her attention. It was important she relax around him.

There was nothing to fake, however. When he slipped a hand to the small of her back to lead her toward the deck, she shivered. But she didn't step out of it. The warmth of her skin seeped through the thin cotton and ignited his blood.

Pain lanced through his head. Crippling pain. He slowed, hoping it was just a flash.

It wasn't. Air rushed by his super sensitive ears. He heard her breathing. And he could smell her, the womanly musk that stuck to her skin and clothes. Fear mingled with her scent, too.

He closed his eyes. She couldn't see this. Not now. Maybe never. "*Perdonarme.*" He released his clenched fist from the back of her shirt and opened the door to the kitchen. Lightning bolts volleyed off the inside of his skull. Fighting it made it worse, but he needed only a moment. Long enough to find Sokhra, his most trusted employee. "I must go," he gasped. "Take the food indoors. Do not let her outside."

He dropped to the floor at her feet. The agony of it tore through his skin and through his lungs. He yelled as the pain worsened, then stopped.

He raced out of the house.

Julia now knew something very strange and *very* scary was going on. Sal had been rendered almost helpless by whatever it was that had seized him from the inside. What medical condition could it be? Her mind had raced as she had watched him limp toward that door. Drug withdrawals? Overdose? What drove a man to the middle of nowhere to study? Labs were plentiful, and usually private enough, anywhere in the world. The more she saw the more questions she had.

A woman appeared. A native. Who was she? After the way he'd touched her, flirted with her, she couldn't believe it'd be his wife. Julia immediately looked for a ring, and found none. Plus this woman almost looked old enough to be considered maternal. She walked barefoot and silent. She didn't speak either, but simply gestured for Julia to follow her.

But what of Sal? Did this woman know he was hurting? Sick? What if… "But—"

"Salvatore… he—" the woman waved her hand as if shooing off a rodent.

"He's gone? He left?" Julia quizzed. Left? In the state he was in? She wasn't sure he could make it to the front door. His face had been white, as if the blood had drained from it. His hands curled, white knuckled. Seeing a man so ripped apart by pain bothered her. "But he looked…sick. Shouldn't you check on him?"

Julia doubted the woman understood her. She turned to walk into the lab.

Hands grabbed her arms and pulled her back. It was Paolo. "Tio say…" he struggled for a word, gave up, and patted his chest.

Fantastic. Understanding even a moment of this was impossible. She could never have imagined this in her wildest dreams. No thought or discussion of her trip to Africa—to a missionary camp in Ethiopia— had ever come close to matching this adventure.

Adventure? Her heart took a U-turn into a downward spiral. Nightmare was more like it. It seemed like years since she was on that plane with her sister, discussing the tribal customs and what they would see.

Her choices were gone. But at least she had a meal waiting. Julia nodded to Paolo and followed him, albeit reluctantly, through the kitchen and into the elaborate dining room.

The house, she realized as she glanced around the huge rooms, was truly a mansion. And from the modern furnishings, it would be easy to forget her position on the globe—nothing here was African except the few people she saw, other than Paolo. He fit in.

He pointed at a chair. She sat down at the elegantly set table and waited while he said something to the young girl waiting at the doorway.

Salvatore and Paolo—she didn't even know their last name— seemed to have a regal air about them. Obviously they had money. Amenities like this weren't cheap to create and maintain, anywhere. But there was something else. She watched as Paolo sat at the head of the table and unfolded his cloth napkin.

Practiced table manners.

The soup bowl was fine china. The silverware real silver, not the stainless steel she'd seen in every household and restaurant she'd ever been in back in the States. The water goblet was probably real crystal, too. But in all honesty, she didn't care. It was a quick observance. The food and water and...wine? She lifted her glass and sipped. The fruity flavor burst on her tongue. Very good wine.

She didn't care about what the meal was served on. Those answers would come later. As would all the others. She'd see to it—later. She was hungry.

✳ ✳ ✳ ✳ ✳

Sal paced the edge of the grounds. A low growl vibrated in his throat. Hunger tore at his stomach. But nothing out here appealed to him. Eating would prolong his absence.

He couldn't run it off. It was too risky. There had been too many recent accounts in town about the white leopard. He followed the high walls that had been built on his property line. Walls to keep out as well as keep in. He had too many secrets. And on a day like today...he lifted his head to look skyward. Things were much more dangerous in broad daylight.

Hindsight was wonderful. Clearly he should have made more temporary antidote earlier, when he'd sent Paolo to town. But he was close, so close to figuring it all out. Then he wouldn't need anything temporary. One last mystery to figure out. Then he could reclaim his life. Or at least control it.

Until then, he'd feel like Dr. Jekyll and Mr. Hyde. A reject, a freak. The spells were hitting him harder and more often. And with no warning. Like today. Normally he could predict it—feel it coming on. The change then would take time. Of course, he always feared Paolo would come in during his body's metamorphosis. He'd learned once—locking the door was disastrous. He couldn't get back out.

Long, loping strides carried him to the other end of the property. A refuge, secluded by man-made walls and thick foliage. There he relaxed, slightly.

His stomach still turned in terror with the memory of that day Sokhra had walked in during a transformation. He remembered the mortal fear in the woman's eyes. And he'd been helpless to move, speak, comfort her. She'd been hysterical. Rightly so. It continued to frighten him.

It'd taken weeks of explaining. She'd remained locked in the house, his prisoner, until she had understood. If word got out, even here in this remote African town, he'd be killed. And he did not wish to be hunted down and shot. Or dissected by some curious scientist.

Finally, perhaps when she saw him chase off the alpha male leopard, she had come around. The cat had gotten in through an open gate and began actively stalking one of his yardmen. He could have killed it then, but such carnage was unnecessary. The animals were protected, even endangered by some people's estimate. And his real work involved protecting and studying them.

But Sokhra had changed. A trust had formed then. In return for her loyalty she and her family would never want for anything as long as he lived.

The thick green foliage along this small tributary would protect him now from the sun. And the prying eyes of anyone or anything that lurked within these few gated acres. Always a price. There was a freedom to this state. It was a powerful knowledge of his own abilities and what happened around him. Even now, if he listened carefully he could hear the slide of a snake's underbelly along the leaves. As a fish rose to the surface, he heard tiny ripples in the otherwise still waters. He could smell, from somewhere within the walls, death. Most likely a bird or rodent having fallen prey.

He did not get up to investigate. Nature had its own harmony. Best not to disturb that.

There were times he wanted to share the awe of it, of being one with nature, with someone. His human mind never ceased to find something new.

He could almost imagine Julia's face, her eyes lit up with wonder as he explained the things no man could detect.

A growl escaped him. Julia. He hadn't chosen her. He'd found her. It wasn't her choice to be here. And after the confusion today, it would be harder than ever to make her want to stay.

He rose, stretched, and lapped water from the still surface of the stream. No, Julia would not be ready to accept much about his life for a while. Especially this part.

He returned, finally himself again, after the golden twilight had faded to darkness. It exhausted him, the changing. He stopped in the lab, as was his custom, and withdrew a vial of blood. He'd study that later, looking for changes from the last time. One more needle, this one a shot of concentrated vitamins. A super shot of energy and rebuilding power. He prepped it as Sokhra walked in.

"Salvatore, she is very unsettled. I gave her a sedative, but now, she has restless dreams. You must come." Sokhra took the needle from him and thrust it into the muscle of his buttock.

"I should be twenty years younger to appreciate this sight." She backhanded him just above the waist. The gesture wasn't sexual, and the words were something she'd said before. Usually it was followed by a remark about him finding a mate before he ended up like her.

He didn't answer, despite the fact he normally would. And he knew why. Julia was in the bedroom directly above them. He lifted his eyes to the ceiling. In his peripheral vision, he saw Sokhra smile.

He spoke Sokhra's language nearly as fluidly as his own. "Let's go see her then."

For hours all he'd thought about was Julia. What to do with her, what to tell her. Maybe he'd listened to Sokhra's hints too often. He could have sent money with the boy and had him arrange a train ticket for Julia to Malakal or even on to Khartoum. He shouldn't have worried about the red tape hell the government would put her through.

Then he opened the door and forgot all those reasons.

He'd kept her alive. He'd brought her here. He could claim it was purely physical. Right now it was easier to.

She'd showered, her face all dewy and clean, strands of her hair spread out on the pillow, still damp and dark. He stepped in, afraid to wake her, yet eager to do just that. He turned away only for a moment when Sokhra pulled the door closed and left him alone with her.

"Julia," he whispered, using the Italian pronunciation. He took in her fresh, puckered lips, smooth ivory skin. She was an angel, his own personal angel.

"Julia," he whispered again, reaching out to push a strand of hair off her forehead.

She moved, shifting the blankets. Her bare shoulder rose above the navy sheets. His mouth went dry. He'd tasted this woman, but now he longed to devour her. Inch by inch, feasting upon her skin.

He couldn't explain the attraction. He'd seen gorgeous debutantes, film stars and runway models. He'd bedded a number of them. But they were quick fucks. A release of pent-up male pressure. He'd never felt this way about them before, and certainly never thought like this after.

The woman asleep in his house couldn't hold a candle to any of them.

He couldn't help but touch her, assure himself she was real. The back of his fingers slid softly up her arm, down the deep chasm to her neck, then along her cheek.

She moaned. He tightened. Release had been a long time coming, but usually he'd handle that himself or work it off with some of the willing women in Italy. But this ache was nothing like it had been before. He knew the truth. Only one woman was going to make it go away.

He smiled and let his thumb trace over her slightly parted lips. It would be his pleasure to thrust himself into her hot, willing mouth, to feel her tongue against him.

Shifting, he withdrew his hand and adjusted his raging hard-on. Not now. Not yet.

But perhaps he could sample just a nibble. He might be able to go back to his room and ease the ache temporarily with the taste of her on his lips.

"*Cosí bella*, so beautiful," he muttered. And dear God, she smelled like vanilla. He nipped her shoulder with his lips. So different than before. This time gentle was the key. The taste on his tongue now was precious skin, not the tang of blood. The feelings that drove him now were purely human, not affected by the drive of a bloodthirsty cat. He kissed the places he knew had been punctured. Places he'd also healed.

Julia twisted in her sleep, muttering something. He didn't care. The sheet barely covered her breasts now, her arms spread wide. An angel welcoming him.

He nearly growled, imagining how she'd feel, so soft and pliant beneath his body. The shadow from the overhead light lay where he ached to. He leaned over to envelop her scent, feel her breath. He reached down and pressed a kiss to the hollow between her breasts.

What he wouldn't give to climb the peak and feel her rosy nipple grow taut beneath his tongue.

He throbbed at the thought. The torture would be too much to bear. Besides, he wanted, needed her awake and receiving when he touched her so intimately.

"Sleep well, Julia." Once more he dared to touch her, sneaking a taste of her sleep softened lips.

What had he done? To himself, much less Julia. He stood just outside her closed door, turned on beyond his wildest imagination at just the sight of her sleeping. For all he knew, she was married, betrothed, or maybe she just wouldn't find him attractive.

And this was something new. He'd done this to himself as well. Found himself full of self doubt. When had that ever happened? He'd never lacked for the confidence it took to land a woman in bed. Hell, they fell for him and begged for fucking all the time. He knew he wasn't bad looking, and he kept himself in shape. Even Sokhra noticed that.

He ran a hand over his stubble roughened chin and closed his eyes. *Mio dio*, what a mess he'd made.

Instead of drowning himself in a cold shower, he threw himself into his work in the lab. He needed to make more antidote anyway. The brewing would take awhile. Then he'd take a look at that blood. Hopefully he could keep his thoughts out of his briefs — and Julia's panties — and on the work at hand.

Julia awoke, trying to understand the luxurious sheets and comfortable bed. Where was she? Then she remembered. The house of the scientist named Salvatore. No need to panic and worry. At least, so far, she'd been treated like a queen, even if the king was rather erratic. And speaking of erratic, that dream she'd had about him had her clutching the sheets to her in a delighted memory.

It was hazy, but she remembered just bits of it. Gentle kisses up her arm, her neck. She touched her lips, knowing that in her dream, Sal had touched them.

A shiver raced up her naked spine. Too bad she didn't remember the rest. Maybe tonight. She stood and stretched, cat-like.

Tinges of guilt dampened her cheer. She shouldn't be happy. The rest of the party she'd left Cairo with were undoubtedly dead. She was cut off from the rest of the world. She pulled on her tattered, but cleaned, clothes. Maybe Sal would allow her a quick phone call to her parents, to let them know she was okay. Especially if they'd already learned the fate of the plane. And Chelly. She bit back tears and resolved to stay strong. How was she going to tell her parents that her older sister had died? She had to. It'd be better if *she* told them, not some stranger.

She pushed her hair off her face. That was her priority then, albeit one she'd dreaded more than anything else at this moment. She needed to take care of it immediately — as soon as she found Sal. She got up to do just that.

The hallway was long, but empty. Nothing but a row of closed doors. She'd been so out of it the night before, she hadn't remembered which way that woman had brought her.

The only thing she dared do was follow the maze around the corner. Surely it opened into a living room of sorts. Something.

For all she knew, it was the middle of the night. It had still been bright outside when she'd succumbed. Wouldn't have surprised her to learn that they'd slipped her a sleeping pill. Nor did she find reason to complain. Sleep healed. And she still had a long way to go. Right now she wanted to learn what time it was. What day it was. Where they were, exactly.

It seemed daunting to know that she was somewhere in northeastern Africa. South of Cairo. That encompassed a hell of a lot of space.

Julia realized she was right about the time. Judging from the lack of light out the living room windows, it was well pre-dawn. There was no noise in the house. Tiny nightlights kept her from walking into furniture. She thanked whoever was thoughtful enough for those.

It wasn't like her to sneak around someone else's house in the middle of the night. Any second she expected some kind of alarm to go off and someone to jump out and demand what she was doing.

Silence. And for the first time, since she'd arrived on the continent, it didn't scare her.

The kitchen was huge, but homey. There she didn't feel guilty flipping on the overhead light. They wouldn't begrudge her a glass of water, would they?

She did her best to be quiet as she opened and closed rich wooden cabinet doors, searching for a glass. She had one poised beneath the spout when she heard the footstep.

"Don't drink the tap water."

She whirled, clutching the tumbler to her chest.

Sal walked up and removed it from her hands.

Her skin tingled with awareness as his fingers brushed against her breasts. She gasped.

"You'll want to drink the water in the refrigerator. It has been boiled and filtered."

"Of course," she nodded, trying to calm her blood pressure.

Sal still wore his clothes from the day before. The shirt was no longer crisp. Now he wore it unbuttoned, exposing the top of his chest. Sleeves had been rolled up to show off muscular forearms.

He'd removed his glasses, and while she'd considered his hair a bit askew earlier, it looked as if he'd run his fingers through it many times while thinking. She flexed her own fingers. What would those strands feel like sliding through her hands?

It was the stubble that was her weakness. Something about an unshaven man had her mouth watering. Sal's lower face was shadowed in it, making it more tempting than his hair.

"Julia?" he asked.

She blinked, and then noticed he held out a half full glass of water to her.

"Sorry," she said, rubbing her eyes. Busted. "I'm still pretty tired. Thank you for letting me stay. The shower and fresh bed were so wonderful after..." She let it end there.

"My pleasure," he reached up and touched her cheek.

She swallowed. God, what was she doing? Turning away, she said, "I need to talk to you." She drank deep of the cold water. Hopefully it would extinguish the fire he'd managed to light. "I need to make arrangements to get home."

"Of course. As I mentioned last evening, I've made a phone call. I will be returning to Florence next week. You can accompany me and then proceed from there."

Relief and then panic flooded through her. "Next week?" She paced. "But I need to go now. As soon as possible."

"I'm afraid it's not as easy to make travel arrangements here as it is in the US. Because I'd already arranged the trip, getting an additional ticket is possible. Pricey, but possible."

Pricey. Great. And she had no money. At least none that she could access before going through miles of red tape back in New York. It was overwhelming what she'd have to do. New drivers license, new social security card, new credit cards. She wouldn't need a new passport because she never intended to leave the good ole US of A once she got back. "I'll repay you as soon as I get home."

He waved her off and lifted the empty glass from her hand. "It has been my pleasure to have you as my guest. You've been through a terrible ordeal. How could I not help you?"

"Thank you," she looked up into his dark eyes. They bore into hers with a gentle kindness she didn't expect.

"Do you often roam strange homes at five in the morning?"

She laughed. His English ranged from stilted and formal to sounding quite natural. His accent was heavy, however, and made the most American sounding sentences sound exotic. "Only if the host drugs me and I wake up at that time."

"Touché," he responded. He looked her over. Standing still was nearly impossible. His gaze touched her, heating her up and making her way too aware of him as a man.

She sighed. These kinds of thoughts needed to stop.

Since he seemed eager to talk, she'd get some answers. "What do you do here?" she looked around.

"I'm a research scientist."

"That must pay well." She chuckled.

"Not this well. I was fortunate to be born into a family with its own money."

So she had guessed. But she was getting answers. "What is it that you research?"

"Genetics."

"Really?" This might be interesting after all. She waited for him to ask what she did. She didn't offer.

"I'll show you my lab."

The prospect sure beat sitting in her room, waiting for the sun to come up. She told herself that she was excited to spend time with Salvatore because he could speak English, and she was craving personal contact. The fact that he wasn't hard on the eyes and had an undeniable sex appeal was secondary to that.

Despite teaching science, she really had never felt at home in a laboratory. In fact, there was little she felt she could do with the degree she'd earned, except teach. But she had the utmost respect for those doing research. It was a time consuming, often thankless job.

"What is it you are studying about genetics out here? In Africa I mean. I assume you're from Italy?" He'd mentioned returning to

Florence, so she could put that with the language she'd assumed was Italian. That and his looks — definitely Mediterranean.

"Florence, yes. At least that's the university I'm currently affiliated with. My family is from Sicily. I received a degree from U of C, Berkeley initially. I've worked in other countries, as well — spent a year in Afghanistan with a special team trying to catch up with the snow leopards."

"So why'd you leave?"

He smiled. "Graduated."

Her heart thudded. Damn that grin was sexy. Made her forget all about degrees and microscopes. She licked her lips and watched him watch her. What the hell was it about him? It was getting harder and harder to believe it was just the language, the need for companionship. She was starting to believe that if he spoke nothing but the native tongue, she'd still find him irresistible.

She smoothed her torn shirt and walked over to the counter. She needed a moment to breathe. "So you're studying the leopards here, as well?"

"*Si*," he said. "This is one of the northernmost habitats in Africa, at least in countable numbers. This subspecies differs from the others in this part of the country. There is much to learn about why."

His explanation wasn't as glamorous as she imagined it would be. Like that he was working on some top-secret project or finding the cure for cancer or something. Made him a little more touchable, though, to realize he wasn't anything more than a man whose job had taken him far from home.

The notes he had spread out on the table were all in abbreviated Italian. She couldn't decipher it if she wanted. Still, she could sense him tense up behind her as she flipped the page.

"Don't worry. Your secrets are safe. I can't read this."

She swore he let out a deep breath, then covered it up by clearing his throat. "This is all boring to you. Sometimes I don't realize that others aren't consumed with getting the answers the way I am. Why don't we go onto the deck? The sun will soon rise."

She let it go. She'd learned from her years at school, both as a student and part of the faculty, that scientists could be moody and were often possessive of their work. He didn't know any more about her than she did about him. It wasn't strange for him to be wary of her reading his notes.

Unless he did have something to hide.

Julia waited until they were out in the open air. Below them, the African version of crickets and other nocturnal creatures harmonized. On the horizon, the first hints of light were visible under the veil of night.

"Sal, I need you to take me to the plane."

She watched his adam's apple bob. He leaned against the rail, long, dark fingers gripping the wood. "No. It's too dangerous."

"I need to go. Perhaps if you go with me, during the day."

"No."

"Why?" It was a simple question, really, and his answer just made her all the more determined. When he closed his eyes and tilted his head back, she knew that he knew something.

"You don't understand the danger there. I will inquire in the village. See if they will accompany me in a well armed group."

He didn't understand. She needed to see it. She wanted to bury her sister. Perhaps her personal items could be found. Local men would not know what to look for. No, she must be the one to go. Laying a hand on Sal's arm, she turned him toward her. "I will go with them. I am not afraid."

She saw it in his eyes as clearly as if he had spoken. *But you should be.*

From afar, she heard the cry of a large cat, one that sent chills up her arms. "You go to them, though, don't you? You collect their blood and study their DNA."

He looked away, nodding. She wanted to demand why this was so different. Why in broad daylight they couldn't go to a site, gather their things and then leave?

When he turned back, his eyes flashed with something dark. "Trust me."

Could she? As the light increased, she could see something more on his face. Lines. From worry? She reached up and touched the one that creased beside his mouth. "Can I, Sal? I'm so confused. I'm so lost and alone and—Oh!"

He caught her fingers in his mouth and suckled them lightly. She swore lightning reached out of the hazy sky and ratcheted through her body. He reached up and held her hand there while he traced around her two fingers with his tongue. She wanted to clamp her thighs together to stop the sudden tingling she felt there. Damn, he turned her on.

His teeth gently nipped at the skin and trailed a line of fire down to her palm. Moisture gathered between her legs. Her knees were going to give out at any second.

"Sal," she murmured.

With a less than gentle jerk, he pulled her to him and laced one hand through the hair on the back of her neck.

She gasped. He filled her open mouth with his tongue, his lips taut against hers. This wasn't about biology or genetics, this was pure chemistry. Every cell in her body went on red alert.

He manhandled her in a way she hadn't expected to like. He possessed her mouth—no featherlike kisses like those she'd dreamed. This was pure demand, pure take. And she took as well.

They barely parted to breathe. Other than his hand holding her captive by the back of the neck, only their lips touched. And it frustrated Julia. The more his tongue rolled over hers, stroking, coaxing, the more she imagined how his tongue would feel on her sensitive clit. She moaned, picturing his dark head between her legs, the stubble scraping against her inner thigh.

Her hands reached up of their own accord and fisted in his shirt. He didn't protest when she pulled his body against her.

He was hard. His erection rocked against her lower belly. That spurred her on, pushing, raising on tiptoe so that she could feel the hard heat of his cock against her throbbing center.

"Sal," she whispered against his lips when he paused for a breath. Words were lost as he lowered his mouth and nibbled along her jaw line. She wanted to beg to be taken back to the bedroom, but was scared he'd stop what he was doing.

Her trembling fingers denied her the ability to free the buttons from their holes. She wanted to touch him, feel him against her hand. She didn't question the need, she responded to it.

Sal's lips were doing magical things to her neck, and then her collarbone. Julia moaned and ground against him, fumbling for the button of his pants. The head of his cock lay directly beneath her palm. She pressed and rubbed.

He moaned and grabbed her hand, pulling it away. She fought against it. She needed to drive him to the edge where he'd taken her, she wanted to get to the point of no return with him, stranger or not. She wanted…

"Oh God," she moaned. Somehow he'd slipped his hand down the back of her pants, slid his fingers down between the cheeks of her ass and inserted the tips of his fingers into her throbbing pussy. "Sal!" she nearly screamed in delight.

He probed at the entrance, not deep enough to ease the ache, but enough to stoke the fire. She was going to melt down and come all over him in a matter of minutes.

"Sweet heaven," he murmured, reaching farther as she rose on tiptoe to give him more access.

Julia clung to him, unable to think as wave after wave of pleasure shot through her body. Somehow she'd clawed his shirt from his waistband and slid hands up over the hard, defined planes of his abdomen. She couldn't touch or explore enough of him, not as he plunged in and out of her, finding ways to go deeper and deeper into her aching core.

"Sal, please," she begged, reaching down between them and stroking his cock. "Please."

"Not yet, *mio bella*," he whispered, raking his sandpaper cheek against hers. "Today is for you."

As rough as the first kiss, he seared her lips again. His tongue drove in and out of her mouth, matching the frantic rhythm of his fingers.

Then he lifted her, somehow balancing her and driving his fingers home. She cried out, knowing there was little more she could take. "Yes, Sal." His fingers fucked her as his mouth possessed her.

The first peak stole the breath from her body. She gasped, closing her eyes to the sensation and grasped his shirt to keep from falling to the floor.

"That's it, Julia, come for me. Come on me." His fingers never stopped their magic. Wave after wave of quakes went through her body. She felt her body tighten around his fingers before another explosive orgasm sliced through her.

She had never come so hard, so fast, so long. A whimper escaped her as his fingers slid free.

He kissed her again, the urgency had lifted, now his lips and tongue made promises she prayed he'd keep. She clung to him, afraid to open her eyes.

Now what? Even in her pleasure fog, she felt...unsure. She'd just had some crazy sex on the back deck of this stranger's home. Damn it felt good, but this wasn't exactly normal behavior for her.

At last he pulled her into an embrace—he stood behind her so both of them could face the sun that had finally broken free of the horizon. Below them, the green of the foliage along the stream glistened with dew. From this view, she could almost imagine she was somewhere else. Some exotic hotel or villa with this wonderful lover, enjoying a languorous vacation. He leaned against her, his cock still hard.

She smiled. Whoever this Salvatore was, he was all man.

Chapter 3

"Salvatore!" Sokhra summoned from the doorway. Sal groaned. Now what? He dropped a kiss on Julia's forehead and followed his housekeeper into his lab.

He knew it was bad when she locked the door behind him.

"Paolo—I see it in him. He's becoming like you. Oh, when will this end? Is it a vicious curse?" She burst into tears.

What the hell was she talking about? His mind was still foggy from the way Julia had reacted to him. But it was clearing fast. "What curse? What's wrong with Paolo?" He'd kill the boy if he'd gotten into something in his lab. *This* was why he needed to send the boy back to Italy, to his father.

"He saw you with her. Jealous, I think. He turned and I saw his eyes. Eyes like yours...when you change." She choked the last word out.

Paolo? Change? How? "Sokhra, that's impossible. I had an accident in the lab. Paolo wasn't there. He couldn't have been affected. There's no way."

"Si, I saw him, I saw the hatred there."

Hatred? Sal pushed his hand through his hair. *Hatred?* Surely she was mistaken. "Impossible." He kicked the trash can.

But what if it wasn't? Julia couldn't read the Italian, but what if Paolo had? There were nights his lab was unlocked. Many nights when he roamed the savannah in another form. Paolo could have done just about anything he'd wanted.

Including making a batch of the serum that would alter the genetic code of those infected with it.

"*Maledicalo!* I get no mercy. This is the first evidence you've seen?"

"Yes." The woman's red-rimmed eyes told the truth. She feared. Hell. He feared. Paolo was a good kid, but this was too much to burden a teenage boy with. Especially one with a rebellious streak like him. His brother, Antonio, didn't realize he'd gotten an email before Paolo's arrival a month ago. Paolo's mother had warned him that Paolo was in a ton of trouble back in Italy. They'd wanted Sal to straighten him out.

This Paolo was not like the boy who'd visited his Uncle Sal the year before.

Nor would he ever be the same again.

Sal erupted in rage. How *dare* he do that to himself? Didn't he read the notes, know the torture? Did he know the end result that would destroy him forever? He could tear the boy limb from limb now, while still in human state.

More than ever, that cure needed to be found. Something to back off the bacteria that caused the synthesis and restore the DNA to human form. And Goddammit, he didn't even know the kid's blood type.

"Paolo!" he bellowed through the house. He stormed up to his room. By God, the kid better be gone or he'd probably do something he'd regret.

He tore up the room. He needed a clue, a hint, something. He wanted to know just how far the transformation had progressed. Needed to know.

He found nothing. A handful of naked pictures the kid had apparently downloaded from the net were under his mattress. Sal remembered Sokhra's observation. Jealousy? Christ. The poor kid hadn't seen a non-African female for over a month. And Julia was an attractive, young American woman. The kid was coming into his sexuality. If he'd witnessed them on the deck…Christ!

What a fucked up mess.

He made the sign of the cross, and headed downstairs to see if anything he had planned was salvageable.

Paolo, according to the gardener, had just raced off in the Land Rover with that lady who'd shown up the day before.

Sal let loose with a stream of curses in three languages. And a few choice words in Spanish and Arabic just for good measure.

He had no choice. He had to go.

"Sokhra," he called as he raced to the lab and jerked open his supply drawer.

The woman came running. Thank God he could depend on her.

"Did you see them leave?" he asked. He knew where they went. Stupid, stupid, stupid.

"Paolo?"

He ground his teeth. "And Julia."

She clapped a hand over her mouth. "You will go?"

He handed her the hypo. "*Si*."

She didn't hesitate. He'd taught her not to. The stimulant was brutal, but effective. He'd avoided it, using it only when absolutely necessary. There was no question about it today.

Sal streaked through the yard to the easternmost corner of the property. The tree there was his gate. Effortless he bounded up the branches, then jumped, landing in the fork of the neighboring tree.

Remaining hidden was important. It'd be easy to cross the open grassland to the plane's wreckage. But it'd also make it simple for someone to spot him. No, he had to play it safe.

Even when his muscles ached, he ran. He needed to circle around and head them off. Julia couldn't go back, she couldn't see the carnage left behind. While it was nature's way, yes, it was brutal. He'd been there. He knew human remains littered the site, now being picked apart by scavengers. The local tribesman had been there, as well, though heavily armed. They had picked through and removed anything that appeared valuable.

There would be nothing left for Julia to find. Nothing but heartache.

He zigzagged through the tall brush. Ahead of him he could hear the hum of a motor. Behind him, however, ran day hunters, nursing mothers, eager for a kill.

Sal leapt into the tire tracks and continued at the exhausting pace. He hoped the sight of him, and those behind him, would force Paolo and Julia to turn around and head back to safety.

Julia sat in the truck, hands folded in her lap. Good thing she hadn't eaten breakfast. Her stomach flip-flopped as she tried to prepare her mind for this. She dreaded it. But she had to do it. She needed closure.

Everything was mapped out in her head. They'd left the bodies of those who'd died on impact in the fuselage. All she wanted to do was dig a shallow grave.

It was so damn frustrating to try to make Paolo understand what she wanted.

Finally, she'd drawn a picture. Then he'd gotten a clue.

So with paper and pen and some strange charade-like sign language, they were able to communicate. Julia felt like it was a huge victory.

Bittersweet as it was.

Paolo hit the brakes.

The truck skidded sideways, shuddering to a halt.

"What?" she screamed.

Suddenly a giant white cat leapt on the hood. It leaned in, nearly pressing its nose against the glass, and snarled at Paolo.

Julia didn't look over at the boy. She slapped down the lock mechanism and made sure her window was rolled up tight. "What does he want?"

Paolo of course, didn't answer.

She expected to find him cowering in fear. Instead it was boy to leopard. An intense staredown.

"Paolo, let's go. He's going to come through the window." She didn't doubt he could either. He was huge. Bigger than she'd remembered, bigger than she thought leopards were supposed to be.

Paolo pushed off her hand when she tried to pull at the steering wheel. "Oh God, please, get us out of here before they kill us."

Two more leopards circled the truck. Females, she noted. But they were no less frightening with their lips curled back and fangs glistening like ivory. She remembered the feel of them as they tore through her skin, even if she had no scars to prove it.

Paolo threw his head back and laughed. Then he gunned the engine.

Julia screamed and grabbed the dash. The horrid sound of nails screeching along the hood ended when the leopard known as Snow bounded off.

He followed them, even as Paolo veered and swerved to hit him.

Bad thing was, she didn't *want* Paolo to hit him. Any of them.

"Maybe we should go back," she said. To emphasize, she grabbed Paolo's wrist and pointed behind them.

Paolo threw off her hand again and pressed harder on the accelerator.

Did he think he could outrun them? There were three, not one, three. And they were much too smart to simply allow themselves to be run over.

They slowed and rounded a small grove of trees. Paolo pointed up.

Julia gasped. At least four more leopards lay in the branches and forks.

Why wasn't he afraid?

The wreckage was just ahead. She could see the broken wing, sticking up in the air like a beacon. Or a temporary gravestone.

She pressed her face to the cool glass and peered at the debris field. Boxes of supplies had been scattered and their contents lay open among the brown tipped grass and patches of dirt.

Then she lost it. Even as she tasted bile, tears welled up. A hyena raced off, a piece of something. *Someone* she realized, hanging from its mouth.

It had been pure carnage. The animals had torn up the bodies. Bones lay scattered around a burned out fire. She covered her eyes. No way could she witness anything else.

"No!" she screamed. "Go, Go, Take me back. Go!"

Not understanding, Paolo stopped the truck.

"No!" she cried again, rocking forward as if to push the truck on pure emotion. "Get out of here, go."

Hysterics were close. She could feel it.

Suddenly, the truck shook.

She heard metal squeal as it bent and felt the force of a blow.

It wasn't enough that they'd eaten her family, her travel mates. Now they wanted her, too.

She reached over and pushed on the shift lever. Gears ground as she tried to force it into something other than neutral. "Go, Vamos, Leave, Home. Something. God, Paolo Go!" she pointed, banged her fist. Why wouldn't he listen? Surely he could understand part of it.

The ramming started again.

Julia lifted her feet to the seat and curled up into a ball. She should never have come here. She should have listened to Sal. Dammit. *Sal, where are you?*

One of the females jumped up on the hood and paced.

Growling and hissing continued outside her window. She couldn't look. All she wanted was for it all to go away. For this to go away. She rocked, just slightly. "Make it go away, make it go away," she repeated, over and over to drown out the noise.

Then the entire truck shimmied. For the first time since they'd stopped, Paolo spoke. And then it sounded like nothing more than some expletive in Italian. She reached over and turned the key. Then pretended to move the shifter. "Go, go!" she pointed. "Go!"

The white cat reared up on the hood of the truck and tackled the smaller one. Paws the size of baseball mitts with razor-like claws connected with flesh. Blood splattered the edge of the windshield.

More leopards were arriving.

"Go!" her throat hurt from screaming. She alternated between tears and hysterical hiccups. No matter what, she wouldn't look to her right. She couldn't bear to see what was left of the plane wreckage. What had she done?

* * * * *

"What in the hell were you thinking?" Sal stood over her with black eyes flashing. "I've been searching all over for you. I didn't think you'd be stupid enough to go out there. Didn't I warn you?"

She'd barely gotten out of the truck. All she wanted to do was go into the house and sort things through. Alone. "I'm sorry, Sal. Trust me, there's no way I could regret my actions more."

"*Non importa.* The grasslands are a dangerous place." He ran his hand over a deep scratch in the hood. "If those cats had wanted in, trust me, *la piccola*, they would have gotten in. Then what?"

Sal's housekeeper intervened. She pointed at Paolo, still sitting behind the wheel of the Rover, his hands gripping the steering wheel, and said something to Sal. It sounded harsh.

Regardless, Julia was more than relieved to have Sokhra lead her to the house and sit her down at the less formal kitchen table. Sal had been poised, ready to pounce just like those leopards had. And she felt just as helpless.

The steaming cup that was set before her smelled wonderful. Tea. Immediately she wrapped her trembling hands around it and took a sip.

"We went to the site. It was so awful. Awful." She drank again, forcing the sweetened liquid past the lump in her throat. "As soon as I saw it, I knew it was wrong. I wanted to go back, but Paolo wouldn't listen. I tried to tell him to stop, to turn around. But then the leopards came again. He just sat there. He wouldn't leave. I kept telling him to go--"

Giant tears rolled down her face. "All I wanted to do was see if there was anything I could salvage. And bury my sister." She pushed the cup away and laid her head down on her arms. "Now there's nothing left. Nothing."

Strong arms pulled her up.

She stood, ready to face the fact. She'd directly disobeyed Sal, went behind his back to get what she wanted. He'd known. Perhaps he was trying to protect her from the horror of it. She couldn't speak, just swallowed and swiped at her tears.

"You're safe now," he said, pulling her to him so her cheek rested over his heart. "All the while you stay in this house, you're safe."

Of course, that just made her cry all the more. She didn't want to be safe here. Here scared her almost as much as outside. Here was starting to feel like a prison.

"But what about—"

"I told you not to go there. There's nothing for you there."

"Nothing?"

"The locals have been there. It's gone."

Every tangible piece of her existence here, wiped clear. Within a week, there would probably be little evidence to even identify the other victims, whether they died in the crash or from the leopard attack. It hurt. She felt hollow inside.

Sal tightened his lips and looked away for a moment before pulling her to an arm's distance away. "I may have to change my plans. The trip to Florence will need to be postponed." She raised her head and pounded a fist against his chest. His voice had been gentle, but she knew what this meant. She was stuck here, at his mercy. He called the shots. "No, dammit. I have to get home."

Strong arms wrapped around her. She supposed he wanted her to feel secure. Instead, she felt like a trapped rabbit. "Soon. Soon."

She didn't believe him. Pulling away, she stared pointedly at him. "Then let me call. Let me tell my family I'm alive and trying to make arrangements."

"No."

"No? Sal, you can't hold me here like a hostage. They'll presume I'm dead when they learn of the crash."

His face wasn't the stony, hard expression she anticipated. He looked almost sympathetic. A rush of hope filled her. "Why?" she asked after a calming breath. "Why can't I call?"

"The phones are tapped. The lines are privately owned. Nothing is secret. And if they learn of an American here without visa or passport or permit…" He scratched his day old beard. "You would not have the luxury of remaining in my house."

"Oh." Basically he said she was his captive no matter what. But there had to be a way. "How do you communicate with your family, with the university? Surely you don't share research information over a monitored line."

Sal frowned. She hoped he underestimated her. She was not going to give up. There had to be a way. And she wasn't sure she believed him about the government thing either. All they had to do was see the site and verify her name on the passenger list. They'd gone through check and recheck in Egypt. Too bad they'd forgotten to take fingerprints — that might be the only piece of identification she still had.

Julia followed Sal into a side office. There sat another phone. And a computer.

"Sweet mother of God. You have Internet access?" she asked. Adrenaline shot through her at the realization. She wasn't cut off.

"Let me email someone then. Let me tell them I'm safe. Please."

Sal pushed a button and stopped the screen saver.

Julia's heart dropped.

Italian. His computer was set to a language she couldn't understand. "Great," she breathed, turning around and walking to the door and back. "You've got me stuck no matter what, don't you, Salvatore?"

"I will send an email for you. I don't like you to think you are my prisoner. You are free to leave, but the village will be much less welcoming than my home. I've already arranged for the trip back."

"But you postponed it!" Why!? She didn't understand any of this nonsense.

"It couldn't be helped. It's not what I wanted either, trust me."

"Fine. But you will send the email?"

"*Si*. Recipient?"

She told him her best friend's address. Then asked him to carbon copy it to her email at work. Sonja would check it there and get it if she didn't at home. "Tell them where I am, at least near what main city. Tell them Chelly is…g-gone. But I am well. And that I've found someone who is helping me make arrangements to get home."

He typed in Italian. She leaned over. "Sal, they aren't going to be able to read that." She pointed to the screen. "We speak English in the US."

"I know this. My program will translate itself automatically. It may be more formal than you'd have spoken it, but they will understand."

She paused, her chest swelling with the relief that she'd done it. She'd made contact. Perhaps if someone from the outside started working, she'd get home much faster. Sal hit a few more buttons and erased the screen. Then he stood up.

She didn't step back. They were nearly touching. She was a fool if she didn't acknowledge the way her body reacted to him, even under these situations. But that complicated things.

"Thank you," she said. "You have no idea how much that means to me."

The slightly rough back of his fingers slid over her cheek. "I never mean to do anything but make you happy."

She bit her lip, remembering what had transpired between them at dawn. She opened her mouth to say something, but couldn't. Sal slid the pad of his thumb over her bottom lip.

Sparks of awakening spiraled through her. Her top lip closed down, sucking his thumb lightly inside her mouth.

His eyes flashed black. She never let her eyes leave his. Storms built behind them, the wrinkles at the corners deepened as she circled the tip of his thumb with her tongue, then sucked deep.

"Julia." The texture of his voice matched his scruffy face. It slid down her senses and set her skin on fire. The way he said it, softening the J and letting it roll off his tongue, like he was making love to the word.

How did he do that? Melt her so quickly? Everything had shifted. The reasons they'd come into the room were a faded memory.

Her eyes fluttered closed as he placed his other palm on her cheek. She felt so cherished, yet wanted in such a primal way. How could it be like that? Why wasn't it just physical lust? It was as if he touched her deeper than her skin.

Sal removed his thumb and replaced it with his mouth. He couldn't take any further torture from that sweet tongue. It was all he could do not to imagine her lips tight around another part of his body.

But he needed to slow things down. This morning had been explosive, unplanned. He needed to make sure that she didn't leave, and all she'd done was accuse him of keeping her hostage. That needed to change.

He shifted his weight and slid down into the chair. He pulled her onto his lap. *Madre de dios.* Did she have to move like that to get settled? If he had his way, he'd get her to try that again with their clothes off. But not right now.

What he needed to do now was build trust. He leaned back, letting her sit, straddling him. "I need to know, Julia, if you've got someone at home waiting for you."

Her eyes widened and that delicious mouth turned into a perfect 'O'. She shook her head. It shook her whole body. Damn if she wasn't driving him to distraction.

"Oh, no." She looked around. "I wouldn't—"

"Shh," he said. That was all he wanted to hear. "You're not a virgin, are you?"

Now her cheeks tinged pink. Beautiful. Another head shake.

"Good," he grinned. "Lesbian?"

"Sal!" she shrieked and slapped him on the chest.

Just the in he wanted. He snagged her wrists and leaned forward so that her breasts rubbed against his shirt. "Well, I'm glad to hear about all that." He let go of her arms, grasped her thighs and stood, holding her against his nearly painful hard-on.

Then he sat her down. Torture. He'd hate himself later for this. "I'd hate to lay awake tonight imagining what it'd be like to make love to you if you were any of those things."

All that beautiful color drained from her face. It pooled as pure desire in his groin. Damn he wanted her. He couldn't imagine desiring her more if she'd begged for it.

"I need to shower and shave. Plus, I'm behind in the lab. Shall I show you my library? I think there's a few books in English in there."

She gasped. He had to turn away to keep from smiling. When he finally got around to making love to her, it'd be worth it. There was no question about that.

Julia followed him from the room. Talk about confused! Maybe she wasn't that attractive to him. Maybe he was gay or taken or...no, she'd felt that erection, both now and earlier. He wanted her.

So what was he waiting for?

Oh God, she couldn't even believe she'd thought that. She didn't go to bed with men she just met. She had no qualms about sex, hell, it was science in pure form and that was her forte. But...this was just out of character.

Then again, when had she felt that way? Never. When had simple touches turned her on to the point of drenching her underwear? Never. She had a feeling that she could come without him ever breeching her clothing — just by his mouth on hers and his body rubbing against her.

Now she was following him as he led her to the library. He acted as if nothing had happened! She thought...never mind what she thought. What mattered is what had happened in there before, anyway. He'd sent the email she needed. Now, if it were possible, she'd try to relax and at least enjoy the luxuries the house had to offer.

And that might just include its host.

Chapter 4

Julia spent the better of three hours reading science journals. The rest of the time she stared out the wide picture window and imagined what it'd be like to make love to Sal.

She'd given up questioning the thoughts. Or being embarrassed by them. The only thing she could figure she'd lose was another experience like this morning. Now *that* brought heat to her cheeks.

Sal, with his wire-rimmed glasses and lab coat, was anything but nerdy. She grinned. What her co-workers back home wouldn't give to have someone like him working in their lab. But Julia knew, even after her limited time with him, he had a presence that would shine through no matter what he wore.

Which turned her thoughts back to wondering what he looked like wearing nothing at all. So maybe it was slightly juvenile. But it beat reading about the side effects of chemotherapy on the circulatory system.

Despite its lack of books that were of any use to her, she knew right away that the library would become her haven. It amazed her how she often forgot she was even in Africa.

The dark wood shelves lined all four walls and were broken only by giant windows and of course, the doorway. Books and periodicals filled every shelf. Hardwood floors with an exotic rug and neutral, but comfortable furniture gave the room the impression of being very old. She felt very comfortable.

To the point of stretching out on the camel colored leather sofa and closing her eyes.

* * * * *

Sal was exhausted. He'd researched until his notes blurred. Then he sat in his office and drafted an email to his brother, asking for a favor and explaining there'd be a delay.

Inadvertently, his thoughts had returned to Julia. That little bit of tempting he'd done earlier had probably tortured him more than it had her. Well, at least he'd been able to concentrate for a little while.

Nothing wrong with killing a little time now. He kicked back and thought about her. His hand slid to his lap and rested there as his penis hardened. When months passed without female companionship, he'd resorted to self-satisfaction. Right now it was a little different. He knew what he wanted, and it was there, his for the taking. And he didn't take. Yet.

His full erection pushed against his zipper. Without hesitation he flipped open the button and eased the zipper down. His exposed cock sprung up against his hand. His fingers slid down the length, but he imagined Julia's lips touching him there instead. Her tongue would tease him, the way it had invaded his mouth and explored there. He traced the head of his cock and rubbed the tip. His balls tightened against him.

God, how he ached to fill her. Pre-come dampened his hand. He used it to moisten his shaft, amazed at how quickly he'd gotten to this aching hardness. Julia did this to him.

He wanted the quick, tight strokes to be her damp pussy clamping down on his cock. He wanted to watch her face as he pushed himself inside of her, filling her up. Just thinking about it had him ready to explode.

He bit back a moan. That something about her had the ability to reach down into his private office even now and intensify his pleasure. He wanted her to be there when he erupted and came. It was because of her.

He thrust into his palm as if he was pumping into her. Relieving himself, even when thinking about one particular woman, had never brought him to the brink so quickly. If he were with her now, he'd likely be unable to maintain control.

She'd whimper into his mouth like she had this morning. Her juices would drench them both as he slid in and out of her. He reached down to cup his balls. He wanted her hands on him. As he stroked, he imagined her flushed face, her eyes closed to the intensity. Watching her come would be nearly as hot as making her.

He'd wanted his cock to be inside her when he'd made her come earlier. He'd wanted to rip away their clothes and lean her against the railing and slip between the soaking wet folds. But this would have to do for now. He slid the pad of his thumb over the tip of his cock. Slippery fluid erupted.

His legs slid apart and he relaxed farther down in his chair. If he closed his eyes, he could picture her climbing on and taking him in.

His fingers tightened as he imagined her interior walls would, squeezing and shuddering against him as she came. He stroked hard and fast. God, she made him hot. He wanted to possess her, to fuck her over and over.

"*Dio!*" He closed his eyes and tensed, his back arching and head falling against the back of the chair. He thrust his hips upward and rubbed himself until he couldn't take it anymore. He called out her name as he shot come into the air.

Sal followed his bit of indulgence with a cold shower. Not that it did any good. If anything, giving into impulse and imagining what it would be like to make love to Julia made him more desperate to possess her. He lathered his body, stroking his still aroused cock more than usual, knowing she'd used this shower last night. He'd smelled the vanilla and saw the small bottle of lotion Sokhra must have given her. Which made him all the hotter.

Julia'd stood where he stood now, naked, with water rushing down her body.

Had she moaned with the pleasure of the hot water spray? Did she think of him when she touched herself? The mental image of her reaching between her legs to explore the ache had him hard and ready.

How was he going to wait? He knew she'd take him willingly, but he wanted it to be more than just sex. It wasn't for him. If it had, his release in the office would have him interested, but not burning up with desire.

"*Che cosa ho fatto?*" he muttered, switching the water to warm and rinsing. What had he done to himself? The only thing that was going to quench this blinding thirst was having Julia.

* * * * *

Who said that? Julia reached out from the dream, swearing someone was talking to her. Or was it her imagination—one gone wild with strange images of wild leopards and a tall, muscular man that she swore was Sal, but who she could never catch up to.

She stretched, surfacing from her sleep as if it had been a long underwater dive. Yet she felt wonderfully refreshed.

"Sal!" she shrieked, finally focusing and seeing him standing directly above her. A dark twinkle reflected in his eyes, an almost-there smile dancing on his lips. Her breath hitched. Damn, did he clean up good. He'd even shaved, which she expected would disappoint. But not so with him. He had the strong jaw line to carry off a truly masculine face even without the stubble.

Still damp hair curled around the top of his ears and onto his forehead. Plus he smelled divine.

Maybe *this* was the dream...

She licked her lips. He frowned.

It took her a long moment to realize why. This was real, and Sal was casting out these little sexual hints that had her body temperature steadily climbing. She covered her mouth, because naturally, she felt compelled to do it again.

Feeling desired—and desirable—was very new to her. A pang of regret came and went—it'd be awesome to share this experience with her best friends. They'd get a kick out of her rendition, and of course, never believe Sal was all she'd describe. But she'd get to do that—later. And when she did, it meant she wouldn't have Sal in her life anymore.

She finally understood the 'living for the now' phrase. He wanted her. She'd have to have been blind to miss that. What she wanted was another story. At least another mental debate. If she did what her body desired, however, she'd have him backed up against the bookcase with his hands all over her.

"Sokhra's set the table. Will you be my guest for dinner?"

His formal request, hot on the heels of her daring imagination, made her giggle. But he remained straight-faced and held out his hand to her.

Julia sobered immediately. So maybe he was serious. And look how she was dressed—still in the tattered clothes she'd put on in New York before she'd left. God, that felt like months ago. Her voice shook with a reservoir homesickness. "I'm afraid I won't be dressing for

49

dinner."

His eyes cut through her without seeing what she wore. The lack of any expression changes actually did comfort her. "You're fine," he said.

Still, she was a single woman accepting a dinner invitation from a sexy man who completely pushed her buttons. If she *were* home, this would be a big deal. Right now she'd kill for a change of clothes and a tube of mascara.

Sal pulled her up, sliding his hand around her hip and rested it on the small of her back. Funny how such a small gesture erased the need for silk or lace. She felt like the luckiest, most beautiful girl in the world.

"What?" She looked back to smiling dark eyes.

"I'm watching you. I could do that all day."

A thrill raced through her. What a charmer. Hell it could even be a pickup line, but she was too far gone to notice. She said, her own grin in place, "You'd fall asleep from boredom."

"I'd find things to do to keep us both awake." His thumb rubbed against the material just above her waistline.

That did it. Her insides turned to mush in apprehension. For a woman who'd never made the first move, she was already calculating how and where to attack. Though she doubt it mattered. He seemed as eager as she did.

They were just going through the motions. What sweet torture it was.

"Like now," he said, interrupting her thoughts. "You're concentrating. When you do, that little dimple appears right here." He stopped and pressed a forefinger to the space between her eyebrows.

She wrinkled her nose. He couldn't have seen that from where he was, walking half behind her.

"Come on," he whispered close to her ear. "Our dinner's getting cold."

He led her past the large dining room where she'd eaten the night before. The table was bare save the long white runner and matching candlesticks.

They didn't stop. Julia was curious where Sal was taking her now. Seems everyday she found a new room—"Oh! Oh!" she gasped. It was like walking into a ball of light.

His timing was perfect. The sun dipped low on the horizon and glowed through the glass that made up three of the four walls of the sunroom. "This is spectacular."

Sal slipped his arm around her waist. She stood there, pressed to his hard chest and stomach, not sure what to admire the most, nature's fiery end to the day or the man beside her.

As the room dimmed, she finally noticed a small, glass-topped table set elegantly and formally. The vase in the middle even held a red rose. Where had Sal found a red rose in the middle of Africa? Did they *have* roses in Africa? In rural nearly desert-type Africa?

The man amazed her to no end.

"What about your nephew?" Surely this elegant setting was meant for the two of them, but she forced herself to remember they weren't the only two in the house.

"He's out. Or else locked in his room. Are you hungry?" he asked. His voice dipped low, just barely more than a whisper. His husky voice fluttered against her temple and tiptoed down to all her private places.

"Yeah," she answered, knowing both the question, and her answer were multi-faceted. But they were playing some primitive game. Something so true to the country they inhabited. An animalistic mating dance, a formal set of necessary steps that was little more than mental foreplay.

He held the chair. She sat. Like good little marionettes they ate. He sighed at least twice when she'd closed her lips around a forkful of linguini. His eyes grew as black as night as she licked her lips, then her fingers.

She'd need more than the bread knife to cut the tension between them.

Tension that had her squirming in her seat. Her senses were so alert, she was conscious of the way her panties lay slick against her. Sal was invisible to her from the waist down. Did he suffer the same fate? Was he as turned on from the simple act of eating a meal?

Finally Julia could eat no more. It wasn't that she was full, it was the literal lack of fulfillment that had her unable to enjoy the food. "Sal? I'm ready for dessert."

She tossed her hair back and lifted her chin, empowered by the way he blinked at her. On a whim she lifted the rose from its vase and brought it to her lips.

Her eyes fluttered closed.

Silverware clattered to his plate.

Julia inhaled, enveloping the scent—roses, spicy Italian food and the musky smell of sex-ripe bodies. Sal whispered her name, the way he softened it gave her the courage to continue.

With her head tilted toward the twilight sky, she caressed her cheeks, her lips, her neck with the petals of the rose. His chair scraped against the floor. But she didn't stop.

She used one hand to unfasten the top button of her blouse. The other guided the rose back up to pass over her lips, the scent of the flower leaving her heady. She'd never done anything like this before. She could only guess at Sal's reaction. It turned *her* on though, her brazen actions, the way she teased her skin into begging for touch.

Petals graced down her chin and the column of her neck, sliding gently toward the exposed skin just above her breasts.

Sal touched her then, a touch lighter than the rose as he finished undoing her shirt and opening it.

"So beautiful," he said. The back of his fingers traced over the swell of her breasts. Then he palmed them through the lacy bra. "Perfect. I knew they would be."

Julia twisted in her seat to face him. She watched him then when he took the flower from her and traced her sensitized skin. He worshipped her. Fingers and flower petals and then soft, promising kisses.

Desperation for the final act had her start this, but now she was content with the languorous way they explored one another. Maybe because the end result was clear, this time. She would know Sal's body, all fine flesh and muscle. She would feel his cock inside her, thrusting and throbbing. They'd get to that.

Right now it was all she could do to sit still while he teased her nipples through the thin lace.

"Take this off," he said, pushing her shirt down her arms. She wriggled out of it, glad to be free of its confinement. Sal's fingers traced up her bare shoulders, leaving a legion of goosebumps in their wake. Everything he did made her more alive, more aware.

"What about you?" she asked, feeling almost shy. But dammit, she wanted to touch him too. This was supposed to be *her* seduction.

Sal pulled the shirt over his head. A gold chain lay at his

collarbone. It glowed against the tight bronze skin of his shoulders and chest. Damn. Moisture pooled in her mouth and her panties. He was what wet dreams were made of.

Unable to bear not touching him, she stood up and reached for him. The muscles just beneath his skin rippled behind her fingertips as they grazed his tight stomach. She'd never expected to be so turned on by just the first innocent steps of foreplay.

"We're going too fast," Sal muttered.

No. They weren't going fast enough. If she didn't move now, she'd lose her nerve. With one hand on either side of his face, she pulled his mouth down to hers. "I want you, Sal," she whispered, then plunged her tongue into his mouth.

His touch went from tender to demanding in the blink of an eye. He hauled her body against his, curling one hand around her ass to pull her against his erection.

"Upstairs." His impatient growl was thrilling of itself. No need to tell her twice. She yanked her shirt back on and tied it jauntily at the waist. He didn't bother to pick his up.

What if one of the staff people saw them racing upstairs for their tryst? What would they think of her? She nearly laughed. Why should she care? All she knew at this moment was that she wanted to get intimate with the man in front of her. And that was going to happen regardless of who they passed in the hallway.

It was a little overwhelming to walk into his bedroom. And awe-inspiring. A king-size bed held center court, a four-poster with rustic canopy railings. A navy cloth wound around it snakelike and dangled from the ends.

The bed was unmade, but also dressed in deep blue.

She was completely outclassed. The only place she'd ever seen a bedroom like this before was in Better Homes and Gardens.

"Change your mind?" he nibbled at her neck as he asked. "We can go back downstairs. Or to your room."

No. She wanted to lie on that bed and feel him climb on her. She wanted to smell his scent on the sheets. She wanted this to be something more than convenient sex. "Absolutely not. Just thinking how this room is so full of possibilities." She waggled an eyebrow. She reached up to touch the corner of his mouth that turned up ever-so-slightly.

"There is only one possibility. What will it take to get you naked and in my bed?"

"Kiss me, Sal. I think the rest is guaranteed."

The tone was joking but the words weren't.

Lightning fast, he lifted her up and placed her on the waist-high bed. She watched her own chest rise and fall with excited breaths as Sal's long fingers untied her shirt and cast it to the side.

As much as she'd wanted to be the one to lead the way, she couldn't stop him. Slightly calloused palms slid over her skin once again, touching only the exposed flesh. When he pushed her, she lay back on the bed. What a sight. When he leaned over her, his hair fell forward and shadowed his face. Would she ever tire of looking at him?

A whimper from her became a moan as he licked her bared stomach. He teased the edges of her waistline—where she wanted him to go, and dropped feather light kisses along the naked skin.

He was torturing her to death. She didn't want to take it slow, she wanted to feel his flesh beneath her fingers, feel his cock inside her. Gone were the last of her shy inhibitions. Dammit, she wanted Sal, now.

"Stop!" she cried.

He jerked up. A frown creased his face.

No, not what she wanted. "It's my turn." She grabbed his arms and tried to tug him down on the bed with her.

He didn't listen. The frown crept upwards, creasing the little wrinkles at the corners of his eyes. Without a word, he shook free of her hands and went to work on the fastener of her pants.

"Sal, no. Wait." Like she really wanted him to stop. "Let me please you."

"You do, my Julia. This pleases me."

My Julia. His words curled into her chest and squeezed. She did belong to him, want to or not. At least for now. And she wasn't going to waste a minute of it.

Sal couldn't get enough of her. The way she fought to take an active role sent him dangerously close to ripping away her clothes and taking her now. He tasted the dip of her waist. She squirmed.

No, if he let her lead he couldn't guarantee he'd be around to finish. It'd been too long, and he'd fantasized too much about this moment. And if she didn't stop—

He leaned over and ground his erection against her damp mound. Damn clothes in the way. To hell with taking their time. They could do that later.

His clothes quickly dropped to the floor. Christ, even watching Julia look at him made him tighten with need. Unashamed, she looked straight at his cock and smiled.

No more waiting. He stepped toward her. Either she was as needy or she read his intentions. He didn't care. Now was the time for possession.

She crawled backwards up the bed and spread her legs for him. Sweet Jesus. Moisture glistened off her opened pussy lips. He followed her on the bed, male in form, animal in thought.

What if he tasted her there? The temptation was too much. He crawled across the bed, feeling much the part of the leopard as his back muscles rippled. Reaching the juncture between her thighs, he heard her sigh.

Sweetness. She wanted him. Wanted him to kiss her there. Taste her.

He dipped his head as she moaned his name.

She shuddered as his tongue swept up along the folds and found her clit. She lifted her hips and ground against his mouth, her pussy soaked with the fluid of her arousal. He wasn't going to give her release this way. He wanted to feel those muscles clamp down on him as he came with her.

He lapped the folds, slid his tongue down into her depths, then suckled her clit once more. She was close. Her body shook in anticipation.

And he couldn't take any more.

He climbed above her and pushed the head of his cock against her. She lifted her hips, letting him slip inside. He had to fight back control.

He swallowed and focused on her face. "Open your eyes. Look at me when I'm inside you."

The moment her lashes fluttered, he thrust.

Velvet tightness enveloped him. Never could he have imagined it'd be this...intoxicating. She lifted her hips and rocked gently. There was something magical happening here. All he could think of doing was burying himself so deep that they became one. At the same time he wanted to wrap his arms around her and hold her completely to him as she came.

"Julia," he gasped. His eyes never left her face. Eyes hooded with desire held his. Her mouth parted as she panted out little gasps. "I need to fill you up. I want to feel you come on me, for me."

"Sal," she moaned, reaching down to where their bodies joined. His body quaked as she touched herself. Christ, how could she make him even hotter this way? He struggled not to explode as her fingers circled her clit and then slid down against where his cock disappeared inside her.

Her head rolled from side to side on the pillow as she moaned. Her finger stroked the slick side of his cock as she pushed it into her pussy. The first wave hit him. He held her hips and rocked against her. Those velvety walls clamped down as everything else shattered around him.

His body tightened as her fingers wrapped around his cock and jacked him off inside her. Her own orgasm followed. She totally abandoned herself to him, sobbing out as she rocked against his groin.

Sal pulled himself up beside Julia and wrapped her in his arms. He had so much intended for them when this finally happened, and dammit, his self-control had flown out the window.

She was a dynamo. He'd expected her to be sensual, yes, but the little things she did had both surprised and excited him. It was easy to plan what he wanted next—to have her straddle his cock and let him watch as she touched herself.

He hardened again at the thought of it.

The next time. Hopefully that'd be in the early morning hours when he awoke to her in his arms. Something deeper than his libido stirred then. He ignored it and listened to Julia sigh as she slid off to sleep.

Sal waited until she had dozed off. He'd heard another door down the hallway open. No way was he going to sleep thinking Paolo was leaving the house, boy or leopard.

He slid on his clothes and shoes quietly, then turned back to the beauty asleep on his bed. He ached to stay with her.

Maybe another night.

* * * * *

As he suspected, Paolo's room was empty.

Where the fuck had the boy gone? His next stop—where he went without hesitation—was his lab. But there was no sign of the boy, even that he'd been there.

His fingers hesitated over the vial that would quickly force his body into metamorphosis. It was over half gone. No. He'd better save it. Just in case.

If he couldn't find Paolo within the property limits he'd come back to the lab to finish another batch. And maybe review his notes. Supplies were dwindling. He'd needed the trip north, for more than just an opportunity to return the boy to his father.

Now it looked like that was postponed indefinitely.

He tasted the bitterness of selfishness when he acknowledged that also meant he'd have Julia just a little while longer. Hopefully he could win her trust, perhaps even her love, and she'd stay.

He didn't just need her for his lab work. She was quickly becoming an addiction in other ways as well.

A few Italian self-insults later he had a handle on his focus. Work. Lab. Paolo. Julia would be for later. He punched a few commands into his keyboard and brought up the formula he'd need to create.

At least he had what he needed to keep himself in stock of the serum to force his transformation. What he lacked was what it took to keep it from happening naturally. The blood tests were clearly marking what he knew would happen. The more often he changed, the more his physical characteristics failed to change back.

He'd need blood soon. And if need be, he'd fly to Florence himself. At least Cairo. Perhaps he could intercept a package there.

He felt the cold sweat that indicated the crippling pain would follow. He dropped to his knees and waited.

Julia jerked up in bed. She'd heard something. She'd swear it had been a yell or a howl or something that yanked her from sleep. Her heart beat double time as she strained to hear it again.

Nothing.

Maybe it'd been Paolo or Sal. The sound had been decidedly male, that much she was sure.

Sal! She felt the bed beside her. But she already knew. He wasn't there.

Trepidation slipped in. Who *was* this man that made love to her until she was senseless then left her in his own bed? Why was he living like a hermit in desolate Africa?

Just this morning she'd found him still up at dawn. She hadn't questioned it then, but even now, her mind made up excuses for him.

She didn't want him to be abnormal. She wanted there to be a rational explanation. Maybe last night he'd fallen asleep in his office, working. Maybe tonight he'd heard Paolo up and went to check on him.

She hadn't seen Sal's nephew since they'd gotten back from visiting the site of the plane wreck. She'd more or less curled up and cried all the way home from that. Then Sal had jerked them both out of the truck and, from the tone of his voice, read his nephew the riot act.

That had been expected. The look on Paolo's face hadn't. Pure rebellion.

Julia threw the covers back and felt for the edge of the bed. Of course, walking in, she hadn't bothered to figure out where the lamps were. There was a window. She strained through the blackness, and found a gray outline where moonlight tried to peak in.

Thank goodness there were no tables or anything in the way as she felt her way toward it. The shade pulled up easy. Did little to help her see in the room, just highlighted some vague silhouettes.

The view was amazing.

The moon was like a giant eye, blinking as the clouds obscured it. Beneath the window she could see the outline of the deck railing, beyond that, not much more than darkness.

A flash of light caught her eye. She shrieked, almost immediately covering her mouth with her hand. The last thing she needed was the household rushing to find her naked at the window.

She had to be hallucinating. She blinked and looked again. Nothing. Just darkness.

Maybe she should go find Sal. A fist tightened around her gut. What if that was the white leopard? What if it had gotten over the wall that surrounded his property?

She found the door, and therefore the overhead light switch. Her clothes were lying in heaps, but she noticed that Sal's were gone. She hurriedly dressed and left the room.

The layout of the house wasn't much clearer to her now than it had been earlier. But she knew how she'd gotten to the kitchen. She made her way there first, watching for a light under a bedroom door. Hair on the back of her neck rose as she looked out the windows that lined the main living room. The moon was shadowed. Visibility wasn't more than a half dozen feet. Anything could be out there, watching her. Hell, she didn't even know what kinds of animals were common here. Except the leopards and hyenas. Real comforting.

She darted to the kitchen and got out a glass for some water. But no Sal walked in to remind her to get it from the fridge. She downed the cold, clear liquid while telling herself not to be disappointed.

Dammit, she was. They'd just had incredible sex. She'd never...given herself so openly, freely—and so quickly. That sinking feeling in her stomach anchored itself in the fear she was making the wrong decision about Sal.

What did she really know about him? He was a research scientist. A geneticist. He studied leopards. So? Most people who studied on site rented a place or worked out of a temporary lab. Unless there was a facility nearby. But here he was, working out of what looked like a permanent home. Sal probably had the most advanced equipment for hundreds of miles.

Why had he put down roots here? Was there that much to study? Wouldn't he travel to the different areas and investigate the leopard populations there? Things didn't jive. It bothered her more than she'd like.

She hated doubt. She poured herself another glass of water and continued her raging thoughts. Back to Sal. She knew scientists. Hell, she was one, by all regard. If she wanted to, she could demand she be referred to as Dr. Haverstock. It just wasn't that important. She had to admit, however, some of her colleagues, and past professors, were certainly of the eccentric breed. She was starting to think that Sal went past that.

Good. The light was on in the lab. Maybe she was making a bigger deal out of this than she should. But today wasn't like yesterday. Now they were involved.

"Sal?" she called out as she pushed open the door. Another trick she'd learned at the university. Never surprise a lab rat.

But she needn't worry. No Sal.

She finally had a chance to take a good look around. The counter stretched along two whole walls, broken only by a doorway. The way Paolo had led her in that first day. God, that seemed so long ago.

Twin refrigerators—had to be commercial size ate up half the space on the third wall. On the fourth was the door to his office and several large pieces of equipment. She walked closer to investigate.

"My God, is this what I think it is?" She lifted the plastic cover and took in the features. She'd never really done much with them, but if she wasn't mistaken, this was a top of the line electron microscope. Where the hell had he gotten one of those?

The other equipment was just as impressive. All reasonably new, which shot the idea that he'd gotten them second hand or as pieces the university had replaced. These would have *been* the replacements—at a huge cost.

The room was bigger than most lab classrooms. Benches and tables were set randomly around the room. On several, notes were spread out and several test tubes holding what looked like blood. She crossed to look closer.

Italian. She slapped her hand on the table. He was determined to remain an enigma to her. So much for that 'doctor' title. She felt as helpless as a high school freshman walking into a chem lab.

Then it dawned on her.

Sal had a computer. She was familiar enough with Windows to change the default language. At least she thought she could. No harm in giving it a shot and maybe getting off another email to her friends and family before heading back up to bed.

Julia nearly ran to the office and closed, but didn't latch, the door behind her. She wanted to hear if he walked in.

The computer was on and open to what looked like a word processing program. It took her eyes a minute after she sat down and stared at it. It was in English! She could read it!

Email would wait a moment, she wanted to see what he was doing.

She started reading.

Then she scrolled up, horrified.

Leopard data.

Some formula for a serum that altered the DNA through bacterial synthesis. Another that she guessed reversed the alteration.

She scrolled down. More data — including age, sex and estimated weight of the leopards he apparently used in the experiment.

She choked back a sob and stood up, knocking the chair to the floor.

Sal was genetically altering the animals — or at least attempting to. The image of the cat pouncing on her fellow passenger played before her eyes. "Oh, God. No." She backed up.

Escape. Out of here. Out of this house. Out of this godforsaken country. Away from this madman.

She ran, half blinded by tears, toward the doorway.

And directly into a solid wall of man.

He let out a roar worthy of the king of leopards. "What the hell are you doing?"

Chapter 5

Julia let out a scream that was immediately muffled by his hand.

"Shh, dammit. Do you want the whole house to come down here?"

She shook her head. *She* didn't want to be down here. Oh, why had she come, why had she read that? Why did things have to be so damn complicated? Taking a step back she said, "I want out of here. I want to go home. Use your computer to book me a trip home. I'll pay you back as soon as I can get proper ID and — "

"Impossible." Sal blocked her in the office. He stood in the doorway with his arms crossed over his chest. Just a few hours before she'd been mesmerized by the tightness of his muscles and — she forced her eyes upward and met his gaze. His eyes were black, unreadable. Probably pissed off that he'd been found out.

She couldn't believe it. He'd been messing with the cats, altering them genetically. Surely the university wasn't paying him for that! It all raged inside her until her blood boiled. "It's not impossible. You log onto the Internet and you purchase a goddamn ticket. It's how I got here."

Sal shifted and leaned against the doorway with one shoulder. He still blocked her from escaping. "I'm afraid it's not so easy."

It was! She knew it was. Yes, it was Africa, but even the modern world had touched it. Look at the fact that he *had* Internet access. Electricity. Running water. She bet there was a big city nearby that would make her feel like she was back in Albany. How could he just stand there and deny her this?

She was a captive. Plain and simple. For all the passion they'd shared, it really came down to the fact that she was more or less in his possession.

"Let me go!" She flung herself at him with a rush of rage. He'd killed them. By tainting the leopards he'd killed them all. Turned the cats into murderers. She'd been the only one to survive. And he was going to kill her too. Somehow, some way. That's what he wanted.

There was no ticket home. She flung that at him. "You lie. You won't take me home. You intend to keep me here. Probably subject me to the torture you're doing to those poor creatures out there. How dare you, Salvatore. How *dare* you?" Her fists ached as they connected over and over with his chest.

He didn't flinch.

Tears flowed unchecked down her cheeks. Why? She couldn't understand it, but the fight was quickly seeping out of her. She was exhausted. Numb. Aching so bad for all the things she'd miss in life. For the sister that had died too early. For her parents who probably still had no solid evidence on the true fate of their daughters. She imagined the helplessness they had to be suffering. And for herself. For the hopeless feeling of betrayal and doom.

He lifted her up. She didn't even open her eyes. Let him do what he wanted. She was past caring. She wanted peace. Sweet peace.

Sal said nothing. That was good. She didn't want to hear lies.

Julia steeled herself against the tender way he held her, cradling her head against his heartbeat. It thudded against her ear. She knew from its tempo that he was anything but calm.

Another surge hit her as she thought about it. Why *should* he be calm? She just pried into his computer and read sensitive information. Information she was sure could cause problems if the university learned of it. He could do anything to her. Nothing would stop him.

"Put me down," she demanded, squirming to get out of his hold. She didn't want the mad scientist wannabe to even touch her anymore.

His growl vibrated against her cheek. The fingers around her thighs and shoulder had tightened. She'd have bruises there. She pushed away harder. Fear, anger, hate, all built up inside her. If she were a man she'd knock him out. If she had a gun she'd have the balls to fire it.

"I should be the angry one, you know. You shouldn't have meddled in my lab. You were not invited to use my computer. You don't understand the sensitive nature of what you found. *Per l'amor di Dio*, you violated *my* hospitality. And you strike at me?" He finished the sentence in rapid Italian. She trembled now, adrenaline turning her reaction from fight to flight.

He carried her upstairs to his bedroom and dropped her carelessly on the bed. She curled into a fetal ball where she fell, and cried. And by crying, she felt more helpless. She'd just shown him how easily he could manipulate her. It was all nothing but a downhill spiral.

Sal left, turning out the lights and locking the door behind him. Locked in, her tired mind analyzed. Not protected—captive. Like an animal in a cage.

Exhaustion held her down like an iron chain. What good would pounding on the door and screaming do? She didn't expect any of the household staff to defy him, especially when she couldn't communicate to them. All a giant mess.

She sighed and realized all she could do was wait. For what, she wasn't sure.

She slept.

Sal stood outside the door and waited. He'd expected her to demand to be let out—to at least try the door, see if she could. It hung heavy on his heart as he walked away. That was one thing he really admired about her. Julia seemed to have a strong spirit. She didn't waste time worrying when she could be doing.

And he couldn't afford that luxury either. Time was important, for him and now for Paolo. He went back down to the lab.

It was clear she hadn't touched anything, at least to the point of disturbing his important research data. On one desk, the top page of a neat stack of papers was askew and the cover of his electron microscope was pulled up slightly. She'd been curious, but respectful.

For that he was grateful. There weren't enough supplies to restart the research he had in progress. Damn. He ran his hand through his hair. He needed to get to Florence. The university would be expecting him. He'd already pushed back his reports twice—mostly due to the lack of control he had on his own transformations. Now that he'd worked up a serum to keep him human—a serum made from human blood—he had been ready to go.

And then Paolo.

The urge to sweep off the contents of his desk forced him back across the room. Damn! Why had she gone in there? Why had he left the notes, translated to English to keep them from Paolo's prying eyes, up on his screen? He'd had enough time to close the program before he'd changed…but he hadn't thought he needed to. He kicked at a stool and sent it sliding across the floor and into the wall.

God only knows how much she read, or what she understood.

Part of it, obviously. She'd been crying and talking. It hadn't made much sense. Just something about him genetically altering the cats.

No! He'd never do that. But now she thought him some kind of heartless...idiot. She probably had him pegged right up there with the Frankenstein doctor. Dammit, dammit, dammit.

Sal sat and leaned his head against his high-backed leather chair. From here, he solved problems. But not tonight. He stared at the screen. This plan was not going well at all. At least there were a few things he could do to prevent this from happening. Something he should have done before.

He keyed in an email and shot it out to his brother. Sal knew Antonio had enough political pull to get what he needed done. Anger welled back up when he added a little lie about Paolo doing well. Hell, Sal wasn't sure who pissed him off more, Julia or Paolo. Definitely Paolo. At least Julia had an excuse.

He finished the note of half-truth then added something else at the top. Best to have a Plan B.

Feeling about one micrometer better about it, but helpless to do more at this time of the morning, Sal kicked his feet up on the desk and fisted both hands in his hair. Tomorrow he'd have the pleasure of once again postponing his Florence trip. But maybe making a short one to Cairo.

Thoughts slid back to the problem he least wanted to face: Julia. He'd need a lot more than just a PhD to figure out women in general. And then Julia strolled in and destroyed what he thought he knew. She made sex something more than just a physical act. That was definitely new. Sex was supposed to be...instinctive, physical — emotionless. She blew that definition out of the water.

Maybe using sex was a real bad idea. He had the means to make her stay, the least of which he used when he locked her up in his bedroom. But that was not what he wanted. He cared about what she thought. He wanted her to *want* to stay.

What a sucker for a tear. He leaned back and closed his eyes. What *did* he want from her? More sex, sure. But he wanted to see her smile. Wanted to walk in and see her looking for him. He wanted to be the one to make her happy. *Therein lies the problem, Dr. DeMartiano.* Giving her what she wanted would more than likely mean the end of him.

He swore. It was hopeless. Best he could do was try to mend the fences and re-earn some of her trust. He would take her home. But not until he could without fearing for himself. And Paolo. Now he had to worry about *him*, too.

The standard science department screensaver kicked in. As he watched a little computer man put together different color blocks to make a chemical formula, he realized there was one easy fix, at least for his computer. Password protection.

Why couldn't everything be that easy? He got up and twisted the key on his filing cabinet. The hiding place was basic. Accessible. And hopefully too easy for Paolo...or Julia, to find. He hated locking them out. But look what happened when he didn't.

Nothing else could be solved now. It was too late, he was too tired. Mentally and emotionally drained, though he'd not admit it to anyone else. A drink might help. Then he'd go up and see if he couldn't find a place to sleep.

In the kitchen he held the heavy glass bottle in his hand. How long had it been since he'd had the opportunity to just sit and drink until he didn't feel anymore? Probably when he was stuck in California at the university, when his father died. He'd nearly blown it then. Pissed off at the world about losing the person that meant the most to him. Didn't sound so different than the way he felt now.

But he hadn't given up then. Couldn't now. He opened the cabinet and reached for a glass. When he sat it on the counter, he noticed one already in the sink.

Julia. She must have come through here on the way to the lab earlier. His chest tightened. Yet another reason he needed that drink.

He should go check on her. He'd been mean when he should have understood. He was man enough to at least admit that.

Christ. This wasn't right. He was Salvatore DeMartiano. Acclaimed geneticist and researcher for the endangered animals. He stayed in control. Stress wasn't supposed to enter his world, unless it was cutting a deadline close.

But no, here he was in his kitchen in the middle of the night, thinking about the way Julia's mouth had wrapped around the lip of the glass. His cock hardened as he recalled how they'd stood in here less than twenty-four hours before and where that had led. When he was around her, last night a good example, he forgot to think about the big picture, the reason he wanted her to stay. The reason he needed her. If he didn't watch himself, he was liable to forget those reasons now.

He put the clean glass away and lifted hers from the sink. He poured in two fingers of the amber whiskey and swirled it.

He drank. The bitter swig of the alcohol temporarily replaced the ache in his chest.

Nearly two A.M. Another night of no sleep. If the damn genetic alterations didn't kill him his destructive habits would.

Fuck it. He picked the glass back up and poured it half full of the fiery liquid. He was going to die, might as well live while he could.

He heard something. Someone. Very slowly opening the glass sliding doors off the deck. "Son of a bitch," he muttered and abandoned his drink.

Ten to one it was Paolo.

He rounded the corner and saw the unmistakable silhouette of a leopard on the stairs. His blood pressure shot through the roof.

"Paolo," he called. No way was he going up those stairs. Not like that.

The cat paused but its long tail continued to slice through the air behind it.

Sal knew enough about their posturing. Paolo wasn't going upstairs to go to bed. He had a plan. It turned his stomach when he thought of the possibilities. Yet, Sokhra had warned him.

Naturally, he couldn't will himself to change. There was no time to get a hypo. He'd have to fight as a man. Hopefully, all it would amount to was a battle of wills, nothing more.

"Get out of this house in that state." Sal did his best to keep his voice level, even.

The cat turned, crouched to watch him.

Sal took a half step backwards but never broke eye contact. "There's nothing for you upstairs. If you want to hunt and play big, mean leopard, you get your ass outside and survive by tooth and claw. Respect the ways of these creatures. You are a danger to them if you don't."

Paolo leapt from the step and crouched about ten feet in front of Sal. In the light that spilled from the kitchen behind him, Sal looked him over.

He still had adolescent features, but already boasted a few scars along his shoulders and sides. Sal couldn't understand the color mutation that accompanied the transformation. Paolo was as golden as a she-lion, yet his features were pure leopard, including the long bared fangs he displayed to Sal.

It was impossible not to be apprehensive. As a cat, even a young one, Paolo could easily kill him. He had to believe that he still had the conscience not to.

The long leopard tail whipped from side to side as Paolo slinked toward him.

"You have no idea what you're doing to yourself. Every moment you remain in that form, the more you permanently change. The mind's the last thing, you know. Soon you'll be stuck in the cat's body, forever. There'll be no way out, no way to communicate. Nothing. Soon the human aspect of the brain will revert to feline and Paolo will be gone. You'll be one of them, no bigger, no better, no smarter."

Paolo growled and continued to advance on him.

"I can help you." Sal struggled to make his tone sound anything but frantic. But he was easily within pouncing distance. "I have a formula that can fight back against the permanent effects. Eventually I'll figure out how to stop the synthesis altogether. Then we can be normal again. Paolo, it's the only way. Come with me to the lab."

He took two steps backward.

Paolo obviously didn't wish to listen. He launched. Sal fell back, kicking his feet up so they contacted the leopard's chest and forced him to back up. Sal then scrambled backwards and into a half sitting position. "Dammit, the last person you need to hurt is me. Do you think anyone else here is going to protect you? You're a freak, a dangerous freak!"

Sal kicked up again and caught Paolo beneath the chin. A paw swiped at him, laying open his pant leg and digging into calf muscle.

"Go on, get out of the house," Sal said, pointing to the door. "You've made your point. We've been through this before. Tomorrow I'll find you, I'll drag you back and if I have to, lock you in one of the cages in the basement."

Another set of razor sharp nails caught him in the shoulder. Damn, he shouldn't have trusted the boy. He put his hand over the blood that immediately welled to the surface. Paolo could have killed him already if he'd wanted to. Sal recognized the sinister look, but didn't find it deadly, even now. It was more about a teenage boy becoming a man, standing his ground. He'd done the same thing, not in such a dangerous form, of course.

Problem was, Sal really was no match for him, and they both knew it. One more try. "Paolo, I'm going to call your father. He can deal with this. I'm done."

The cat's snarl relaxed. Good. Sal knew he might have leverage there. After Antonio kicked Sal's ass, he'd really lay into Paolo. It'd happened before. Different circumstances, of course. He really didn't *want* to be around when Antonio found out. Neither, apparently, did Paolo. He backed off, tail down in defensive posture.

"Get out of here," he said. The floor creaked above him. Don't let her be up. Don't let Julia start pounding on the door. "Go, now."

Blood rolled down his hand and stained the tan carpeting. His shoulder and leg burned.

The cat turned tail and strolled out of the house. Sal resisted the urge to shout after him. He struggled to his feet and followed him, closing and locking the glass door. He was sure that wasn't the only unlocked way into the house, but he wasn't going to worry about it. There really wasn't any way to lock out Paolo the leopard without locking out Paolo the boy. And he couldn't do that.

He limped as far as the stairs leading to the second floor and collapsed. It felt like a thousand tiny knives were being thrust into his leg with every step. His arm hung limp from the shoulder. Surely the muscle there had been torn. At least his body's system had rendered the area partly numb.

And the blood. Dammit. Sokhra was going to finish the job that Paolo hadn't. A dark trail indicated just where he'd traveled on the light tan carpet. It pooled at his feet even now. He needed to get to the lab to fix it in a hurry. He couldn't afford to lose blood. Especially with Paolo out there. He didn't fear for himself. Paolo was after Julia and he couldn't figure out why.

The stairs looked like a mountain. It pissed him off to be weak like this. He pounded his fist against the step. He couldn't go up there. She'd probably tell him he got what he deserved. That it served him right.

Damn, he hated this. Biting the bullet, he stood and half-dragged himself to the lab. Paolo wouldn't defeat him. Julia? He exhaled. He had no time for that. Their sexual relationship had been great for the eighteen or so hours it had lasted. He wasn't going to play mind games. He had shit to do. Starting with using his own body as a case study yet again.

* * * * *

Julia jerked awake at the sound of someone fumbling at the door. Sal? She held her breath and gripped the sheet she'd finally pulled over herself. What now? She'd woken up several times, once even getting up to try the door when she'd heard a crash below her.

Everything seemed surreal. The incredible sex, what she'd found in the lab, and the confrontation in his office. Her groggy mind couldn't remember what was real and what was dream.

She was supposed to be mad at him. Because of the leopards. What *was* he doing to them? The more she thought about it, the more preposterous it seemed that he did something as basic as inject them with steroids or another basic drug. How would he get close to them? Wouldn't they attack him? And then how did he track what was happening if they ran free?

A scientist, albeit not a practicing one, she understood all the gaps in his research, if what she suspected was true. He seemed much more thorough than that.

Sal opened the door and flipped on the light.

Julia moaned and squinted, shielding her eyes until they adjusted. When they did, her whole body jumped into motion.

"Sal, oh my God. What happened?"

He limped. His pants were bloody from the mid-calf down. Not just spotted—soaked in blood. His shirt was torn from the collar to mid bicep. A white bandage hid whatever damage lay beneath, but it too showed signs of blood seeping through it.

So much for the theory that he didn't deal with wild cats. He'd obviously lost a battle—and luckily not his life—with whatever did this to him. She pushed her opinions and theories aside. This was no time to hurl more accusations or question him. Sal was hurt. His face had lost its color. She grabbed his hands. Icy.

Julia helped him to the bed and pushed him down.

The bandages were sloppy, but did their job of slowing the blood flow. Her own heart pounded at mach five as she lifted the corner of the one on his shin. Three long welts looked like surgical incisions down the side of his leg.

"These need stitches."

"No. No stitches. No scars." His accent slurred so she could barely catch the words.

"Scars? You're worried about scars? You've got to close the wounds. Tell me you had the common sense to clean them out."

He stared at her blankly. Shock. If his shoulder looked anything like his leg, he'd lost a ton of blood already.

She closed her eyes. There could be billions of tiny organisms and bacteria thriving in the seeping flesh. "Stay still. I'm going to get some hot water and soap. I may not be an expert, but I know enough to get this closed up."

Sal grabbed her wrist and held it in a surprisingly strong grip. "No. Just sleep. Lock the door. Will all heal."

Heal? Sleep? There would be no healing and he'd sleep all right. If infection set in, he'd sleep forever.

"Let's get the clothes off, at least." As much as she'd like to take control, there was really little way she could physically force him to do anything.

She swore he grinned. The shirt was easy. At least, it looked that way. As her fingers connected with his bare chest to push the material off, it felt like an electrical current raced up her arm. She wanted to trace the outlines of the muscles that tightened as the shirt slid over them. His breath hitched.

"Am I hurting you?" she asked. But she knew better. The two of them had been extremely aware of each other from the beginning. And there was no switch either of them were going to be able to just turn off. Even under these painful circumstances.

Sal shook his head. He kept his eyes closed as she finished with the shirt and dropped it on the floor beside the bed. She wouldn't look at the hardened black blood rivulets that dried in the light hair of his arm. Or the streaks his shirt had smeared into his chest.

The pants had to come off as well. The leg wound was serious.

"Help me," she fumbled with his zipper.

His hand slid over hers and pushed it against the semi-hard length of him. Great. He was half-conscious, bleeding and horny. "Not now, buddy. I don't think we need to get your blood pressure up any higher until these scab over."

She watched his face. A corner of his mouth turned up. Beneath his pale cheeks, the shadow of his fast growing beard seemed a stark contrast. She didn't want to notice things like that. Sal was hurt.

"Sal, lift your hips," she instructed, using her best teacher voice. "Hold them there, like that while I slide these pants down." He obeyed. Made it so much easier. And she only had to focus on the bulge in the front of his underwear for just a moment.

Not that his muscular thighs were any less distracting. "Are you listening? Stay awake for me." It felt like she was talking to an elementary school student. Geesh. She cleared her throat. "Don't relax, not yet. You've got to talk to me."

"Julia," he moaned.

The texture of his voice slid over her skin. She shivered. Another bad idea. "Okay, listen. I'm going to get your good leg free, then I'll pull this around the one with the bandage. You are listening, right?"

She was on the floor now, kneeling beside his ankles. She couldn't see much beyond his knees and the edge of the bed.

"Sal?"

No answer. Great. Well, then she needn't worry about hurting him. She tugged down pants over both legs and let them fall.

A little bit of the earlier anger crept forward. Here it was, once again, the middle of the night. She hadn't gotten a decent night—or days—sleep since she'd landed here. She was exhausted, on edge and right now she didn't trust Sal any more than the leopard who'd done this to him. And now he'd fallen asleep and left her to tend to him.

It was bullshit. She got up and looked at him. Bad move. Relaxed in sleep, he was beautiful. His features were aristocratic--carved by Michelangelo himself. His dark hair was still too long. And damn, was it sexy as it curled slightly across his forehead.

She reached up to push it out of the way.

Sal's eyes shot open and he grabbed her wrist.

Julia jumped back. "Hey!" Damn, he'd scared her. She took a deep breath and tried not to look panicked.

"Lie with me. Sleep."

"I can't Sal, I've got to clean these out. Do you have a first aid kit? If not stitches, maybe I can use some tape and try to use makeshift butterfly closures. We've got to get them tended to or you'll have more than just scars."

"They'll heal. Need sleep."

He pulled her with his good arm until she was nearly stretched across him. Either that or fight him and end up with a dislocated shoulder.

No. She wasn't going to sleep with him. She didn't want to roll over and bump him...anywhere. "I can sleep on the floor, or even go back to my —"

"No!" Sal struggled to sit up. Color flowed back to his face.

Great, now he'd get his blood flowing and break open the wounds. "Would you just lay down? What are you, some sort of masochist? What animal did this anyway? Why aren't you dead?"

Calm and even, he asked. "Did you want me to die?"

Blame the time, blame the fact that she couldn't hold the damn wall up between them under these circumstances. Damn her for caring. "No." She could answer that honestly. "I didn't want you to die, but why didn't the cat? Was it a leopard?"

Sal's hand still held her wrist in a tight grip. "Leopard, yes. A young one I never would have expected to attack. You'll have to be careful."

Her? Hell, she hadn't anticipated being able to leave the house. Surely she'd be safe within these walls. She wriggled to get off him. The feel of his body, his scent, his breath near her temple. It was too much to keep her from thinking...remembering.

They may have already been lovers, but that was then, before. Now she knew more than she wanted, and realized she didn't know enough to make a judgment call. It was normal for any female to have a mothering instinct. She simply responded to that.

Now why he'd responded to her with the sizable lump in his underwear? She pushed away and averted her eyes.

Her mind ignored her attempts. She fussed about the room, busying her hands with folding up the stained pants while her brain remembered what had happened here—in this room, with this man just a few hours earlier.

Her nipples hardened against her shirt. Her own body was starting its betrayal. It was getting hot in there. "If you won't let me take care of those wounds, then I'm going to my room to see if I can get some sleep. There's still a few hours left. It'd be a good idea if you get some rest, too." Let his housekeeper or whatever she was take care of him. That's how things would be if fate hadn't intervened and stuck her there.

"Julia," Sal whispered. "Don't go."

She'd expected another forceful "no" like the one he'd gasped out a moment ago. Instead he played her like a marionette. And she couldn't resist it. "I need to sleep." She yawned and rubbed her eyes as if on cue. "You have no idea how tired I am. I could just fall over and pass out from it. You can't expect me to just take care of you. And don't *even* think about sex, Salvatore. Though thinking and doing are two different things. And I don't think you're exactly capable of much right now."

She was babbling. God, what a mess she was. She craved a warm bed and a pillow more than air. The frustration of everything she'd endured—the fact that this strange nightmare never seemed to end—it nearly had her in tears.

"Stay with me. I'm cold. Don't go."

Her ears weren't hearing that. Her heart did. This was like straddling the fence. In front of her was what she wanted. The body of a man she'd taken as a lover to curl up next to. A comfortable bed. Safety. Peace.

And with his injuries, she shouldn't have to face the temptation of his seduction. Even if he woke up amorous, by then he'd be hurting so badly he'd forget all about her.

She was so confused!

"Give me a hand," he asked, blinking at her. His dark eyes still didn't seem to focus, but he had surprising strength when she helped him swing his legs up and position himself on his half of the bed. "I want you to stay. Please?"

Sal spoke softly, almost like a pleading little boy. Dammit. How could she just walk away from that?

"All right." She threw up her hands in defeat. "Only because I'm too freaking tired to find my room. And because I'm worried about you." She laid the back of her hand on his forehead. "At least no fever. Good."

And what if he'd had one? Then what? She flipped out the light and felt her way back to the other side of the bed. She didn't undress. Tomorrow she'd either borrow something of Sal's or even Paolo's...and as a last resort, figure out how to put on the native long dress Sokhra had offered when she'd arrived. Tonight clothes would be one temporary barrier she'd put into place.

She lay flat on her back and folded her hands over her stomach. Sal didn't touch her, but she could *feel* him there. A hundred things raced through her mind. He should have taken a pain killer. The leg should be elevated. Shoulder, too. And she never had cleaned it out, even with plain water. She wasn't much help, was she?

Exhaustion was taking over. Her thoughts rambled as she tried to imagine how Sal had escaped the leopard without losing a limb, or his life. The last thing she remembered was the snarling face of the white leopard.

Chapter 6

Julia dreamed Sal was making love to her. She didn't want to wake up, not yet. Not until she'd had her release.

It was like the first time. Only they were lying down. Sal reclined beside her, his hardened cock pushing against her hip. His fingers were the magic, stroking her clit and diving into her pussy. He'd start slow, then speed up until she was nearly wild for wanting him. Then he'd stop, wait, teasing her opening.

Her hips ground upward against his hand. He cupped her with his palm then, rocking his fingers in and out of her.

She moaned and reached for him.

Her eyes shot open.

It wasn't a dream.

"Sal!" she pushed his hand away and pulled the covers over her naked body. She couldn't make words come out, they were caught in her throat at the shock of it.

"Good morning, *l'amore.*"

He reached for her.

She turned away from him and lay on her side. How? How had this happened? Why? She knew how. She craved his touch, the crazy way he set her on fire with just his fingers. Even now her body trembled in anticipation, ready for his thick cock to fill her and take her to the edge.

She didn't get up. Should have, but didn't. Sal was like an intoxicating drug and she needed it, despite the risks she knew she'd take. She took a deep breath and was about to turn to him when his fingers probed between her buttocks and found her core.

A gasp escaped her. Yes. She wanted this. Her body needed this. She pushed her ass at him and relaxed her thighs so he had ready access.

She couldn't keep track of what he was doing to her. She didn't care. All she knew was his fingers were torture and sweet pleasure all at once. He slid them into her, then over her, grazing her clit and slicing electricity all through her. It wouldn't take much more of that before she was begging for release.

"Fuck me, Sal. If you're going to do it, I want you inside me."

He growled and flipped her onto her belly. He was rough, driven by urgency. It made her hotter yet.

"Please Sal, put your cock in me."

He slid one hand under her, pushing through her curls to spread the moisture that dripped from her eager pussy. Then he lifted her onto her knees. Even as the air rushed over her damp skin, she trembled. The wait was killing her. "Now, Sal, fuck me. Please!" she knew she sounded desperate. Dammit, she was.

He slid up onto her, his skin already slick with sweat. The head of his cock rubbed against her ass. She reached up between her legs to position it. When it touched her opening, she nearly cried out with the pleasure of it. "Now," she instructed, bracing her arms as he pushed into her. "Oh!"

Her body contracted and shuddered as he entered her and then began thrusting with urgency. Neither of them could have stopped if they'd tried.

Julia pushed back against him, taking his cock into her as far and hard as she could. He held her hips, yanking her back as he half growled-half moaned. His balls slapped against her, touching her exposed clit. It drove her upwards faster and faster.

"Oh, Sal, I'm coming, fuck me faster. Harder. Sal!" she arched backwards taking him all in and collapsing around him. She panted out moans as her body rocked with spasms that spurred more shocks of pleasure.

Blood roared past her ears. Her pussy trembled and contracted with aftershocks as Sal continued to ram himself into her. "Come, Sal, fill me up. I want to feel your cock explode inside me." As she spoke, she reached between her legs and touched where their bodies joined.

Her own body bucked at the feel of her fingers. But it was for him, not her. She stroked him as he slid in and out of her, then cupped his balls, rubbing them against her clit with each forward thrust.

Her own desire built again. It had never been like this. Never had she been ready and wanting so quickly, with such force.

Sal noticed too. He pulled her up, until she was sitting on his lap.

His breath scorched her neck. "I feel you tighten around me. You make me want to come."

Julia reached down again and touched them both as Sal pulled her up and down on his cock.

"Touch me, touch yourself. God, I love to watch you touch yourself like that."

She obeyed, rubbing her clit then encircling her finger around his slick cock. He moaned.

"Touch yourself, Julia. Make yourself come while I fill your pussy up."

She leaned forward again onto all fours. She wanted him deep, deep inside her. She wanted it hard and fast and incredibly brutal.

"Fuck me, fuck me. Sal, harder!" Julia was out of control. Every ounce of her being had slid down between her legs and all she wanted was release. Frantically, her fingers thrummed her clit. Sweet God, she needed to come.

Sal grunted as he thrust. It almost hurt as he arched into her body with such forcefulness. And she wanted more. "Sal, please, now."

Her body contracted. Sal roared out her name. His fingers cut into her hips as he held her against him with his cock buried deep inside her.

It took several minutes for her labored breathing to slow and for the room to come into focus again. She blinked against the dull morning light and tried to find her bearings.

He rolled over but kept her body against his. Her eyes fluttered shut. She could almost glide back into a peaceful, relaxed sleep.

Damn, Sal was incredible as a lover. But that wasn't supposed to have happened. She hadn't stayed in his room last night for recreational purposes. It was because—"Sal! Oh my God, your leg, your shoulder." How could he have done that? There'd been no indication whatsoever in his lovemaking that indicated he was favoring his wounds.

"They're fine."

Julia winced. The tone wasn't fine. It was short, curt and with it, he'd gotten out of bed, gloriously naked, and walked to his closet doors.

Try as she might, she couldn't see any blood. Even any angry, pink skin and darkened scabs. His bandages were gone.

And, it appeared, so were the injuries.

"Sal?" she asked, fearful now. What was he? Who was he? What happened? Something clicked, which kept her from questioning if she was losing her mind. She had been attacked, bitten by the wild leopard. Yet her wounds had disappeared by the next day.

Sal's had vanished as well. Just like that. He'd turned and she could see both shoulders clearly as he pulled up his pair of pants. From this distance, there was no way to even guess which arm had been laid open by a vicious animal.

To preserve some sense of sanity, she threw back the blanket and inspected his pillow. Reddish brown streaks were there, albeit hard to see against the dark blue of the sheet. Fear notched higher than her curiosity.

"You need to explain some things to me. But I need clothes." Julia hoped her tone of voice left no room for questions.

"What things?"

So that's how it was going to be. She was his little sex toy who shouldn't question anything. No fucking way. "For starters, I want a full explanation why the slices on your shoulder and calf are completely healed today. That can't have been, what? Six hours ago?"

He shrugged. If she hadn't been naked she'd have rushed at him and slapped that mysterious grin off his face.

Sal stood at the door, completely dressed now in a green polo and khakis. As he opened the door to leave, all the magical connection she'd thought they'd shared during their lovemaking emptied.

The door clicked shut. A lock turned.

She threw herself face down in the pillow and screamed.

There was no feeling sorry for herself in her reaction. Mostly frustration. And while she wasn't embarrassed by the way she'd given her body to him, she knew it wouldn't have happened if she'd have known he'd be like this now.

Julia got up and circled the bed. Her clothes lay there in a heap. How had he gotten them off of her without her knowing? Luck? Whatever it was, she'd just have to make sure it didn't happen again.

And what she wouldn't give for one of her suitcases right now. Fresh clothes. She sighed. A clean pair of jeans and a shirt that didn't stick to her would be awesome. Another shower was in order, as well.

There was a bathroom—with a tub, but no shower—adjoining the bedroom. If she was going to be stuck in here, she was going to use it. Enjoy it even. She set the water to hot and inserted the plug. No sweet smelling body soap in this bathroom, but that was okay, she'd make do. The water alone would feel heavenly.

But probably not as good as Sal had made her feel.

Could she not have one predictable thing happen to her? Was it so bad to have some say over her own destiny? In an act of rebellion she did something she'd never even imagine doing as a guest in someone's house. She yanked open the bi-fold closet door and assessed his clothes.

Holy crap! She'd expected a row of dress shirts, semi-casual pants or khakis and long white lab coats. What she found was a variety that rendered her speechless. A tux? Where the hell would he wear a tux here? There had to be a half-dozen suits. She didn't check the tags, but bet they were brand name. And he had jeans! Why didn't he wear them?

The closet was meticulously organized. That was probably the only thing that wasn't a surprise. Shirts on one side, arranged from dress to casual. She fingered through the t-shirts. Surely he wouldn't begrudge her—

"What the hell are you into now?"

Julia screamed and pulled out a shirt to clutch to her bare breasts. Thankfully it was long enough to keep her from feeling entirely exposed. "J-just looking."

He lifted a thick eyebrow.

She pointed to the bathroom. "I'm…going to take a bath. I, uh, wanted something clean to wear."

"Then go ahead."

No way was she going to walk past him like that. He'd watch her bare ass as she walked across the room. But if she didn't do something quickly, the tub would overflow. "Do you mind?"

He straightened and crossed his arms over his chest. Obviously, he did.

She sucked in a deep breath, turned around and pulled the shirt over her head. A little shorter than she'd like, but if she kept the hem stretched down, it should cover just enough.

His laugh followed her to the bathroom.

God, she wanted to be majorly irritated. In a way, she was. In another, she knew it was almost like flirting. He treated her like his lover. There was no lack of respect in this little spar, despite the way he'd roared in. After all, she would have done the same thing.

She closed the door firmly behind her and smiled. Not that it'd matter. She didn't even bother with the lock. Sal would barge in regardless. It wasn't going to stop her from enjoying the hot, relaxing water.

"Julia?" he called through the door just as she stepped into the steaming liquid.

"Hmm?" Those bubbles would come in handy now. That way if he did come in she'd have some sort of cover. Now? The water probably worked like some distorting magnifying glass.

"I was hoping to talk to you. There are a few things I should explain."

She chewed her bottom lip and debated the sharp retort on her tongue. She had always had a bad habit of striking out. She wanted answers, yes, but even more so, she wanted what they had together, without this complicated stuff messing it up. But it was a little late for that.

"Julia?"

She stared at the tiled ceiling. And they said women were impossible to understand. Had to have been a man that made that comment. She took a deep breath. "Go ahead and come in, Sal. Just talk—that's it. Don't get any other ideas."

Sal steeled himself against the vision he knew he'd find when he opened the door. After last night and this morning, he should be at least temporarily satisfied. Hell no, he wanted her more than ever. And well, now would be good.

Only there was something he needed to confess. His conscience had beat him up over it. He felt guilty as hell. He needed to make her understand why he'd done what he'd done to her.

Plan A was history. This was no simple seduction. Didn't know why he'd thought it would be. Plan B was simply getting her to trust him. Not quite an easy feat at the rate he was going. Hopefully, a little honesty would start mending their out-of-bed relationship. If he played it just right, he could even convince her to help him out.

He pushed open the door and kept his eyes on the floor. At least he tried to. The light hitting the water created a reflective play of light on the walls and ceiling. And he looked.

Bad, bad move. He'd seen her naked before, yes, but only while he was driven by lust and had one single motive. Not that that motive didn't exist—it was alive and well and residing in his pants. It was a little different now. She lay with her head back, eyes closed. Or maybe not. Her eyelashes fluttered just slightly. No, she watched him. As he appraised her, she watched.

"Go ahead. Bathe. I won't touch you. Even though I'd like to." He figured it was what she needed to hear. He didn't want to touch her. He wanted to *be* the water that glided smoothly over her skin. He wanted to kiss where her knees emerged like mountains above the ocean. The water that lapped her breasts would have the slightest tang from the salt in her skin.

He'd taste that. Someday.

"Are you done staring?"

He loved that. She had a spark that hadn't gone out, despite the pile of dirt life had shoveled onto her recently. He knew she mourned. One look at her and he could see the shadows that never left, even when she smiled. And she'd cried at night. He hadn't meant what had happened this morning. He'd gotten close to hug her, comfort her. But when their bodies touched…he sat down on the closed toilet lid and glared at the door.

Concentrate, Salvatore. This isn't about your cock. This is about honesty and the truth, no matter how bizarre she's going to think it is.

"About the leopard last night," he started, rubbing at a shadow on his pant leg with his thumb. "It, uh, well, you saw the damage."

She sat up. He covered his eyes. If he looked at the way the water dripped off her breasts…he licked his lips, wishing he could take those rosy nipples in his mouth. "Either stay under that water or get out and get dressed. You have no idea how distracting you are."

He had to shift the way he was sitting. Damn it. How could he talk when she was naked and wet and not six feet away from him?

The water splashed. She'd gotten out. He wouldn't look. It'd kill him, but he wouldn't.

"Okay."

Christ Almighty. Long, wet legs stuck out from beneath his T-shirt. It was damp in places and stuck to her body in a way that should be illegal. Even her face was beautiful. She seemed totally unaware of how sexy she looked with the way her hair curled up where the ends had gotten wet.

"There's some drawstring pajama pants in the third drawer of my bureau. Go put them on."

She started to lean down to let the water out. He stopped her. No way was he going to be able to take it if she bent over in front of him. "I'll see to that," he said. "Get dressed."

So this was payback for earlier? He shouldn't have left, but he was in no condition to talk then, either.

At the rate things were going, talk wasn't what they were going to do.

He popped the plug, picked up her towel and counted to ten. That should give her enough time to get decent. Then he'd stand with his back to her so she couldn't entice him any more. At least not until he got what he had to say out.

"Sit down," he said as he walked into the room. He sighed in relief as she jumped up on the bed and sat cross-legged.

"You know as well as I do what happened yesterday."

"Last night, you mean? No, Sal, I don't. I know you came in here with half-ass bandages over cuts that would take months to heal completely. Those wounds, whatever they were, were red and bleeding and needed stitches. Then this morning you've barely got a blemish. It's not right. What the hell *are* you?"

"A scientist. I want to talk to you about what I've discovered."

"The miracle cure-all?" She threw back her head and laughed. This was what he feared. This reaction. Not just from her, from everyone, everywhere.

"What if I said it was? What if I said that it's what had cured you when the white leopard bit you?"

He hated the stab of pain and shock and denial that flashed over her features. Blood drained from her face. Her eyes widened before she closed them against him, but he could have sworn he saw the glisten of tears. Worked like a sword through his side. He wanted to take it all back and pretend it hadn't happened.

"You said it hadn't—"

He expected that. "No, I asked you to prove that it had."

"Why? Why did you, if you knew it attacked me and you were the one to cure me of it? Why did you—you bastard!" Julia stood up and stormed up to him. With a finger pointed at his chest, she continued, "You sent Paolo to town to 'rescue' me, didn't you. You dropped me there and then made yourself look like the big hero. Oh, my God. I can't believe this."

She whirled and paced the room. "So who's the damn cat, Sal, your precious pet? Did you sic him on me? So then you could be some other big hero? Oh wait, I got it, you wanted someone to be your test dummy. Someone that it wouldn't matter if it worked or not. Because if I died, you'd just throw me to the leopards and claim I got killed in the plane crash if anyone asked, right?"

He hadn't worked it out like that. Part of it, yes, but he knew the serum wouldn't kill her. But he doubted she was receptive to hearing that. He wasn't real interested in answering her. He had to bite his tongue to keep from lashing out verbally as it was.

"So, was it your darling pet, Snow, that turned on you?"

"No," was his flat answer. He couldn't tell her about Paolo. Not yet. "Can I explain?"

She'd slowed her pacing and paused, leaning against the raised mattress with her arms crossed. "Oh sure, go ahead. I'm sure you've got some fabulous speech planned."

He bristled. He wasn't violent. Never had been. But he wouldn't get knocked around either. And she was starting to really push buttons. "About the serum." He unclenched his teeth before continuing. "It's really about the leopards here. They have an amazing healing rate—the natives swear one actually regrew a leg that had been torn off by a trap."

"Oh get real."

"You think I'd set this up to study one pack of about thirty or so leopards?" He waved his hand. It had cost him a bundle to build this place. More than money, he'd spent years fighting for the right to study right here. "Regeneration in mammals. That's incredible. How could I not learn the language and listen to legend and watch for myself?"

She shook her head. "So then what? Obviously you've got it bottled. Why isn't it on Wal-Mart's shelves?"

"What?"

She frowned and shook her head. "A store. Get to your point."

Was she not listening? Of course, he was talking scientist. What made perfect sense to him probably sounded like Greek to her. This wasn't a lab partner or colleague he was talking to. "I gathered information, I took blood and fecal samples. Even ran a few DNA tests.

In the end I found the enzyme that's present in these leopards but no others."

"Really?" Julia leaned her chin on her hand and looked like she believed about two percent of what he was telling her. Still, he should have done this in the beginning.

"Never mind. I know that stuff doesn't interest you anyway. Just know that I'm not anything special — we both just got a sample of the drug that's going to change the world."

She blinked. At least she had the decency not to laugh — this time. "You really think it's what you say it is?"

Sal jerked up his pant leg. "You're denying this? What about your shoulder? You mean you didn't feel that? You don't remember what it felt like to have those teeth sink into you?"

Julia cringed. "Why didn't it kill me, the leopard, I mean? Why didn't the one who attacked you kill you? They killed the others." She tilted her face into her hands and shook with tears.

That answer would come. He knew even these basic details about what he'd discovered — the magic cure-all, she'd called it — would be too much for her to handle hearing. The idea was preposterous; even he failed to comprehend how it would impact daily life and health care. He just knew it'd be big. And he wasn't doing it for the money. He had enough of that, thanks to his father. He swallowed. Too bad he hadn't figured this out before his father got sick. This might have — would have — helped.

He plunged into the rest of the story, knowing he had to. "About Snow..."

No, he didn't have to. He could keep it a secret and let it go. She'd never figure it out.

Julia lifted her tear-streaked face. "What about it?" Her anger worked like a flare. She started with a white hot flash and then settled into a steady flame.

"The white leopard, remember?"

"Yeah, Snow. Why do they call it Snow, anyway?"

"Do you think many of these people have seen real snow? I mean, unless they travel up into the mountains, there's not exactly a large amount of snowfall in Africa."

She rolled her eyes at him.

"Because a pure white leopard is as rare as snow. It's just never seen. And obviously the color helped it get its name."

She nodded. "Listen, I'm sorry. But this is...I don't know. I just want to go home. I want normalcy. I want predictable. My job, my house, my routine. I miss that."

He didn't doubt that for one moment. He'd mentally imagined what it'd be like in her shoes a time or two, and he honestly couldn't imagine dealing with what he'd expected of her. "And I'll get you back soon. I've just had a few setbacks. One of which relates to the white leopard."

"See? I knew he was your pet. You've got him at your beck and call, huh? Or did he turn on you?"

"He is me."

"You *are* crazy, that cat doesn't think, rationalize like we do. Our pets are pets — they can learn tricks and obey commands and even read our body language, but they can't think like we can."

She didn't get it. His blood turned to ice as he said it again. "No, Julia. I am Snow. I am the white leopard."

He expected shock, wide-eyed, open-mouthed shock. Perhaps a scream. It wouldn't have surprised him if she'd launched at him or ran from the room. None of those things happened. When he looked up, he saw her blink at him. Her eyes glittered, then the corners of her mouth turned up. She finally threw her head back and laughed.

"You?" she gasped. "The leopard?" She hopped up on the bed and wrapped her arms around her middle. "You've got to be kidding me. What do you think I am, some child?"

He didn't find her reaction at all amusing. There went his blood pressure. Again.

"You know, Sal," she said, still muffling her laughter. "Perhaps you should see a shrink when you get back to Italy. You're starting to think some pretty weird stuff. I mean, I understand how you want to believe this miracle cure stuff, but I just can't buy that it's that simple. As far as you—" her hair fell down around her face and hid her features. Her shoulders shook.

"Dammit, Julia, I'm trying to be serious here."

"Serious, Sal? Then tell me the truth. The truth. Or is that too freaking top secret? Are you even legit? I mean, what I read of that crap on your computer is full of holes. How can you possibly do research without test animals, without ground work, a control. Even if you tell me that precious white leopard of yours is your control, I'm sorry to say you've let him become tainted — because I've seen him running loose on several occasions."

What had he started? "Maybe I should start at the beginning."

"No, Sal, I don't think you need to. I know enough to realize that I can't believe anything you tell me anyway. So far you've lied about going home, hell, you probably never sent that email — you wrote it in Italian, remember? You've lied about knowing about the white cat attacking me. You've admitted to injecting me with some experimental drug with God knows what for side effects. And now you say to me 'it's the breakthrough of the century and by the way I'm a freaking leopard myself'?"

She got up and stormed out of the room.

Chapter 7

"Julia, wait."

She was gone.

"Why?" he asked up to the empty room. What a fool. Had he lost his mind? Why had he even begun to think she was ready to hear something so...off the wall?

Because he wanted her to accept him for who he was. For what he was. Maybe to help him escape that curse. Because somewhere in his fantasy driven mind, he'd imagined a life with Julia there.

Not with her back in the United States where she wanted to be.

And she was dead right about what he'd given her to hold on to. He'd intentionally kept everything he could from her. Yeah, protecting himself. From what? He didn't feel so safe now.

Thing was, he knew his decision, initial decision, had been sound. What he hadn't counted on was finding he cared what she thought of him, what she wanted. He hadn't planned to care. No way was he going to hurt over this.

Yet he did — a physical pain weighed heavy on his chest.

His stomach turned over. No. Couldn't be.

Her clothes lay in a pile beside the bed, where he'd dropped them after slipping them off her. She'd been so asleep, like an angel. Doing that had been wrong, yes, but how could it be when it was so right between them? She hadn't complained in the end. She'd begged for him.

He picked up the shirt. The shoulder still bore the tears the leopard's, *his*, teeth had made in the silky fabric. He shouldn't have told her about that.

Sal tossed the clothes back on the floor and looked around. How it happened, where it happened, he had no clue.

But he was in love with Julia.

* * * * *

Julia raced from the house as if demons chased her. Or leopards. At this point, there wasn't much difference to her.

She ran past a beautiful flower garden. Exotic to her, probably native to the region. But she didn't want to see pretty things. In all honesty, she didn't know what she wanted — or where she was going.

Half of her screamed for solitude — a small dark capsule with no stimuli. Then maybe she could sort through all the messes in her head. And her heart, dammit. No way could she make love with someone and not involve her heart. But what did that mean in this case?

She stopped about thirty feet beyond the edge of the manicured lawn, and leaned against a tree. The density of the foliage, at least, offered some protection from the heat. It was peaceful here. Because, she realized after a moment of thinking, it felt familiar. Her parents had retired to Florida when she was in graduate school. She'd spent many vacations there, helping her father clear walking or horse trails in the wooded acreage they'd bought. If she didn't concentrate too hard, she could almost fool herself into believing she was there, just off one of the side walking trails, waiting for her parents to catch up.

But she wasn't. They weren't coming. And she wasn't home in Albany, New York either, where houses and buildings replaced the towering trees. She was stuck. *Stuck.* More than an ocean away from all those things she craved. It'd be different if she had the option of going home. Or if she knew for sure there was a way home. Then maybe she could consider herself on vacation and do a little sightseeing, maybe learn something about the culture. The things she had planned to do on her visit with Chelly.

Julia choked back a sob and ignored the sharp bark against her back as she slid down into a sitting position. Chelly was gone. Julia hadn't been able to say the things she wanted to. Chelly hadn't gotten to live — she'd just been married. She and her husband were so alive with talk of starting a family. Nothing left. Nothing.

As if mourning with her, a bird screeched somewhere over her head. She looked up, but the brightness of the sun shining through the trees blinded her and made it impossible to see anything in the shadowed canopy right beneath it.

Slowly the rest of nature came alive around her. Maybe she'd just tuned in. Maybe the creatures around her had accepted she wasn't going to harm them. If that was the case, they were entirely right. She was nothing but a helpless fool. A danger only to herself.

Ants marched past, carrying leaves and twigs on a mission to somewhere. A bush about six feet from her feet moved. She shuddered. No way was she going to look to see what it was. She'd freak if it were a snake, even one fleeing her. Surely she'd scream and then Sal would have to save her...again.

She groaned. Sal.

She knew her thoughts would eventually settle on him. How could they not? Unlike the ants, she didn't *have* a mission here. Her life had always been driven by an ultimate goal. But now she had none, other than getting home. She'd been biding her time, enjoying recreational sex... Who the hell was she fooling? Up until he'd started babbling about the miracle cure and being a leopard, she might have admitted she was starting to fall in love with him.

Now she just felt like the helpless prisoner of a madman.

Julia picked up a stick and threw it at the tree to her left. Something small scurried away. Okay, so maybe she wasn't harmless, and perhaps not helpless either. After all, she'd just saved herself from being eaten by the African version of the chipmunk.

She smiled. On the right track now. She should be ready to survive in the open savannah any moment.

Thing was, she *was* a survivor. No one ever doubted that she'd get done what needed to be done. That she could overcome all and succeed. Failure had never been part of her vocabulary. Yet she'd already failed to see the danger in getting her heart involved.

So how to keep this from turning into the biggest failure of her life?

Defining what it would mean to succeed.

That was supposed to be the easy part. Like mapping a course. Usually the goal was what gave people drive, motivation. She got up and walked toward the sound of water.

Her only goal was to get home. And that was quickly becoming about as possible as getting to the moon. Not that she'd give up, no, but that quest alone was no longer enough to sustain her. She couldn't trust Sal. So she'd have to find another option. That would take patience.

What could she do in the meantime?

In front of her, the stream forked. The thicker branch wound its way behind the house — she'd seen it from the window. The smaller arm was little more than a bubbling brook. As she followed it, looking for a place to cross, she noted that the rocks and roots that rose up to disturb it didn't keep the water from continuing on its destination.

See? Even the water had a place to go. And nothing stopped it.

She hated the lost feeling.

She hated being someone's marionette.

And she hated not being able to say that she hated Sal, despite all he'd said and done.

She reached up and rubbed her shoulder. How could he be telling the truth? Why hadn't anyone else ever discovered this miracle cure? How had *he* found it? This was major!

Of course, political and economical uproar would accompany it. And that would be major, too. Years of whispers circulated about the cure for cancer being available but not released because of the loss the doctors and hospitals would feel because of it—this could potentially be worse.

But that was all U.S. stuff. Who knew if there was any truth to it. Sal was from Italy. Maybe they'd handle things differently.

Julia bent down and let the water roll over her hand. *If* he were telling the truth. *If.* Then she should try to learn as much as she could. Just in case.

The in case what, she didn't care to think about. Julia stood up, satisfied with creating a small goal for herself. Now she'd need to figure out the 'how'...but that would be fine. It would keep her busy. Until she could leave. And then maybe she'd take more than memories with her.

Still, she was reluctant to head back up to the house. She didn't want to face Sal. Not yet. Not until she was sure she could without remembering the passion between them. She needed to be sure she could face him without her body reacting.

And it wasn't that she didn't want to continue their physical relationship. Her body ached for him even now. He took her to places she'd never experienced. Something in the way they connected caused her to expose her entire soul to him. She couldn't continue to take the risk that went with it. Sex alone would be fine...if it could remain simply a physical act, nothing more.

It was already too late for that.

Two goals now. While neither was completely compelling, it did give her renewed confidence as she followed the deeper water upstream. As she expected, she found the wall. High walls made of clay bricks that either protected or encased Sal's property. Why? So many questions. Still, logically, anyone living in a place as wild as this would want protection. Without the walls, she'd never feel safe walking as she did. They'd be in danger of any number of predators every time they left the house.

Maybe she was making too much of it. Maybe she was seeing things where things didn't exist.

She hated the doubt, the unsure perspective. She wanted to reach up and rub Sal's influence right out of her eyes so she could see things the way they were. Then understand and decide—for herself—whether to accept or reject them.

Julia leaned against the cool wall and closed her eyes. At the rate she was going, she'd end up back at the house more confused than settled.

* * * * *

"Go away," Julia shouted at the door when someone knocked.

Truth was, she was dying for company. Even a good book—she could care less what genre or if she'd read it before. But answering the door would not satisfy her quest for companionship. Only Sal could provide it at this point and there was just no way she was facing him right now.

She'd been asleep. Dreaming.

Erotically dreaming.

Only this time she hadn't woken up to find him teasing and pleasing her body to heights she hadn't known existed. No. She'd awakened tight and tense with wanting. The way the seam of her pants slid across her fluid-slicked clit as she pushed the covers back with her feet had her moaning.

Her sexual imagination wouldn't win any creative awards. But that didn't matter. What was missing was from lack of experience rather than lack of interest. And already Sal had taken her to levels she'd never known before.

While sleeping, she'd imagined the feel of Sal's tongue against her inner thigh, teasing, taunting. She'd moaned and begged, pushed against his head to make him kiss the folds and ultimately, her swollen bud.

Her hand slid between her waistband and skin damp from sweat. If she couldn't have him, she'd do it herself.

Whoever was at the door knocked again.

Dammit! She got up and straightened her clothes. The bedding was twisted around her ankles. The nap she'd taken in hopes of recharging had only managed to short circuit her ability to think about anything but her own starving sexual appetite. And it was her own fault—she had to deal with this because she told herself she couldn't have it.

Julia pushed a hand through her hair to get it out of her eyes and jerked the door open. A girl she hadn't seen before blinked at her.

"What?" Julia barked. Then closed her eyes. Last thing she needed was to take it out on the people there to help her. The poor girl held a tray of food. "I'm sorry." She opened her eyes and tried to smile. "I'd fallen asleep. Nightmares."

Of course, the doe-eyed girl simply blinked. At least she hadn't thrown the food and run.

Julia accepted it and locked herself back in the room, the bedroom she'd occupied the first night she'd stayed in the house. No way was she going to stay in Sal's bedroom. Even if it had its own bathroom.

She ate, satisfying one hunger. The other gnawed at her. The more she tried not to think about it, the more the images in her head went from flashbacks of earlier lovemaking to possibilities for the future.

Finally, she'd flipped on every light in the room and started investigating.

As she expected, the room was more sterile than a hotel room. At least if she had pen and paper she could take notes, start documenting or at least journaling her days in Africa.

Dresser was empty—cleanly empty. Not even a dust bunny to keep her company. Nightstand the same, except for a spare light bulb. At least she wouldn't be stuck in the dark.

Another hour in this room and she'd be stark raving mad.

But no way was she going to face Sal. Maybe, just maybe she could get Paolo to understand what she wanted. Paper and pen. It'd be a start.

She gathered up her dishes and escaped to the kitchen. It looked as clean and unused as it had in the middle of the night. Made her half homesick for her cluttered countertop. Dammit, she missed living out of the dishwasher. She missed being able to go straight to her stash of chocolate when she needed it. She wanted to go home.

One thing it didn't look like Sal had equipped this castle with was a dishwasher. And for once in her life, she was glad. If she went slow, she could kill what? Ten minutes cleaning up her used cutlery and bowls? Sure.

Halfway through her menial task, something out the window caught her eye. Something white. On the other side of the hedges.

"No," she breathed even as she stood on tiptoes and strained to look out. Then let out the air in her lungs. No, it wasn't the white leopard. Just a gardener with a white shirt. "Good," she said out loud while scrubbing the pattern off the bottom of the bowl.

Damn, was she a mess.

She rushed through the rest of the dishes and wouldn't dare look outside again. She was absolutely not disappointed it wasn't the leopard. Of course, at this point, she wasn't sure the leopard existed. Snow, anyway. And if it did, it was nothing more than a genetic anomaly. An albino. Rare, sure, but there were white tigers, why not white leopards, right?

Julia opened every cabinet in the kitchen while putting the dishes away. Not a damn pen in sight. Or paper. It was as if they were intentionally keeping her in this sterile prison and she hadn't realized it yet. Well, she did now.

The clock on the wall indicated just how much time she'd wasted. And how much left to go before it'd be reasonable to go to bed. No TV, no books, no paper, pen, telephone, computer, people.

Was this what it was like in solitary confinement? Was someone trying to break her? Why?

* * * * *

Sal listened to Julia as she banged around the kitchen. He'd gotten to the door, ready to ask Sokhra what the hell she was doing, but then heard Julia's voice. He'd waited. But never heard anything in return.

Talking to herself?

He'd done a lot of that lately himself. Since she'd arrived, his concentration had disappeared. Today started with spilling a vial of the precious pure blood that he had so little of. Which meant he'd ruined what potentially could have been two treatments for Paolo. With that his sour temper had further deteriorated.

Now the reason he couldn't focus stood merely five feet from him and was separated by a few pieces of thin wood. He could yank open the door and snatch her into his arms and hold her there. Let her fight. Let her cry. Let her deny that it was where she wanted to be. He could take her and possess her and make her his. If he wanted, he could keep her here forever.

He could. But he didn't.

It'd be a bittersweet victory and he had no earthly idea what he'd do with the trophy. Right now he needed to get her out of his head so he could make headway. So much to do.

Sal looked back over his shoulder. He'd printed out every note he had made on the serum that reversed the transformation. The key was to stop the synthesis of the bacteria that had been injected into the body. As long as the bacteria were there, working, the changes were happening. And any time he...or Paolo...was in leopard form, the synthesis happened even faster.

Easy in principle. He'd had no trouble figuring out how to retard the bacteria's effectiveness. But to stop them, eliminate them? This wasn't like a common cold...wait a minute. Sal leaned against the doorframe and closed his eyes.

Why wasn't it? Was he stupid or just trying too hard?

Shit. He had work to do. And of course, none of the supplies he desperately needed. Supplies. It'd cost him more than he'd normally be willing to pay, but it wasn't about himself anymore. It was about Paolo. And there was little he'd be willing to sacrifice to save the boy, regardless of the kid's disregard for himself.

First things first. He needed to get the items in his hands, immediately. Sal swallowed and looked toward the door. Damn it. Antonio would question getting two emails in one day, but he didn't care. He needed fresh blood, several antibiotics, general supplies and what else? Normally he'd have a list nearby to work from. He wondered if he should get some items for Julia...no, he didn't have time for that. He punched up another email address, to his sister-in-law,

Carlotta, this time. He needed a few favors anyway, and didn't she know someone in customs? He'd have to call in all his favors to pull off what he was thinking.

He typed in his request, noting that he'd already sent a standard supply order to Antonio. He'd have to sound like this was a normal correspondence. He had to mention Paolo. Tricky to word that to sound positive without lying.

Then his fingers paused over the keys. Bad thing was, he didn't know what Antonio had told Carlotta about Julia. Chances are, he'd said something when Sal had asked for a third return ticket.

His hand shook as it poised his finger over the send button. He couldn't figure out why he was so rattled. What was the issue here? Was he that afraid his brother would see through his requests and question why he needed those supplies, faster than immediately? Or was he concerned that they might guess about his relationship with Julia?

He clicked send. Fuck it. So what? Like he couldn't take a little ribbing from his big brother. Sal had never committed himself to life in a monastery. Antonio may have an opinion, but really no say in what he did with his private life.

That done, he sat back in his chair and kicked his feet up. Like he had time for leisure. He ought to be out there, getting as much done—both in general lab work and in paperwork instead of lounging. But for the first time all day, he felt a little more in control.

Sokhra woke him from that position nearly two hours later.

"Your woman, she's locked in her room, crying. What is going on? You are not working, things are not right."

Sal rubbed his eyes and dropped his feet to the floor. "No, they're not right. I'm low on supplies, which means I don't have enough to treat Paolo even if he'd let me. I've informed his father he is up to his rebellious ways. I'll be going to Florence soon, or at least Cairo to pick up supplies. Perhaps as early as tomorrow. And I'm not sure what to do with Julia."

"But—you can't. What if..." her voice trailed off. Eyes were wide with shock. He knew what she thought. What if he became a leopard? On the plane? In the airport? It could be a sure death for him.

"And Paolo? I fear for him too," she continued. "My boys may never come back. Then what?"

"I'll come back, Sokhra. I always do. Paolo won't be going this time."

Sokhra tapped her foot and crossed her arms. Not hard to determine that stance. "And the lady? You will take her or leave her behind?"

Ah, the question of the hour. "I have no papers for her yet. If I leave now, how will she go? They will not let her into the airport without identification."

"It is wrong, Salvatore. You cannot force her to stay here. We are not her people."

He repeated, tired of running through this in his head and now out loud. "I don't want to force her to do anything, but how will I get her out of here? You know how strict it is, she has nothing. No identification, no passport. And I did not report her to the Sudanese government as a survivor of the plane crash." He hadn't admitted that to Sokhra, but he assumed she knew.

"Why?" Her voice held no surprise.

He'd have to come up with a good answer for that. Why indeed? Julia's answer would point out the convenience of not having to worry about a trail if she died from whatever he'd inject her with. That, he knew, was as false as could be. But no way did he want that question to even come up. He didn't experiment on anything—other than himself. And that was purely out of means of survival. And even that was taboo.

So what would he tell them?

Or how to get around telling them?

"Sokhra," he teased, trying to steer away from the interrogation. "You sure know how to make a bad situation seem worse."

She didn't bite. "Your vision is clouded with the presence of that woman. Keep to your priorities. Your nephew, he needs you."

Sal bit his tongue as she left. He probably deserved that. And no way could he deny that she was one hundred percent right.

He got up and stretched. His back ached from too many hours standing over a microscope as he'd stared unseeing at the bacteria there. Things were stalled. He needed to make something happen.

Chapter 8

Sal opened the door but couldn't make himself go any farther.

Damn he hated being torn between wanting to do something, needing to do something and realizing what he couldn't do.

Even if he went upstairs to try talking to Julia, he'd fail. She'd made it clear that she didn't trust his words. Hell, he'd admitted something vitally important and she'd laughed at him. Trust? There was no trust there, despite his misconception that there had been.

He stepped back out of the doorway and closed the door, locking himself in the lab. He couldn't fix Julia's problems. His problems. He shook his head and stared out the window. There was nothing wrong with Julia. Hell, in reversed positions he'd act the same...no, no he wouldn't. He'd be violently demanding to go home and make a royal ass of himself in the process.

Someone else had problems too. Paolo. The day was fading. Sunlight would disappear in just over an hour and Paolo would wake up and start his roaming. Sal was worried. The boy wouldn't come near the lab on his own. And it wasn't like Sal was going to get close enough to administer the shot while his nephew was in leopard form.

So he'd have to do it by force. Ethically wrong, but fuck ethics at this point. This was his own flesh and blood. He loved Paolo like he was a son. The rebellion had hurt, but nothing compared to the way he was self-destructing right now.

Sal stomped across the floor and yanked open the refrigerator. It sickened him to see it so bare. As soon as he dealt with Paolo, he'd exhaust all his raw materials to make more. He prayed his brother came through for him soon.

With the hypodermic loaded and ready, Sal climbed the stairs and paused in front of the first door. He didn't like that Julia had returned to this bedroom. Paolo was too close to her. The boy, or leopard, could get into her room before Sal had a chance to know what was going on.

And what the hell did Paolo want with her, anyway?

A door opened farther down the hall.

Paolo looked half his age as he groggily blinked. "What's with the way you pounded up the stairs?" he growled and then slammed the door.

The picture of Sal's parents regarded him from the end of the hallway. "Forgive me," he muttered in their direction, knowing he and his brother challenged them in the same way Paolo did him.

Without hesitation he pushed open Paolo's door.

"Get out!" the boy yelled.

Sal froze. The room was destroyed. The walls were scored with nail marks, the bed and pillow shredded. Dresser drawers had been pulled from the base and their contents covered the floor. Where the light gray carpet showed through, he could see blood and mud stains.

Sal relaxed his hand before he broke the needle in half. What he'd rather do was break the boy into several pieces. But that wouldn't solve anything. "This..." his voice wavered. "This is not acceptable. This is not your house—"

"And you're not my father."

"No, Paolo. I'm not. If I were, I'd probably be even more pissed and less hurt. Be glad of that. Be very glad."

"Like I'm scared."

Sal rocked back on his heels and forced his breathing to remain easy. Christ, he remembered saying the same thing. And nothing came to mind about what answer would thwart this sudden hate toward him. "Thing is, Paolo," he said, hoping at least part of his speech got through the boy's thick stubborn skull. "I am scared. Of you? Sure. You're reckless and dangerous and have no business screwing up your body the way you do."

"But—"

Sal jerked up his free hand. "Wait! You are going to give me the 'I'm a man' speech. Trust me, I tried it too. It doesn't work. You're *almost* a man, Paolo. Physically, you're almost grown. Mentally? Right now Paolo, you're rebelling like an adolescent. Real men look at the future and base their now decisions on long-term goals, not short-term bouts of fun."

"So that's why you kidnapped Julia and are using her as a fuck toy."

Sal lunged at Paolo. No way was the boy talking to him like that. Not now, not ever. A freight train roared through his head, followed by a sharp pain that sent electricity arching through every cell in his body.

Sal had to get the serum into the boy. Now. Before it was too late. If he could get the needle deep into the muscle, it'd be good enough.

Weight gave Sal the benefit. Paolo must not have thought Sal would attack the way he did, because he defended himself rather than striking back.

Time was running out.

Sal lifted the hypo and plunged it into Paolo's thigh.

He got about half the liquid in before his fingers failed to work. Half. Was that a success or a failure? He screamed the final stage of the change and fell to the floor.

Paolo swore at Sal and yanked the needle from his leg.

Sal stretched, catlike, but never took his eyes off the boy. There was a sharp hint of the boy's fear in his nostrils. The tides were turned.

He'd never strike out the way Paolo had at him. But Paolo didn't know that. Sal left the next move up to his nephew.

Paolo started talking. Stuttering.

"All that preaching and look at you. You're just like my dad, nothing but a hypocrite. That's all I hear at home: Can't do this, can't do that, but then I get to sit and watch my father do it right in front of me."

Sal lifted a paw and licked it. He'd heard about this before. Knew it was a dead end argument.

"And what's with the girl anyway? You gonna kill her? Turn her into one of us? I kinda wish you would, I might get to mount her then. You get all the fucking fun." Paolo spit out the last part of the sentence and hurled the needle toward his uncle.

Sal sidestepped the hypo and eased forward. The room was small. The mess made it even harder to negotiate. For Paolo. Not him. He let his tail twitch in a way Paolo would interpret as offensive. He couldn't let down his guard, no matter what.

"Jealous? Afraid she might like me better than you? You think because I'm only sixteen that I couldn't please a woman?"

Sal knew Paolo was working him to get his temper roaring. And it worked. There was no reason for talk like that. Yet he started to see some truth in the wild eyes that remained locked on his. Paolo was jealous. Both of him and of Julia. It was about attention. About being number one to someone.

Jealousy didn't make it right. But there were no lessons to be taught by intimidating a teenager. Sal backed away, but kept his muscles bunched and ready in case Paolo turned on him.

The boy ranted about the unfair way he was being treated. Sal didn't even blink when the big 'I'll tell my Dad' speech started its fourth chorus. He took in the room.

No other cats had been in here. That was good. Paolo had changed and gotten locked in. That was his guess. Too afraid to break out the window, but incapable of turning the doorknob. He knew the feeling.

* * * * *

Julia knew she wasn't crazy.

She'd heard the scream. Yell, really. Same as she'd heard before. A single vocalization and nothing more.

This time it forced her up from the corner she'd slid into when tears of self-pity had taken over. Her pride hadn't let it last long, but it had been enough to leave her with swollen eyes and a reddened nose.

She sniffed and rubbed her raw cheeks. This was the last time she'd allow herself to sink to that level. Especially when she needed to stay alert for times like this. Something weird was definitely happening in this house. And no amount of feeling sorry for herself was going to make it go away. It was hard not to be caught up in the fear that accompanied that fact. To survive, she had to be ready to take the initiative. That's what forced her up and across the room.

Another noise from across the hall. Something that spurred her to go out and investigate. Sounded like a thump. A thud. Nothing vocal this time.

There were three doors in this stretch of hallway. The bathroom was dark, the door half ajar. Unlikely she'd find anything there.

The doorway across from her had a yellowish hue spilling onto the carpet. Occupied. The other was dark.

She crossed the hall and paused. Even under the circumstances, Julia couldn't convince herself to yank open the door and demand to know what was going on. It wasn't her house. No way could she invite herself into someone else's room. Even if she had heard unusual noises.

But now that she was in the hallway, she could hear a voice. Rapid fire Italian. Very angry tone. But it wasn't Sal. She breathed a sigh of relief. Had to be Paolo.

Who was he yelling at?

She leaned in, one hand on the doorknob, and listened closer.

She couldn't hear a response. Even a mumble. Was he on the phone? Entirely possible.

There she went again, making something out of nothing. The yell she heard might have been Paolo reacting with laughter or a whoop about something the other person had said. Nothing unusual there at all.

So maybe she *was* crazy. She shrugged it off in relief. Her muscles relaxed. It was all in her head.

Julia walked down to the bathroom. At least that little bit of almost-excitement had broken up the monotony of doing nothing. If she didn't have a book to read, she could probably create some bizarre story about the what ifs that ricocheted around in her head.

Damn. That idea had to be of the utmost torture. If she did write a story about her days in Africa, Sal would play a leading role.

She splashed cold water on her face and looked up in the mirror. She looked like hell. Her fingers were a poor substitute for a comb, and there was nothing in any of the cabinets that would help. Sal had to be crazy too, to want her like he did. Had. Hell, he was probably bored and would've fucked anyone that walked into the house. It didn't mean she was so special. Her own vision had been clouded—here was a sexy man who was basically offering her a free ride home and then didn't hesitate to let her know he had some pent-up sexual frustrations she could help him with.

Well, he didn't actually say that. It'd be so much goddamn easier to handle if he had. No, instead it had to be this intense avalanche of chemistry and emotions that had snowballed into something neither of them had been able to stop.

Still couldn't. She didn't trust him, but that didn't stop her from wanting him.

A door down the hall quietly opened, then clicked closed.

She froze where she stood, with both hands gripping the edge of the vanity top.

If Sal walked into the bathroom right now, she knew she'd be torn.

Her senses were already stretched like fine wires. He'd cause them to break and she'd lose rational thought. And either go off on him and try to kill him for the way he manipulated her or melt into his arms and beg for him to fuck her again. She lifted a hand to cover the small smile that played at her lips. While the first was certainly better for her morale, the second sounded much more fun. Why couldn't she have left her heart out of it? Why couldn't it have been just sex?

Ah hell.

She reached over and flipped the lock on the door. This was for her. She turned and leaned against the low counter and let her fingers slide down the front of her pants.

She wore no panties, and the immediate moisture dampened the thin material.

Sal's fingers had been magic. He'd known just how to touch her—just how much pressure, just how fast to thrum her clit. She remembered how she'd opened her eyes and found him watching her. As if his only concern was pleasing her.

The memory, more than her own light stroking, had her breath already coming in pants. This wouldn't take long.

Her eyes closed as she imagined it was Sal sliding the waist of her pants over her hips. Would he kiss her there again? Her fingertips lightly stroked, mimicking the movements of his tongue. The image of his mouth on her, suckling her clit, stroking in and out of her pussy with his tongue made her blood heat to nearly boiling.

Two fingers slid inside her soaked opening. She gasped and clutched the counter for support. She moved them in and out, mentally calling out to Sal to fuck her, begging for his swollen cock to push inside her and fill her with pleasure.

Sal stood outside the bathroom door. He hadn't gone looking for her, but when he noticed her bedroom door open, he had to make sure she was okay.

What he hadn't expected was to stand in the hallway and listen to her get herself off.

Torture.

In cat form there was nothing available to ease the immediate tightening of his balls. His cock was rock hard and all he could do was listen with ultra sensitive feline hearing to her pant and moan. Between them stood nothing but a thin wood door. Had he been human, he wouldn't have cared about the damage and broken in to at least watch her.

The image seared his mind. The idea of that was almost too hot for him to handle.

He listened as her fingernails scraped the porcelain of the sink. The little moans made him crazy. It should be him, dammit. He should be in there pleasing her, pleasing himself.

Why was she locked in there doing it herself?

Because she didn't trust him. Because he had lied to her or at least kept the truth from her. But dammit, he'd tried! She didn't understand that he wanted, needed to go home as soon as possible. He wanted to take her to Florence, convince her to spend at least a day or two with him in the beautiful city.

She moaned and gasped.

He needed to go before she opened the door and found him there. But he couldn't tear himself away from at least hearing her reach that pinnacle of pleasure. *Do it for me. I want to be the one to take you there, amore.*

It was easy to close his eyes and imagine her standing there, eyes closed, hair tossed back, body naked and beautiful, even in the bright overhead light. He wanted to see her cup her breasts and take the nipples between her fingers. Would she ply them lightly or squeeze until she gasped with the painful pleasure?

Sal's tongue flicked out instinctively as he imagined her licking her fingers and then dampening the rosy tips of her breasts until they glistened. Then she'd slide her moist fingers down into the thatch of hair between her thighs.

He growled and stepped away from the door.

No way could he take any more. He had to go. Run it off, something. Anything. Hell, if he could change back, he'd go take care of it himself.

He darted down the hall and to his lab.

* * * * *

That night and the next day dragged endlessly. What Julia wouldn't have given for a deck of cards. Anything. Mid-afternoon she'd sat in the library and read one of the books of Italian out loud. And ten minutes into it, the laughter at her butchered attempts turned to tears.

Women used to do this. Spend all day idle. What, maybe a hundred, two hundred years before, the women of status spent their day in the drawing room stitching. Hell, she'd kill for some stitching to work on. Though that probably wouldn't last. No patience. Which is why she was desperate for anything to do. Anything but think of Sal. Wonder what he was doing. She didn't want to picture him leaned over his research, unshaved morning beard and ruffled hair teasing her senses. God help her if he turned those eyes on her. She'd melt.

She walked to the window. Outside the sun had nearly set on the grass it had baked all day. Anything daring to venture out into the heat was thoroughly browned. This was the heat she'd been expecting to find in Africa. But she hadn't figured it'd just add to her extreme boredom. Even returning to walk through the heavier tree cover lacked appeal. When the sun set, however, perhaps a few hours on the deck would be nice.

She could go out there now, but she'd heard Sal leave by the sliding doors when she was on the steps coming back down. Last thing she wanted to do was look like she was following him.

Julia leaned against the wall and stared at the watercolor picture that looked suspiciously like a Monet. She scoured the picture right after breakfast, but couldn't find the signature. The names on the other pieces of art in the room weren't familiar. She'd done it all. Looked, read, thought, reviewed, stared, counted and measured. She'd be able to walk through the main rooms of the house blindfolded and find anything she needed.

A lot of good that did for her mental health.

"Will you at least have dinner with me?"

She jerked upright at the breath that grazed the back of her neck. "Wh-what?"

"I know you're mad." Sal shrugged and walked around to face her. "But we both need to eat and dinner will be ready soon. Can't we share a meal and talk?"

She blinked. Talk? About what? She had little she was willing to share and she didn't want to hear anything else from him. There was no way she could believe it.

And then there was another issue. Even though he stood right on the border of the personal space she would claim as her own, teetering in every so often as he shifted balance, he couldn't have felt closer if he'd have touched her. He'd showered recently. She could smell the woodsy scent of his soap. She didn't want to notice that.

Her eyes remained on her fingers as she pretended to pick at a chipped nail. It beat looking at him. He'd mesmerize her into saying "yes" when she should be screaming, "hell, no".

"I love your hair up like that. You've got a beautiful graceful neck. The women of Italy would be envious."

She had a sarcastic retort at the tip of her tongue. *Count to ten.* If she reacted it would show how much he *did* affect her. All she'd done was pull her hair up into a French braid and tuck the end under so it was all off her neck. It was there for function, not fashion, and here he was treating her like she'd done it to attract him. "Um," she said, knowing she had to. "Thanks. I think. About dinner—"

"Right. Let's share a glass of wine first. It'll calm you. You're shaking like a leaf." His hand slid along her lower back and he pushed her forward toward the dining room.

"Whoa, wait, wait." Julia dug in her heels and tried to ignore the sparks that shot directly to the sensitive spot between her legs. "This isn't a good idea. I'll just take a tray in my room like usual."

"You can't live in that room."

That was button number one. "I can't? You say I have to. Oh, yeah," she waved her hand. "I have free rein of the house. But what can I do here? There's no radio, television or other entertainment. I can't read any of your books and I don't even have paper and pencil to write with."

He stopped with her and had the cajones to look shocked. "You could have asked for something to write with. I hadn't thought of that."

She bit her lip, but the words broke through. Three days of pent-up pressure spewed forth. "No, obviously you're not thinking of me. Why am I here, Sal? And what am I supposed to do during the day? Tell me you wouldn't go crazy sitting around with zero stimuli. Maybe you've forgotten. I crash-fucking-landed here. My sister's remains are scattered across the savannah and I can't even bury her. Nobody even knows I'm alive." She pushed away the tears that streaked down her face. "Dammit. I hate crying. I hate you. I hate Africa. I just want to go home."

She twisted away from him.

"You're not going to run away."

"No kidding," she spat out, caring less what he thought. "There's no place to run." Still, she tried to walk back toward the stairs.

Sal snatched her arm and spun her toward him. Now he was dangerously close. As in kissing close. Why did she have to think like that when she should be thinking sucker-punching close? Her breath hitched. At least she could blame that on the tears. "Let me go."

"*Per favore*, have dinner with me. No more of this. I'm sorry, Julia. Truly I am. Tomorrow morning you'll come down to the lab with me. I'll translate some notes or you can just write them and I'll put them in Italian later. I promise that you'll get to go home. Soon."

She dared not hope. Dared not look him in the eye and become mesmerized by his words. And dammit, he managed to sound sincere. Almost pleading. That she hadn't counted on. But still, there'd be no proof that he'd done anything to hasten the trip. As far as the lab? That hurt. Talk about an opportunity. She'd be able to see first hand what he was doing and even take notes. Most importantly, she wouldn't be desperate from another day of sensory deprivation. But that didn't mean she had to eat dinner with him.

"I'd really rather—"

"I insist."

"No."

His lips found hers before she repeated it. His kisses were never brutal, regardless of the intensity. And this one was intense. The fingers he wrapped around her upper arms wouldn't bruise her, but they didn't allow her to step away. And he pulled her right up against his chest. His heart pounded right against hers. She swore she could feel it as it reached in and claimed it as his. There was nothing left but the two of them. His kiss did that to her—erased everything but what she was feeling that very minute. He destroyed even those fleeting thoughts as his tongue slid between her lips and stroked her tongue with velvety sweetness. Her body tightened. The texture of her shirt scraped against sensitive nipples. She wanted his mouth there. Wanted his mouth everywhere.

Dear God, how could she fight this? Why did she want to?

She couldn't. He pulled out the heavy artillery. One hand slid up to touch her cheek. So reverent. He cupped her chin and held her mouth still while he did wickedly vicious things with the swipe of his tongue. She nearly lost her balance as his mouth left hers and traced down the hollow of her throat.

She fisted her hand on his shirt just to hold herself upright.

Her body might have overridden her mind if he hadn't spoken. Up until that point, she was putty. "Please?" was all he asked.

It was enough. She should not be doing this. She had to stop, keep from doing any more. "No, Sal. This is a mistake. It really is." She couldn't bear to look at him as she turned around, yanked her arm away and walked off. He didn't stop her this time. Probably stood there with his bottom lip stuck out and sad eyes, just so that if she turned around she'd be helpless and agree to everything he'd ask.

No way. She was standing her ground this time, even if it meant more torture. She'd have a chance tomorrow to have the interaction—platonic companionship only—she craved.

* * * * *

Julia paced the room. Her food was cold. She'd picked at it for a bit, but the hearty stew and steamed vegetables did nothing to satisfy her. What did she want? Seemed like she was reevaluating that on a regular basis and nothing stayed the same except that she wanted to go home.

He'd promised that *again*. The effort he'd put out there, trying to get her to have dinner. It hadn't gone over her head. The shower—he'd cleaned up for dinner. For her. The way he teased her by just hovering at the edge of her personal space, the apologies that certainly sounded sincere. It had been too perfect when he'd simply reached over and kissed her. Tenderly, at that. God, she was a mess.

Julia turned toward the window. Sex wouldn't have solved anything. Might have kept the boredom from coming back for what? An hour or so? And then she'd have to deal with all this confusion again. Best not to go there.

If she were home, she'd be committed. But in plain English, how could she desire the man so much, yet hate him for the way he manipulated her. Why did she want his approval, react when he gave her the slightest bit of attention and yet become irritated after just minutes in his company?

He stood for what she wanted and couldn't have.

There. She repeated it out loud.

What she wanted. A man that melted her from the inside every time he looked at her with those hooded dark eyes. Someone who encouraged her to open up her full self. She'd done that with Sal. Done it without thinking. And he hadn't ever abused that. Try as she might, she knew that the things that upset her the most had nothing to do with the direct way he treated her. Excluding his delusional statements — but those didn't reflect on her.

Perhaps, she realized with a shiver, what made him all the more desirable was the way he gave himself to her. On that level, in a way that words didn't explain, it was clear their souls had connected. And he didn't retract his, despite it all.

Fact was, he was doing bizarre research and making bizarre claims. He was Italian and living in Africa. She was American and wanted nothing more than to go home to New York. With him.

But wouldn't that spoil the fantasy?

Bingo.

Figuring that out had been harder than passing psychology class back at the university.

No glowing lightbulbs appeared over her head. Nor was she suddenly transported to a feeling of peace and contentment. Hell, she didn't know what she'd do with the knowledge. So far, everything else she'd thought she'd figured out had fizzled out. So much for plans.

Julia picked up her tray and carried it to the door when she heard the knock. Probably the girl that Sal had sent up here with the laden tray. "Come in," she said, figuring whoever it was would assume that was an indication to enter.

"Hi," Sal said as he filled the room with his presence.

Julia's hands immediately started shaking. What was he doing here? In here. With the door closed behind him. "Sorry, thought you were—"

"You've eaten nothing." He lifted the tray from her hands and put it on the dresser. "You have to eat. Last thing I need is for you to get sick."

She hadn't meant to be sarcastic, but he knocked her so off balance she blurted, "But you can just heal me with your magic potion, right?"

The narrowed gaze was anything but tolerant. "Listen, I've screwed up a ton in my life and this ranks right up there with the worst of it. You...I...well, things weren't supposed to be like they are—"

"Were," she interjected.

"Were," he repeated. "I can't help how I feel about you. That's some big bio-chemistry miracle I don't intend to explore."

Julia could only stare at him. How much wine had he drank with his dinner?

Sal took a step toward her.

She stepped back. "Sal," she warned.

"Stop. I'm not going to bite you." Then, as he realized what he said, he smiled and added, "again."

"Out." She pointed. "Get out and let me be. I'll come down to your lab and pretend to be your secretary or assistant or whatever just for the sake of my sanity. Not as a particular favor to you. Not until I see my ticket back to...wherever. I just want to get to someplace where I can make arrangements to get home."

He sighed and looked her up and down. "We could—"

"No."

They stared at each other, neither blinking.

"*Sono spiacente...*I'm sorry, Julia, I didn't mean *that*. I just wish you'd listen to me."

"I have. I'm not real sure what to believe so I'm going with believing nothing. Easier that way." She crossed her arms and lifted her chin.

"On me? Or on you?" His hand sliced through his dark, unruly hair. "Good night."

Abruptly he left the room, rattling the door with a derisive slam.

"Fine," she tossed at the door and dropped herself on the edge of the bed. How had he managed to twist that again? She fell backwards and closed her eyes. God, he was the perfect man until he started talking.

"Fuck it being easy on either of us," Sal said as he stormed back through the door.

Julia struggled to sit up in time to watch him turn the lock and drop the key on the dresser. "Sal?" She backed up on the bed. His face was hard, all chiseled and...intense. Her breath hitched when his half-closed eyes caught hers and he advanced.

"You want it, I want it. We're going to get it, *amore*. Get it good." Sal got on the bed and crawled on all fours until his face was inches from hers. "I won't take what you won't give me, Julia. I won't hurt you. But I want you."

His mouth picked up right where it'd left off earlier. The pressure of his lips forced hers open and his tongue plundered directly inside. It went straight to her core—a jolt of electricity hitting ground.

Her responses were lost in the moans he elicited from her. Truth is, she didn't *want* to say no, even though everything she knew said she should.

She'd never tire of kissing him. He anticipated her wants perfectly and turned kissing into something that filled her entire body. His hands hadn't so much as touched her yet, but she squirmed with the need to have him inside her.

"You can't deny it, can you? We have something together. I could never get enough of you. Ever." His mouth was feather-light against hers. He teased her lips with tiny kisses. Her hips arched up to reach him as he snared her tongue in his mouth and suckled.

Please! Where had all this need come from? She reached for him, trying to pull his welcome weight down onto her. She wanted to feel him, hard, strong, heavy against the length of her. Wanted to feel his erection straining to find its place inside her.

"Please," she begged when he lifted his head.

He watched her. She held his gaze as he shifted his weight and brought one hand up to her breast.

"Don't close your eyes, *amore*." He leaned down and kissed them. "I want to watch you as I touch you."

She obliged, anything to make him touch her heated skin again. And all those clothes still between them. She'd die before he ever gave her what she wanted.

"Look at me," he said, dipping his head low to kiss the nipple that pushed against her shirt.

Pleasure coursed from the sensitive nub to the center of her ache. Moisture pooled between her legs. Her pussy throbbed with need.

Sal's free hand replaced his mouth. His palm covered the nipple and he rubbed her in light circular motions. "Oh, oh," she gasped, then moaned as his mouth descended on her other breast.

They had to move faster than this.

She fisted his shirt and forced him down on her. He complied, his own eyes black and hooded with straining desire. He shifted so the head of his cock pushed against his pants directly at the opening to her pussy.

She ground against him.

Clothes. Off. Now. Julia wasn't going to wait. She yanked up the edge of Sal's shirt and slid her hands between them to fumble with his pants buttons. He kept his erection rocking against her, destroying her concentration.

"Get these clothes off or it'll be over before it gets started."

"No it won't. It'll never be over." He captured her mouth in a kiss that bordered on painful. It just ratcheted up the pace.

She gave up on his button and released the fasteners of her own clothes. Last thing she wanted was to have him shift his weight from her, but it'd be necessary, temporarily, to get his hot, naked body against hers.

A mini spasm rocked her body.

Sal finally got the message. His teeth nabbed her lip and raked it through his with a groan that said it all. Then he rose up and nearly tore his shirt from his body.

She whimpered as she took him in. A thin sheen of sweat covered his skin. Tight, tan skin that trembled when she touched it.

Her fingers slid over his navel and followed the thin hair that led below the waistband. He grabbed her wrist. "*Dolce Dio*," he said. He rolled off her then and discarded his pants. She did the same.

He couldn't go fast enough, but she paused to enjoy the view when he crouched over her — on all fours again, his thick, engorged cock sprung loose and pointing to the spot she wanted it to go.

"Sal," she gasped and reached for it.

Her hand guided it to her as his eyes bored into hers and directly into her soul. She could see that he had his control on tight rein. "Let it go," she whispered.

As he slid into her wet pussy, she arched up to meet every inch, every fraction of an inch she could take. The muscles there immediately clenched onto him. All he had to do was move, and she was coming.

He must have sensed it. Must have known it was that way for both of them. "My sweet," he muttered into her hair as he slid out and drove back in again. She started flying. Nothing existed but Sal. Not the bed, not the room, nothing but his body and hers.

Sal held still for a moment. "Oh, please no. Please don't stop," she begged, thrusting her hips upward. So close, so close. Almost…

He completely withdrew.

She gasped and trembled. The muscles inside her quivered with unsatisfied need. "Please Sal, Please. Oh God. You have to give it to me."

She squirmed and rocked her hips as the head of his penis slid against her lips. No matter what she did, she couldn't get him inside her, where she needed him. "Please," she begged again.

"Look at me, Julia."

God, please, anything! She opened her eyes and focused on his. They were dark, clouded with desire and one more tangible connection.

She saw his whole being there. He was giving her his whole self.

"Sal," she cried as he plunged deep into her and shattered her world.

* * * * *

Now that had been productive. Working with Julia in the lab was going to be a huge mistake. How could he concentrate when she settled those big gray-blue eyes on him and then said something he'd never have expected? Like that final comment before she'd drifted to sleep. He played it over again, smiling. *We shouldn't have done that, Sal. But I'm really glad we did.*

It'd be pure torture to slide his arm from under her sleeping form and pull the covers up over her naked body. The night was dark, but he already had pictures in his head of what she'd look like bathed in moonlight.

Coffee. He needed coffee. "You play, you pay," his father said. In a not so different context, to be honest. So now it was pay time. And he had a lot to do.

Sal knew it'd be another long night, but since he'd made that split second decision to bring her into his research, he had to be ready for her. What he'd really gone up to the room to do was get a feel for what she'd learned from her night of snooping. Things with Julia just never worked out the way he wanted. He pulled the door slowly until it clicked. Then he turned the key. Not locking her in, though she'd think so. She could get out if she wanted. But no one could get in. Like Paolo. But he couldn't tell her about that yet.

From the beginning, he'd admired her spirit, but he was sure he was seeing the core of it now. Sort of like backing a dog into a corner to see how much fight they had in them.

Well, Julia was definitely a fighter. Too bad she'd chosen to fight with him instead of beside him. He scratched his head. Still couldn't quite figure out what he could do to fix things, other than just send her home. Wasn't likely she'd tell him without clawing his eyes out first. And that'd be a shame because all she'd allowed him to do now was enjoy looking at her.

Sokhra stopped him in the kitchen. "Your nephew is upstairs nursing his wounds. Came in pretty beat up about a half hour ago. Can't you stop him? Can't you keep this from happening? Why won't you stop it?"

He gripped the housekeeper's shoulders as gently as the frustration welling up inside him allowed, and waited until she looked up at him through tear-filled eyes. "He doesn't want to stop. I tried. Nearly broke the needle off in his leg trying. It's going to have to be voluntary or else I go after him with the tranquilizer gun."

"No."

"It's the last resort. I'm waiting on a confirmation on a shipment, then I'll be going to Cairo, like I'd told you, before the end of the week."

"Alone?" she lifted her dark eyes rimmed in shadows.

He hated the way she worried about this. "I have to."

"But Paolo. He..." Sokhra pointed upwards to where the bedrooms lay. "I don't like the way he acts about her."

Sal narrowed his eyes at her and leaned back against the kitchen counter. This was not good. "Has there been something new, something I've missed?"

Sokhra shook her head, but her eyes were dull. "I fear for her. If you're gone..."

He pounded the counter with his fist then pinched the bridge of his nose. "I have to go. I can't trust anyone else. You'll have to do your best to keep them separate. I'll call and get back here as soon as I can. It's all I can do. If I don't go…" He didn't want to think about it. "I have to go. There's no question there."

Sokhra nodded and reached up to tidy the perfectly dusted china figurines in the cabinet. Her prized possessions. He'd have to get her something new to show his appreciation. She deserved the world for putting up with him.

"Sokhra? I haven't told either of them I'm leaving. I won't, until I'm gone. It would only make things harder."

She nodded again but didn't look at him.

Great. He knew she disapproved. If it had been up to her, Julia would have been shipped back to the United States immediately upon her recovery. Bad thing is, he probably should have listened.

The lab needed some serious attention. He'd spent way too much time chasing other, fruitless endeavors and not enough time working. All he hoped was that having her in the same room with him wouldn't backfire on him the way he feared.

"I'll be in the lab if you need me." He didn't wait for a response.

* * * * *

Sal fell asleep around two. At least that was his last blurred memory of the clock. He'd translated what he thought Julia would need into English, enough to work with but not enough to hand everything over. And each step he asked himself if he could trust her.

He rubbed his eyes. It was almost six now. His back and neck ached from sleeping face down on his desk and the hours spent leaning over microscopes, papers and keyboard. He rubbed his neck and stood up. What he wouldn't give for a pot of coffee and a long, hot shower. Or a weekend in the Mediterranean where he could forget about all of this and relax near the water.

Soon. He'd have to before he burnt himself out.

A yawn escaped him. Going to bed last night might have been a preventative for that. Now he had to deal with his nerve endings being on constant alert from the presence of a woman that managed to keep him guessing. He rubbed his hair. Who cared what he looked like? Why should he bother to shave? They were working, not dating. She'd made that clear after last night's incredible sex.

He stood up and stretched, then reviewed the screen he had open. Good. For starters she could sit here and key in the information he had about blood enzyme differentials in the various leopards he'd had a chance to sample. While he worked in the lab.

Sal sat down again. One more thing. Opening his email program, he prayed the answer was there.

Two new messages. One from Carlotta, one from Antonio. He clicked on the latter. "Yes!" he punched the air. Everything he asked for was enroute to Cairo. He needed to be there tomorrow evening.

Tomorrow. Shit. Well, he had to do it. He'd just make it a short day in the lab.

He clicked the other email open.

Carlotta wanted her son home immediately. Suggested sending him on by himself from Cairo. Sal's stomach knotted. How does one explain to a mother that her son had turned himself in to a leopard? He erased the message, preferring to postpone dealing with it right now. Paolo couldn't go anywhere, but Sal'd be sure to make sure Paolo knew his mother was looking for him to return soon. And he wasn't going as he was.

"Good morning."

Sal hurriedly closed the email and turned toward Julia. Damn.

She offered him a mug of steaming liquid and then wrapped both hands around her own cup. The dark smudges under her eyes and the lines around her mouth told the story. She wasn't sleeping any better than he.

"Rough night?" he asked, sipping the coffee. Was a little sweet for his taste, but no way was he releasing the cup.

"Nightmares," she responded. Her pink tongue slipped through her steam-swollen lips and licked off the coffee residue.

His body responded. He shifted in his chair and intentionally scalded his tongue. Their conversation felt like a chess match. He made the wrong move, said the wrong thing and he'd end up paying for it. But dammit, it was hard not to notice how her lips curved around the ridge of the cup and her creamy white throat undulated as she swallowed. The dreams he'd had weren't as sweet as the vision before him.

The pants he wore were getting mighty tight. "Listen, Julia. I was just setting this up for you to input some of my data. Are you familiar with this spreadsheet program?"

Bad, bad move. He'd stayed seated to keep his now throbbing erection hidden and she walked up behind him. And leaned over. Close enough that he could smell the mint of the toothpaste mixed with the scent of coffee on her lips. A strand of her finger combed hair fell against his cheek.

And she didn't seem bothered in the least. "I think so. Very similar to what I've worked with before."

"Good." He swallowed. "Does this make any sense to you?" He pointed to the paper he'd used to record the data. His Italian values had been crossed out and replaced with English. He handed it up to her.

He had to turn around to watch her read. But it gave him a good chance to study her face. He could find no fault with her features, yet she wasn't a great beauty. He could hear Antonio now. "Her? Salvatore, what are you thinking? There are a dozen women at home who'd drop everything to be with you who all look better than her."

But Julia wasn't ugly. Not by a long shot. She just wasn't the glamorous type he'd normally used as an arm decoration when home in Florence. But none of those women would wear a smile on their face when reading his research paperwork either.

"What?" he asked.

"I hadn't given you credit. You are thorough."

"Huh?" So why did he feel clueless at this moment? Like a horny teenager sitting beside a pretty girl in chemistry class.

And the one staring down her nose at him was the teacher. "Did you get any sleep last night?"

"I don't need much sleep. We've got work to do. Like I was saying, you'll key that information in here and let me know when you're done. I'll get started out in the lab."

Anywhere, just not in the same room with her while his libido was calling the shots.

"Sure," she waved him out of the seat and sat down. "Okay, um, Sal, the menus on here are still all in Italian."

Great. Roles were reversed. It was pure hell to reach over and smell the faint whiff of shampoo. Impossible to concentrate on the computer screen. All he could think about doing was burying his face into her hair and nuzzling her neck. And then continuing down to taste her shoulder and —

"Sal?"

He straightened. "What?"

"Are you even listening to me?"

"Of course I am." He couldn't see her face, but imagined a scowl.

"Then what did I just ask you?"

"Something about the menus being foreign."

Her blown out breath must indicate wrong answer. "I figured that one out on my own. See? What I asked was if I should save this to your hard drive or disk."

"Definitely hard." He cleared his throat. "Hard drive for now. I'll back up to disk later. Sorry. You're distracting me."

"Me?"

He was still half leaned over and could plainly see that she had indeed changed the menus to English. Damn, she was good. He'd have to be careful with what he let her into on the computer.

Then again... Julia spun the chair around to face him. "Me?"

If he tilted a little to the left, he could taste her lips. "Yes," he whispered. "Just like now. You're taunting me by being so close. All I can think about is what it's like to make love — "

"Stop!" she hissed.

He smiled. She was trapped. Beneath him. If she stood up or even tried to, she'd be in his arms, up against his chest. *Come on, try it.*

"You've got work to do," he said instead. "I'll be in the lab if you need me. Or want me." He winked and walked out.

Chapter 9

Julia took a deep breath when Sal finally left the room. There just wasn't enough space in the office for both of them.

When he'd leaned over her, she'd nearly lost track of what she'd said. And he wasn't shy about admitting what was on his mind. Why did that have to be such a turn on?

She imagined Sal took advantage of her to increase his work output. But having her work in the lab wasn't a one sided situation. For her it was preservation of sanity. Or so she thought. Dammit. Sal still got the benefit of it all. If he had wanted a secretary he should have hired one, not driven her to taking the job and acting like it was a gift.

So she needed to take something out of this. She smiled as she turned back to the keyboard and flexed her fingers. The familiar buildup filled her chest and pushed away impulsive thoughts. Anger was good. Anger was productive. Anger kept her out of trouble.

Anger drained everything out of her. By lunchtime her shoulders hurt, her wrists were cramped and her eyes burned. Who would have thought data entry work was so trying? The knowledge that she helped him on whatever genetic research he was doing on these cats didn't escape her. Of course, he'd not translated any of the important stuff. Just basic data. So while she typed, she wondered, was he injecting them with some enzyme steroid to boost the quantity of his alleged cure-all? Was he toying with the genes in these animals? She couldn't bear to think it.

Sal invited her to eat with him in the lab while he finished something he was mixing together. No way was she putting her food on the same table as his test tubes filled with colored liquids. It would be too easy to taint something she was going to eat.

Flat out, she didn't trust him. Not with his experiments or with her.

She ate out on the deck. The heat was murder. The ice in her glass melted almost instantly. Breathing took major effort. But it beat tucking her tail between her legs and returning to the "I told you so" she'd heard when she announced her destination.

The cat approached from behind her. Her peripheral vision caught it when it was already much too close. She hadn't heard a thing. At first she thought it was a lioness or a cougar. The exact features that differentiated them were still blurred to her. But its posture and overall body shape made her think leopard. She'd gotten an up close view of that particular species. This had to be one of them, even without the telltale spots.

And while she tried valiantly to remain calm and think about her options, her body started preparing for fight or flight. She had to put down her glass of water because her hand shook so badly she nearly spilled it. If she dared eat another bite her stomach would revolt.

It paced the yard just beyond the deck. Watching her. Its eyes would sear into her between the slats in the wood railing. She could feel him assessing her.

So should she throw the hunk of chicken out to it? Should she slowly stand up and walk inside? Surely she could make it before the cat pounced. Right? The door looked about eight feet away. The cat was at least that far away from her. Screaming seemed like a good idea.

"What do you want?" Julia blurted.

Of course, there was no answer.

"Go away. Go back outside the walls. God only knows what Sal would do to you if he caught you."

The last part of the sentence was muttered to herself, but she almost believed the cat heard it. It let out a loud growl and displayed teeth in a way that blatantly said, "I'm not afraid of him."

She forced her lungs to take in fresh oxygen. What next?

There were stairs leading to either side of the deck. The leopard rounded the length and stood plainly at the bottom, looking up at her.

Why hadn't she listened to Sal? And why were these cats constantly after her? The man who worked on the garden was outside every day. Why did this one want to come right up to the house and attack her?

But it didn't attack. It laid down and curled its tail up to the side of its body. But she didn't trust it.

Julia was calmer than she expected to be. Perhaps she was getting numb to it. A month ago and she'd be on edge just standing at the zoo and here she was actually able to get her muscles to move with a wild, probably hungry leopard merely a dozen feet away.

It cleared the steps as she slid the glass door open. Her fingers wouldn't move fast enough. She dropped her plate and cup and raced toward the lab, screaming. "Sal! Sal! Hurry! A leopard's after me!"

He jerked open the door and yanked her behind him. "Where is he? *Il vigliacco*, the coward."

Long, purposeful strides took Sal out of Julia's reach before she could ask why he was calling the leopard a coward. Maybe she misinterpreted. Maybe *she* was the coward.

Well, she'd just show him. Marching with the same determination, she turned back toward the deck.

Sokhra grabbed her arm before she made it to the doors. "No, no," she said, then rattled something off in her own language.

Julia wasn't sure what to think about that. Initially she wanted to jerk free and go out there anyway, but it *was* a wild leopard. Sal would know what to do. She hoped.

Then she nearly laughed. Despite her skepticism, she did trust Sal to handle himself in the presence of those animals. Even if he had been mauled pretty seriously just a few days before.

Seemed like weeks, even months ago that had happened. She cringed at the thought it could happen again. What if he was hurt badly enough that he couldn't get back to the lab for his magic cure.

The cure. The lab. Currently unoccupied.

She ignored Sokhra's surprised look and raced back to the lab.

* * * * *

Sal's scribbles made little sense to her. It was the sketches that had her amazed. Whatever he was working on, it was certainly big. It showed cells morphing or mutating or something. She wished she'd had more microbiology background so she could figure out the differences.

Did this show the effects of that magical healing serum on tissue? There were three slides near the microscope. The writing wasn't clear, but the dates matched the sketches in the notes he'd made.

"Julia." Sal's breath on the back of her neck caused her to jump out of her skin.

"Don't do that," she said, slapping a hand over her heart. "You just scared me."

"Think I was that leopard coming to get you?"

At least he had a smile. "No, but I didn't hear you walk in."

He winked. "So," he said, rocking back on his heels. "Find anything interesting?"

Julia searched his face, waiting for a sign of his anger. Surely he didn't want her looking at this, snooping in his research. Finding nothing but dancing amusement in the light in his eyes, she shrugged. "I can't read it."

An eyebrow lifted. "But you looked in the microscope."

She swallowed. Heat burned her cheeks. "Curious. Couldn't help it."

Sal reached out to her face. She pulled back, catching her breath. He scared her, plain and simple. It'd be just like him to be nice and then let her have it. Then again, just having him touch her so gently was torture itself. Why couldn't she have met him under normal circumstances?

He waited until she relaxed again, eyes never leaving hers. Then his fingers reached up and tucked a stray hair behind her ear.

She sighed. If this was the way he treated the animals, they should be eating out of his hand.

He said, "Pull up a stool over here. Maybe you'll have an idea."

Not only did she not remove her hand from over her heart, she clenched the material of her shirt in her fingers. "What?" She hadn't heard him right. No way.

"I'll tell you a little about what I'm working on and you can tell me what you think." He did, she noticed, push the notes aside and pulled up another set of papers.

"Hey, um, Sal, what happened with that leopard?"

"He's gone."

His lab coat was wrinkled, but not torn. No signs of blood anywhere. Or grass stains. Whatever had happened had been minor. She digested his short answer as she rolled the stool over to his current work area. She was careful to situate her chair to keep breathing distance between them. "Just gone? Did you hurt him? What happened?"

"He ran. Anyway, here, I want to talk about these cells. These are damaged, see?"

She looked up under her eyelashes as he tried to divert her attention in order to tuck the other notes away.

"What are those?" She pointed.

"The other experiment. That one can wait. This is the one that's important." He waved it off, but the quick darting of his eyes indicated things weren't as he said.

She widened her eyes and nodded. No sense pissing him off when she'd come this far. "Okay, I'm looking for damaged cells, right. Damaged how?"

"How?" he repeated, knitting his eyebrows.

Either he thought she was totally clueless or she was dealing with a moron herself. The other, and probably correct assumption was that he only wanted to share with her what he thought she'd need to know. Forget big picture. Well, too bad. "Yeah, how was it damaged, trauma, disease…?"

His lips tightened. "Trauma."

From his reaction, she'd better just go with the flow and stop pushing buttons. "Show me what an undamaged cell looks like, so I can compare." She knew, of course. She hadn't decided if or when to break it to him that she was a little more familiar with what he was doing than he gave her credit for. It wasn't that she was intentionally keeping it a secret, but blurting it out now gave her no advantage. No, she'd wait. Who knew when she might need to play that card.

She peered into the microscope. When he covered her hand to show her how to focus it, she let him, even if she didn't need the instruction. Just the contact of skin against skin caused her body temperature to start climbing. She fought to stay focused with him so near. "And what kind of cells are these?"

Sal shrugged and moved in to replace the slide on the scope. She backed up to put at least a foot of space between them.

She couldn't believe she was disappointed that he hadn't closed the space or touched her again. He simply answered, "Basal cell. Skin. I took them out of my cuts the other night."

He looked up then, and pushed her chin up until their eyes met.

"You were a wonderful nurse. So careful to undress me without damaging...anything."

She blinked and backed up again. "Do you always take samples of your wounds?"

They each took another step. Him forward. Her backwards. Eyes remained locked.

"Yes."

"Why?" She shifted direction when her hip bumped the table behind her.

He didn't stop coming. "It's proper scientific procedure to get a sample before treating a wound with an experimental medicine."

"Ah. Did you take a sample of my shoulder?"

He took two steps forward and was nearly chest to breast with her. Oh God. Her nipples reached out toward him. How could they betray her like that? "No."

She wasn't going to give in, even if it meant doing backwards laps around the lab. "Why not?"

"You weren't in my laboratory and I had no materials with me."

She lifted an eyebrow. "Really? So I was an *undocumented* experiment?"

"Would you rather I left you to die? You could have been attacked by another animal, a hyena perhaps that was drawn to the scent of blood, or simply gotten an infection. The river's loaded with bacteria. I did what I had to do. And you weren't the first experiment. I wouldn't have done that to you."

"But you didn't bring me back here. I don't understand your motives."

"I knew you'd be in the way. Asking too many questions and compromising my ability to work. I was hoping you'd find a way home. And I'd be an anonymous benefactor."

Now that was a story. "Whatever, Sal. That doesn't make sense."

"Maybe I felt guilty for abandoning you like that. So I sent Paolo after you."

Julia was against the door now. She pressed as flat as she could against it and fumbled for the knob. He slipped his hand over hers.

"I had to see you again. I need you." He pressed close, the heat from his body instantly causing hers to react.

"Sal, no. Don't do this."

"God, woman, I love it when you beg." And as he had so many times in the past, he quieted all her demons and left nothing but the hungry woman inside. It wasn't that she didn't want to fight against the way his mouth covered hers perfectly and his tongue dipped in to taste. She couldn't. No more than she could help her own tongue twisting against his with heat and promise. No more than she could stop her mind from reminding her how it felt when his fingers traced over her body and he slid his cock inside her welcoming pussy.

His lips left hers then. She stared at him, blinking to focus.

With a crooked smile, he dropped her hands and stomped back to the microscope.

She stood there, lost. For one moment there she'd been on the verge of giving in. The verbal exchange and constant eye contact had been almost as arousing as physical foreplay. And it had affected him, too. She'd felt the evidence against her hip when he'd held her against the door. She chewed her bottom lip and watched him read over his notes, wondering what she could have done differently to have him pinning her, naked, against the door.

"Well?" he looked up and asked. "Did you intend to stand there for the rest of the afternoon?"

She really could claw his eyes out without remorse. She hated the way he manipulated her, both externally and internally.

One moment she felt like the woman he couldn't keep his hands off, the next minute she was a child being admonished for out of line behavior. All the while he seemed unfazed by it.

"So exactly what do you think I can do to help?"

Another stare down.

"Sal, you asked me to help, no...told me to help. I'm here. I'm trying to help. So far you've avoided my questions, then backed me up across the room. How am I supposed to react?" She had a feeling 'get mad' wasn't his answer, but that was too bad. Her patience had disappeared a long time ago.

And why did he have to stand there looking edible? He hadn't turned to face her, so she could see his back and side. As he reached up to scratch his head, the lab coat tightened around his broad shoulders. Too bad the coat hid his backside. It would have been nice to look at him, if only for a consolation prize for this joke of a day.

She had a flashback to grade school when the boy that liked her made a point to hit or kick her every day. This was just a grown up version. She bit her lip to keep from smiling. So that was it. He didn't know how to act so he acted out.

With that new knowledge, she sauntered back over to him. Fine then, two could play. All she had to do was tease him a bit and then toss a big no in his face. That'd teach him he didn't have ultimate control.

But she didn't stand a chance. Sal turned, smiled, let out a half growl and swooped her up. He sat her on the counter and nudged her knees apart. "We're not going to get any work done."

No, no, no. She caught her breath as his fingers slid up her thighs. "We have to, remember."

"I'll do it tonight, when you're not here distracting me."

No, no, no. There was nowhere to go when he leaned in to nip at her neck. Not sure she wanted to leave either. "Sal, please," she murmured. She meant for him to stop, but he reacted as if she'd agreed to it all.

Yes, yes, yes. The pace went from playfully seductive to demanding. He ravaged her mouth, plundering his tongue inside in a way that she couldn't deny. Her body reacted as if she'd gone for years without a man's touch. Excited spasms already shot up through her body from the muscles of her pussy clenching in need.

He rubbed hard against her. Fingers gripped her thighs and held her tight. The absolute dominance was thrilling. But she wanted her say. Julia slid her hands up into his hair and pulled his mouth away from hers. "I want it up against the door."

Sal's eyes dilated until they were smoky black and all humor was erased. She slid her hands down to frame his face. His unshaven beard made him look such the bad boy. Today she wanted bad, bad things from him. To hell with everything else. What they did here now wouldn't get her home any faster or keep her here any longer.

Her lips curled up into a satisfied grin as he watched her remove her shirt—another of his borrowed shirts. In the depths of his eyes, there was fire. The flames burnt her skin as his eyes caressed her bare breasts. She teased the material over her swollen nipples, touching and flicking them as the shirt exposed them.

"Wanna taste?" she asked. She couldn't wait to feel his hot mouth on her, suckling, pulling, even biting the sensitive skin. More juices flooded her pussy at the thought of it.

He turned the tables. She didn't fight him. He pulled the shirt back and kept her wrists entangled in it behind her. Her skin tingled as the air hit her nipples. Despite being captive, she felt wonderfully free. Only he had ever made her feel that way. Tiny gasps were all she could manage when he came so close, but didn't touch her.

"You're so beautiful." He used one hand to trace along her ribcage and then up the valley between her upthrust breasts. She couldn't arch any more. She needed him. "Please Sal."

"Beg for it."

"Kiss me. Touch me."

"Where?" His breath felt like a thousand electrical currents racing up her belly.

"Everywhere," she moaned. "Touch me everywhere Sal, I need it now." She didn't care about anything as long as he touched her.

And he didn't, yet.

His hips shifted just slightly, rubbing against her sensitized clit and causing her to bite her lip in pleasure.

"You like that?"

With satisfaction, she knew the roughness of his voice was equally needy.

"Yeah."

"Tell me what you want, Julia. Beg me to love you."

"Fuck me, Sal. I want your mouth on my breasts and then your cock in my pussy. I want you to make me come. I need it now."

He laughed, a husky sound that reverberated between them. "You're in a hurry, *amore*. Let's start with one thing at a time." With that, he bent his head and took one swollen, pink bud in his mouth.

She was doomed to melt into a pile of goo on the counter. His mouth was heaven. His tongue flicked up and down on the tip until she squirmed to press her aching pussy against him. If she could just rub against him, she might be able to release the sweet pressure that built up there.

And then he slowed, his thumb replacing his tongue and eventually pulling back entirely.

He stood up straight and cupped her breasts in his hands. "Get dressed, Julia. Someone's coming."

And it should be her! She had to blink and really think about his words. How had he had the peace of mind to listen for footsteps or whatever it was that he heard? She watched him pace to the end of the room and back. No, he was affected. His face held the slightest tinge of ruddiness and his pants still boasted the obvious.

She shrugged her shirt back over her shoulders and slid off the counter.

"Who's coming?" She watched the door and smoothed her hair. She couldn't imagine anyone just walking into the lab without knocking.

"Stay here." His voice didn't provide her an option.

He pulled off his lab coat. Sweat beaded on his forehead. She could see it plainly from three feet away. His eyes looked glassy. What the hell was going on? Was he upset? Who was out there?

She started to walk up to him.

"Stay," he growled.

She blinked, still reeling from the way things changed so damn quickly.

He was gone.

Julia stared at the door.

What had just happened? She'd failed, that's what. Where had all that take-control bravado gone?

Stupid, stupid, stupid. She'd known from early this morning what he wanted. He wasn't playing games, she was. And she lost.

Probably a good thing too.

She swallowed, pride being a bitter pill stuck in her throat. Obviously, this was a learning experience. Not unlike Sal's trial and error methods in the lab. Control did not mean throwing herself at him and begging for—her face burned. Oh lord, had she really said those things out loud?

Fresh air would do her good. Besides, Sal had gone out that way.

"Sal?" she called.

The bright sun was more than she'd expected and for a moment, she was blinded. The blast of heat was firelike against her skin. Her lungs were in a vise. And it wasn't like she hadn't been hot already, but the huge temperature change had sweat forming out of every pore her body possessed. The shade over the deck earlier hadn't prepared her for this type of onslaught.

How had Sal walked out and disappeared without so much as pausing to get his bearings? How could anyone get used to this? She wiped the sweat from her forehead and shielded her eyes from the sun. He had to be out there somewhere.

Wait.

Her eyes had to be deceiving her. Standing there along the tree line, staring at her, was the white leopard. "Snow?" she said.

The cat shifted posture, bringing its chest down and front legs out. Hind legs coiled. That was strike position. The growl confirmed that.

Julia remembered those teeth—long, white fangs under snarling, pulled back lips. Golden eyes that pierced right through her.

Wait. Golden eyes? She stepped back in the doorway and held each side of the doorframe and squinted at the cat. It didn't come any closer, and it was too far to really see. Golden?

That shot her idea of it being albino. Albinos lacked pigment. Everywhere. Eyes should have been pink. Not yellow. So was that why Sal was studying them? Did this batch of leopards have unusual coloring and he wanted to see the genetic alterations? Or was he doing it himself?

"Sal?" she called out one more time. The cat slunk forward in response.

She slammed the door. Sal had gone out there earlier when she'd seen the one on the deck. Obviously he could handle himself. She wasn't about to take any unnecessary chances with any of the wild, native animals.

* * * * *

Julia stood over the microscope. Now what had he been talking about? Damaged cells? She looked at the most recent slide. Yeah, he was showing them to her, but was he going to get into details on how that particular concoction worked?

One ear tuned to the door, she fished out the paperwork he'd moved aside. It was definitely a different study. Just comparing the drawings she could tell that. But interesting...there were some strange similarities between the damaged cells she had on the microscope and the center cells in the progression of drawings on the paper she wasn't supposed to see. So maybe the studies weren't so separate at all.

She gasped. Maybe the serum was causing changes in the cells that it "healed". Damn, she wished she could read what he had down in his notes. She tried to recall everything he'd told her about his studies. Why hadn't she paid more attention?

Because she was thinking of him as a man and not a scientist. It was true, she'd all but discounted him as a rich playboy wannabe geneticist. And there was a good possibility she was dead wrong about that.

The least she could do, while she had free rein in the lab was gather notes. And she was going to start with the computer. He'd opened up the program and even translated it. It couldn't get better than that.

Until she sat down and the screen saver literally laughed at her when she couldn't produce a password. That was in Italian too, but she could understand the empty blank box in the middle of the screen with a big yield sign. Might as well have been a stop sign or dead end.

"Bastard," she muttered and kicked the chair. Only thing she had were the papers he'd given her to enter. Like she really could do much taking home a list of all the leopards he'd been able to track. Right.

She didn't bother. Instead she headed for a shower and a nap. Sal still hadn't returned, but worrying about him was a thankless job, and she just wasn't up to it. Not today.

* * * * *

Sal carefully opened the door and slipped the note on the dresser. The way she lay there, moonlight spilling in just enough to give her an ethereal glow, reminded him of that first night. He'd been a goner from that moment forward, thoroughly taken in by her tough innocence, though he hadn't realized it at the time.

Now he knew so much more about her, good and bad, and still felt the same way. Touching her earlier had been like a dream come true. The way things had been between them, he didn't think he'd ever get a welcome like that again.

But physical reaction wasn't enough, and he could sense she was holding back. The physical only release would certainly satisfy his carnal cravings, but would undoubtedly leave him hungry for that something else. He'd realized then that sex was not enough. He wanted her, all of her. And before he could encourage her to open up, nature had a laugh on him. The change had hit him once again without warning. He'd barely made it outside before falling to all fours.

Then he'd watched her stand in the doorway. Paolo had been out there too, anxious to catch her unaware. The talk he'd had with him after lunch was as fruitless as pissing in the wind. But he'd gotten another hint of Paolo's thinking. He heard a tinge of jealousy when Paolo accused him of favoritism by letting Julia work in the lab.

God, he hoped he could make it to Cairo and back without something major happening. Would Paolo actually strike out at Julia? Would he hurt her? Rape her? He couldn't see it, couldn't imagine his nephew — his own flesh and blood — being so...bad. But Carlotta had warned him. And up until Julia had arrived, Paolo had proven her wrong.

Sokhra had strict orders. And a loaded gun. Tranquilizer — she wouldn't accept the handgun. That he'd left loaded in his nightstand. Hopefully Julia wouldn't be afraid to use it if she had to.

The plan was to leave now, just before dawn, get a ride to Malakal and hopefully hire a ride to Khartoum. From there he could fly to Cairo. Best case scenario was a two day trip. Two nights of a hotel bed while Julia lay in his. Two nights in which he knew Paolo'd roam restless. It was a shame he couldn't trust her enough to bring her as far as Khartoum. She could stay in the resort there and relax by the pool.

He closed his eyes and imagined what that would be like. He could dart over to Cairo, get his shipment and then return to the hotel. Perhaps they could even stay an extra night, getting a little R&R for himself.

The idea had his body screaming for a taste of that. Peace. Quiet. Free of stress. He'd found that once, when he'd first gotten here. Before...

Back then he'd had the chance to fly home on a whim to spend a weekend or a month relaxing on some Sicilian beach.

Julia rolled over and mumbled something. He watched her, aching to push the hair off her face and envelop her in his arms. He'd pass up every beach in Italy to have her.

Sal turned and left the room, locking the door from the inside and closing it quietly. He needed to stop thinking like that. The only context Julia would come into would be the extra blood he'd need. He had to get her willing to help him on that front. Once he got back it was all going to be strictly business. The antibiotics were all available but had a short half-life. They'd have to move fast if he wanted a chance to cure Paolo, and himself, of this dreaded transformation.

He paused at Paolo's door with his hand on the knob. The wood there, too, had distinct claw marks. He was surprised he hadn't noticed them before. His chest tightened. The boy was destroying himself at a rate that was almost irreversible. Unless he *did* lock the boy up and force the serum on him, which he would do, the end would come faster than he'd ever expected.

Nothing could solidify the necessity of this trip more than that.

He let go of the doorknob, listened for a moment, and headed back downstairs.

* * * * *

Julia wadded the paper up and shrieked through her clenched teeth. She didn't care who heard her or what they thought. The bastard! How could he leave? Cairo. That was far enough. She could make it home from there.

She hurled the lightweight missile toward the lab door. It fell short. Just like every-freaking-thing-else. Tears welled up. Damn him. Sal wasn't going to let her go home, was he? She couldn't even fathom staying here another week, another month. No way would she make it a year, unless she learned the language. She laughed, but tasted the salt of her tears. Not likely. She had no teacher and really, no motivation.

Sokhra said something from the kitchen doorway. It put an exclamation mark on what she was dealing with. She couldn't communicate with anyone now that Sal was gone. Paolo was hardly ever around, not that he knew more than a dozen English words. She figured he must have friends in the village or his own duties. Hell, he might have gotten to go to Cairo. But she couldn't.

Julia waved Sokhra off. Not like she could explain, right?

Didn't help. She didn't care if it was childish. She wanted to stand up and stomp the floor and punch the wall and...she sucked in a deep breath. But of course, she wouldn't. Never had.

What she would do, if she could manage it, was reread the note after she finished breakfast and then formulate a plan. The stirrings of one already had started to replace the smoke from the fire Sal had lit. She could go back to the lab. She had questions. She would *find* answers.

She swallowed her toast and honey without tasting it. It was simply food. Sustenance. Free food, really, and she should be grateful for it. Same with the ability to stay in this nice home. Compared to anything else she'd seen so far in this part of Africa, this was a castle.

Why?

Julia got up, kicked the paper and dropped her dishes in the sink. Then, because she couldn't *not* pick it up, she retrieved the letter and smoothed it out. It was typed, but looking at Sal's signature and remembering his notes from the lab, she could understand why. His handwriting was a strong but violent portrayal of letters. See? He'd thought of her and made sure she could read it.

Her mind was a traitor. She wanted to be pissed off so bad, and yet for every bad thing she came up with, she focused on something good. Without trying.

Okay, so Sal wanted her to stay in his room. There was no retort to that. What harm would it do? He had a master bath, a big plus. And her room was empty, almost sterile. She might even find a clue to the mystery of this man somewhere in his room.

She ignored the sentence that mentioned the lab being off limits. *We'll pick up where we left off when I return,* he'd written. He probably worried she'd mess with what he had. She wiped crumbs off her lips and left a smirk in its place.

This may be the biggest challenge of her life, but she was going to figure out what he was doing in there. He'd given her a foot in the door and she was, no way, no how, going to let that door slam on her. It was probably good she hadn't told him what she did for a living. She could only imagine that he'd completely lock up everything so she couldn't discover exactly what he was studying.

Chances were rather high that Sokhra and the others had strict orders to keep her out. She wasn't going to be able to get up and walk in there.

She'd need to bide her time, find something to do until after lunch, and then take a late afternoon nap. Tonight, she vowed. She could slip in after everyone else had gone to bed.

Julia leisurely washed her cup and plate. At one point, she felt someone watching her, and turned to see the housekeeper in the doorway, an eyebrow lifted.

So she smiled. Sokhra smiled back.

It was a start.

It was time to get serious. Julia climbed the steps to the second floor. Time to revert from a helpless victim and take what control she could. It was painfully obvious the only person she could trust was herself.

Sal's room seemed as good a place as any to begin. She wasn't sure what she was looking for. Information about him. Who was he? Why was he here, other than the leopards? It was time to turn off the giddy schoolgirl feeling he'd managed to resuscitate in her and think like a scientist. Undoubtedly she'd find things she didn't want to know. Men this hot and sexy didn't hang out in a desolate savannah. Sal should either be married or living the high life—the rich bachelor that he was.

The idea that he acted so…interested in her had her stomach doing flips. She wasn't his type. Not a glamorous trendsetter or even a beautiful intellect. She was okay looking, she stayed in shape, but in truth she blended with the wallpaper. There was something she was missing.

So much left to learn. Scary how she'd let him into her bed without knowing much at all about him. No way would this have happened at home. It was the close quarters, the clinging need she had for him. Realizing that with newly opened eyes didn't make her feel any better.

But that would change. She was a survivor.

Chapter 10

Julia stood in the doorway that framed a room full of so much emotion. The room had been a prison and a parlor of delight. She nearly laughed at that thought. It hadn't been shallow like those terms portrayed. Perhaps easier to think of it that way, but she really did know better.

Sal had made love to her, not fucked her for some uncontrolled urge. She knew the difference. Sal wasn't all bad. She couldn't make him the villain, but she couldn't lay down and play victim anymore either.

Here, in this room, she had been. She'd listened to stories that were so out of this world she knew they were lies immediately. Why had he even thought she'd be so dumb as to believe them?

The white leopard biting her seemed like a far away dream at this point. It wasn't out of the realm of belief that she had been drugged or given some local drink that caused her to hallucinate it.

And his wounds? She had been so sure they were real, but it was clear now that they weren't. Way too hard to believe in a medicine so potent. Wasn't going to stop her from investigating...just in case. But right now she was quite skeptical.

Julia locked the door behind her. Probably best she work scientifically about this, as she'd been trained to do.

She started at his dresser. The items had been there before, but she hadn't regarded them as much as she should have. Two photos stood there in matching wrought iron frames. One of an older man with Sal's features. A snapshot, taken at something formal, Julia guessed. He wore a tux and the lady beside him a beaded floor length dress.

The picture beside it made her heart flutter just a bit. It was a posed picture. Sal and what she could guess was his family. He was younger. Probably twenty or so. About the age of the college students she taught. And while she recognized his features, the expression was completely new. He was happy. Not smiling or satisfied, but genuinely happy. All of them were. She could imagine the boisterous gathering and the joking and laughing as they posed for the shot.

It filled her with something. Longing? Yes, while it certainly made her miss her family, it also made her wish she could see Sal in this same mood. She wanted to watch his eyes sparkle as the corners crinkled with laughter. God, she'd never really heard him laugh.

It was a shame she knew so little about him. Fascinating. Frustratingly so, but nonetheless, it was true. And as much as she wanted to maintain how pissed off she was, she realized this was a golden egg — being able to find out more about the man than he'd ever offered.

She put the picture down and moved on. Her thumb brushed over Sal's face as she removed her hand. Something twisted in her gut. She ignored it.

Sal was very neat. He'd stretched out two necklaces on the dark wood of the dresser top. One all gold with a heavy filigree cross. A diamond accented the middle. Julia bit her lip. She could *not* imagine Sal wearing that. But then again, this was about learning new things. Apparently that visual of him had been wrong.

The necklace beside the gold was much more Sal. In fact, she'd seen Paolo wearing one similar to it. The chain was actually tightly woven fabric. Almost felt like a rawhide strap, but it was more intricate than that. It tied rather than clasped, and held a black charm. Onyx? Dyed ivory? It was a little carved leopard. A black panther. Now that suited Sal with his dark good looks.

She laid it back down neatly and picked up a little wooden box. Empty. That was disappointing. But there was so much more to find. Julia checked each drawer. Mostly clothes. One had a shoebox, but it contained receipts. Nothing in English.

In his nightstand she found a gun. After a split second of shock, she realized that many men in the US kept guns nearby and were probably safer than Sal was. He may not worry about someone breaking in, but the gun was probably handy to have on his back when venturing outside. With him gone, it somehow made her feel safer. Even if she had no clue how to even fire it.

Besides a few spare bullets, a journal also lived in the top drawer. Naturally, written in something foreign. Probably his native Italian. Just another thing she really had accepted in passing. His English seemed so perfect. But then again, he'd admitted to spending time at an American university. His accent drove her crazy. And she'd never been one to admit she found any particular accent sexy. With Sal, it was different. Not suave. Sincere. Part of who he was. When he used American slang it sounded so...strange. She was sure she'd never hear anything like it again.

As she tossed it onto the bed to work with later, a photograph fell out. Another family picture, this one a snap shot.

The boys looked to be about the same age as the posed picture. Early twenties or so. They were on a beach somewhere, Sal and the one who was obviously his brother. They each had a bikini-clad girl beside them. The man from the picture on Sal's dresser looked on, a beaming smile on his face. Dad, she guessed.

A fiery prod reached under her rib cage. She looked closer. The girl beside Sal hung on to his bicep and pressed her breasts against his arm. The smile on his face indicated he didn't mind one bit.

"Bitch," she muttered, and tossed the picture back into the drawer. *That* was an example of what she wasn't looking for.

Scientific, Julia. Not emotional. Or personal. Get a grip. Her field skills were rusty. She retrieved the photo and tucked it into the beginning of the journal. Last thing she wanted to do was throw up a red flag. Clean, scientific. Practice what she preached, that's what she needed to concentrate on.

Two hours later, Julia could recite Sal's shirt, pants and shoe size, knew he preferred the long, tight boxers as underwear and had a drawer full of white crew length sport socks. That was vital.

She rolled her eyes at her own sarcastic attitude. No skeletons in that closet. She'd scoured every inch of it.

Half of her felt relieved, half disappointed. But undoubtedly, the good stuff was all in the lab. And at nearly noon, the house staff wouldn't just let her waltz into his office and start rummaging through his files.

She'd do that later. First she wanted to make some notes.

It was going to be a long day.

* * * * *

Sal looked down at the mountains below him. It'd already been a

137

long day. The drive into Khartoum, a bumpy, tedious trip on a good day, had been riddled with a flat tire and an argumentative driver. The heat had caused a minor delay at the airport. He'd skipped lunch. Dinner wouldn't be happening until he was checked in to the hotel. His brother would probably give up and wait until morning to meet him and deliver the goods. Then he'd repeat this trek back to Sudan. Needless to say, his mood was shot, and he knew it.

The small commuter plane doubled as a sauna. A dull pain throbbed like a bass drum behind his eyes. Sweat had already soaked his clothes and now threatened to drip off his chin.

And his biggest fear was not being able to tell the change was coming on until it was too late.

He worried the hypodermic in his pocket. He had another dose tucked away in his luggage. He prayed he didn't need either. It had been a nightmare of a day. Only attempting traveling in the rainy season was worse. He'd long learned to avoid that. It was approaching quickly, however, and he still needed to spend at least a week in Florence. Time was running out for him.

Going to Florence meant letting Julia go. He stared out the window, angry that there were emotions tied to that thought. Loneliness had never even raised an eyebrow at him before. Paolo had come for at least a month every year and he had a house full of servants.

But Julia showed him that he *was* missing something, dammit. Something he didn't want to need. And he wasn't even thinking about sex, though the thought drew a smile to his face. Sex with her was amazing.

"*Dio*," he muttered. Now that was something he didn't need to complicate things. Trying to escape it all, he pulled out the list of supplies he'd requested.

He didn't even know what time it was when they finally landed, but there stood his brother, waiting on the tarmac.

"Salvatore," Antonio greeted with a kiss to the cheek. "You look tired."

"*Si*," Sal answered and let his brother take the extra suitcase. "It's not as easy as a quick jaunt from Florence to Sicily, that's for sure."

"A trip to Sicily would do you good. A few weeks on the beach, some R and R. You work too fucking hard. You need to get away."

"I wish." The airport wasn't where he wanted to fill Antonio in on the latest. He wasn't sure how, or if, to breach the Paolo incident. Incidents. The dread in his gut lanced razor sharp. What could be happening back home now?

"You need a drink. Or two. And perhaps some female company. Damn, boy, I don't think I've seen you this beat up in a long time."

Sal shook his head. Alcohol and sex used to be their answers to everything. Wasn't a bad temporary fix. But not tonight. He just wanted to get what he needed and get back before what he found matched his imagination. He waved off his brother's hint. "I've just got a ton going on and running low on this shit isn't helping. I'll get to relax when I get it done and make it up to Florence."

"Consuela's been calling about you."

Caro Dio. Consuela Diaz had been his almost-fiancée and held the record for holding on to his leash for the longest amount of time. And then, strangled, he'd fled, using his work as an excuse. He adored her, she certainly was entertaining in the bedroom, but he didn't miss her, hadn't ever missed her. "Tell me you're joking."

"She even flashed a rock the size of Gibraltar and whispered something about a last minute fling before she got married."

"Christ." No way, no how. Thank God he had come to his senses.

"While we're talking about your women..."

And Sal knew this was coming as well. Quite surprised his brother and his formal conversation ways had taken so long to get to the subject of his houseguest. "What?"

"I've seen her picture. It's wrong, Sal. Wrong."

"What the hell are you talking about? Wrong? I've been trying to get you and Carlotta to help me get her something — passport, ID, anything to get her out of Sudan. You know how strict they are about visitors. She has nothing."

"She had the basis of the plane crash to get her home, immediately. But no, you kept her around and now you've got this mess."

And unless he told his brother everything — now — there was no way to explain that he needed her. And then he'd have to admit he hadn't yet asked Julia for a donation of blood, leading Antonio to let loose a barrage of questions, starting with *why*.

That, he wasn't prepared to answer.

"So where's the hotel?"

Antonio's lifted eyebrow said more than he could. The grilling would come. Otherwise Antonio would have sent someone else to Cairo to meet him.

"Need to call home and check in?"

Sal leaned over and punched his brother's arm. He was too tired to argue and there was no reason to deny it. His older brother had never failed to yank the truth out of him, be it by threats or brute force. This wouldn't be any different.

"Let's go then, loverboy. Seems you've got a bunch to tell me. I'll let you off the hook tonight, though, because I'm pretty tired myself. But you'll be buying me a drink tomorrow and spilling it."

Thankfully Antonio led Sal back to his rented car and drove him on to the hotel with small bits of catch-up conversation. Carlotta was doing well, she'd started painting again, which, Antonio swore, worked like an aphrodisiac.

Like Sal wanted to know that. It of course, led him to think about Julia. What would work on her like that? He didn't know. There was a lot he didn't know. They'd skipped all that, thrust together as they had. He knew from the moment he'd seen her that he had to possess her. There had been something there in the way she was so vulnerable yet had fought so hard for life.

"Salvatore, we're here."

Antonio had parked and turned off the car while he'd been remembering her raw spirit. "Yeah, yeah, I'm beat, man. Tell me this place has room service."

"You know it does." Antonio yanked the suitcases out of the trunk. "And there's a room reserved in your name. I did it when I checked in. Just in case."

"Appreciate that, brother. I owe you."

"Just get up there and take it easy. I'm going to call Carlotta and call it a night."

Antonio slapped him on the shoulder and continued upstairs as Sal paused at the desk in the lobby. As his brother indicated, a room was already booked, and paid for, in his name. He was too tired to argue over it and accepted his key.

"Do you need my credit card to enable me to call home?"

"Italy, sir?" asked the fluent desk clerk.

"Sudan."

Sal smiled at the way the clerk's eyes widened. It would have been easier to call Italy, that he knew without a doubt. He'd never bothered to make the call home on his short jaunts to Cairo. Mainly because it was usually a day trip. Even short overnighters didn't require him to check in. But with Julia and Paolo both there, mostly unsupervised, well, he knew he couldn't sleep without knowing all was still okay.

"Sir, it's very expensive and…"

"I know. I need to check in. Money isn't important." Sal handed over a credit card drawn off an Italian bank.

"Yes sir. You'll be able to dial direct when you get up to your room. Will there be anything else?"

Sal tipped him. "Thank you and good night."

It was going to be a long night.

The phone rang and rang. What the fuck? His roast duck dinner sat on the tray beside his bed getting cold as he dialed again.

No answer.

"*Dio!*" He slammed the receiver back onto the cradle. Now what was he supposed to think? Had Paolo gotten to them all? Was Sokhra out? She better not have left those two in the house alone.

Fuck! He picked up his fork and stabbed at the meat. His appetite was freaking shot now. Dammit. He just knew shit like this was going to happen.

He hurled the fork across the room and grabbed the phone again.

On the sixth ring a sleepy voice answered. "Hello."

"Julia?" he sat down and finally took a breath of air. "Are you all right?"

"Sal?" she asked, then cleared her throat. "Where are you?"

She didn't sound right. "Are you okay? You're not hurt, everything's okay there?"

"You're scaring me, Sal. What's going on?"

He wanted to reach through the phone and grab her shoulders. He forced himself to inhale more cool air. "Answer me."

"I just woke up. Now what the hell are you talking about?"

He leaned back against the wooden headboard and closed his

eyes. Right. Sleep. That's exactly how she sounded, with her voice all throaty. She was asleep. In his bed.

"Sokhra should have answered the first time I called. Do you know where the hell she is?"

"Your housekeeper? Haven't seen her." Her tone was blunt. She was awake now.

"Where did you answer the phone?" he asked. The only phones were in Sokhra's room and the lab.

"Your office. Is there another phone? You didn't let it ring long enough. I tried to answer, you know, being that no one else did."

She was babbling. This wasn't going well. Not that he expected her to be glad to hear from him. He'd just wanted confirmation from Sokhra that it was another quiet night.

"You're right. Fine. Just make sure you close the door when you're done." He wanted to tell her not to try calling anywhere. Best he could do was hope she understood. "These phone lines aren't private, Julia. So don't launch into me about anything now. You can yell all you want when I get back."

"Why should I yell? I know what I am now. You've made it clear you've just hired yourself another servant."

Her tongue was a powerful weapon. Dammit. He wished he had something else to throw across the room. "Shut up and listen. Stay away from Paolo. Whatever room you're in, lock the door. Hang up with me and go to my room and lock yourself in. I mean it."

"Sal?" her voice shook. Anger faded to something else. Fear. Confusion. Dammit. What he wouldn't give to be there to protect her. At the same time, he knew he'd probably wish he had someone to protect him *from* her.

"You'll be fine. Just take that precaution since I can't be there. Promise me, Julia."

Silence.

It absolutely killed him to be so far away and helpless. He should have told her, made her listen. Something. This fleeting control was not to his liking. "Julia?" he growled.

He heard her sigh. Sweat beaded at his temples.

"Listen to me. I can't stay on the phone any longer. Just do what I say. I'll tell you everything I can when I get home. Go upstairs right away." He tugged the hypo out of his pocket and popped the cover off the needle. It was hitting him fast.

"But Sal—"

"Do it for me," he whispered.

Julia stared at the receiver that had gone dead in her hand. That bastard. What kind of message was that? Worse thing was she wasn't sure what to think. He had certainly sounded weird.

She chewed her lip. The phone had jolted her from a sound sleep. She'd been dreaming of Sal, but also dreaming of being home. Yeah, like that would happen. If they were someplace civilized he'd never give her another look.

The phone had cut in and ripped away that fantasy might-have-been. But this was another new option she hadn't considered. How easy would it be to place a call home?

Worse thing about it all was that she knew the phone was there, on the desk the whole time. Looked so...normal there that she hadn't given it a second thought. Gah! She was missing opportunities. But not this time.

She picked up the handset and stared at it. Then put it down. What was stopping her?

So was it monitored? Tapped? She picked up the old-fashioned looking base and peered underneath. Like she knew what she was looking for.

When she lifted the receiver again, it was dead. Had Sal not hung up? Why was the connection still open? Was that his way of blocking the phone or had something gone wrong there?

She barely knew him. In truth, they were still strangers. Intimate strangers, but it amazed her how little of their personal lives they'd shared with one another.

"That's because you're gullible and you fell for his games." She leaned back in the chair and stared at the black box. It should be her ticket home.

Truth was, she was scared.

Of Sal, of what she'd heard on the line, and then what she'd failed to hear. He'd just...disappeared. Bad connection. That had to be it.

Still, she got up and locked the door anyway. No sense in letting someone walk in.

And this is what she'd planned anyway, a late night information scouting adventure. Files, Internet, paperwork—at her fingertips.

Anticipation, exhilaration, hope…it all bubbled around her as she hit the power button on the modern computer system. She was going to do it. Somehow, she'd get word she was there.

But then it asked her for that stupid password.

She picked up the phone receiver. "Sal, dammit, you there? In case you are: I hate you for this."

Silence. A goddamn dial tone would be nice. At least she knew then he couldn't have heard her. "I can't believe you. Why are you doing this to me? Why?"

The receiver hitting the base echoed in the small room. Her breathing was labored. God, he pissed her off. She shouldn't let him, but he did. Probably because it was so foreign to her to have someone take her into his bed and make love to her—not just a quick roll in the hay—and then basically keep her captive without any signs of remorse. It wasn't right.

She slammed her fist into the keyboard. "Son of a bitch."

She tried the phone again. Nothing worked. She punched numbers and rattled the button to disconnect. Absolutely nothing.

Now what? All her hopes, dashed just like that. A password? What was he hiding?

He'd warned her to lock herself in. He said to be careful.

Horror sliced through her. Why? Why had he done that? Why was he concerned? And he was. She truly believed she'd been able to read his voice well enough. Were there leopards loose in the house? Or worse? Why *hadn't* the housekeeper answered the phone? And she hadn't seen Paolo. What if…?

Julia pushed the chair back against the file cabinet behind her and drew her knees up to her chest. Who the hell was Sal anyway?

Chapter 11

It didn't make sense.

Julia sat in front of the microscope Sal had used the day before to show her the damaged cell. The slides in and around it now were different than what they'd looked at before.

Similar, yet different. How many experiments was he doing at one time?

Why hadn't she had the foresight to take Italian in high school? Yeah, right. That made her snort, which echoed in the eerily quiet lab. She'd only turned on the lights over the counter where she worked. Last thing she wanted was to alert the rest of the house to her presence here with five hundred watts of brilliant light.

But with her skin still crawling from Sal's strange long-distance panic and then his cryptic warnings, she wondered if sticking around in here was such a good idea. The corners were terribly dark. Something— someone could crouch there and she'd never be able to see them. It sucked to be scared of something and not even know what it was.

She turned back to the papers she'd spread out on the desk. There was no time for fear, she had things to learn.

As she compared the data, she found three clearly different specimens. The first she knew as human. Those were the ones Sal had said he'd taken from his injury. Skin cells. There were others, as well, blood cells, maybe? What she wouldn't give for a biology textbook, in English, of course.

The second was labeled *Panthera Pardus*. That was Latin, not Italian, and it didn't take a scientist to know what it meant. Best guess she had there was that the four cells represented were also various samples from a leopard. Skin, blood, muscle? She squinted as she held the slide up to the light. Didn't matter. Unlike the first set, these demonstrated no changes. Almost as if they were there as a constant.

It was the last set that held the most interest. They were labeled one through six. Which led her to believe they were a sequence. The first cell appeared normal. And each cell after that showed slight changes until the ending cell only resembled the first in basic structure. Something was altering the cell.

Whatever they meant, it was clear that the two sides of the equation were not equal. If there even *was* an equation.

The more she learned, the more confused she got.

One thing she knew for certain. When Sal got back from Cairo or wherever, she was going to demand to know the truth. And then she was going home.

Three hours later, Julia was on the verge of banging her head against the desk. The obvious was right there. A catalyst.

She was still stuck on the last set of slides. Those had been the ones Sal had been quick to tuck out of her way.

She had way too many questions. Where had they come from? Why did Sal have them and what did it have to do with his magic cure serum? And now, what catalyst prompted these cells to morph?

For having a doctorate, she sure felt stupid. If she would have been able to get Sal off her mind she might have prevented herself from wasting so much time.

She flipped over the next page in the legal pad she'd borrowed from his office and listed more of her observations.

Someone tapped her on the shoulder.

She screamed. If she could have run, she would have, but she was trapped between the stool and the counter and whoever stood behind her.

Julia put a hand over her heart at the sight of Paolo. "God, you scared me. What are you doing up at this hour?" It had to be two or three in the morning by now.

Paolo just stared at her.

Of course, he didn't understand her. She shook her head and touched her temple. "Sorry." So how was she supposed to prompt him to reveal why he just scared the crap out of her?

The look in his eyes finally registered with her. Instead of relaxing, her body tensed once more.

Watch out for Paolo. Sal had said. *Lock the doors.*

She hadn't. Not the main lab door.

"Paolo?"

Empty eyes stared at her. Nothing friendly there. Or confused. They were like cold, black ice.

She backed up against the counter. Fear left a metallic taste in her mouth and caused a clammy sweat to coat her body. "Paolo?" she asked again. Why wasn't he at least acknowledging her? If he'd come to kick her out of the lab, why didn't he point to the door? "What do you want?"

He blinked.

Then smiled.

Julia gasped in horror. Tears sprung to her eyes. As his lips curled even farther into a snarl, his teeth glistened in the light.

Not square, straight human teeth.

What she saw in his mouth caused an image of another set of teeth to flash in her memory. Long, white canines dripping blood. Her blood.

She blinked. She had to be seeing things. It was late; her mind was tired.

Paolo took a step closer. And she hadn't been mistaken. Where human teeth had been, hideous leopard-like teeth were.

She screamed. Then took a breath. And screamed again.

There was nowhere left to go. No place to run.

* * * * *

He'd been gone too long. Worrying about Julia and Sokhra and even Paolo had kept him on edge and unable to enjoy even a few minutes of his trip. Despite trying to call, he hadn't been able to reach anyone for two days. He wondered what he'd be walking into when he finally did arrive.

He cradled the package on his lap and stared out the window. Any other time the trip would have been glitch free. Not this time. Not when he was desperate to get home. Customs had a fit about the materials he was bringing into the country and his credentials had to be checked and double-checked by at least six different personnel before he was granted clearance.

Normally he would have complained. For show, he put up a few token protests at the airport, but he was too tired, too damn impatient and too worried to put forth the effort to fight it like he should have.

He had hoped to be home by now. At this rate, if he got lucky, he'd make it there by late afternoon. He'd been gone for three days. He hoped that dry ice held up that long. But there were things that worried him more than that.

The truck bumped along, exaggerating every pit in the road. He couldn't sleep if he wanted to, despite being one step beyond exhausted.

The temperature outside had to be a near record high. Inside the vehicle, packed with the suitcases he wouldn't dare tie to the top of the truck, it was almost unbearable. They drove with the windows barely open. The roads were quickly turning from hard packed dirt and gravel to dust and sand in the baking sun, and it whipped around and into the truck as they lumbered over the trail.

A surge of pain hit his feet.

"Pull over!" he shouted to the driver in Arabic.

The driver let off the gas.

"Pull over now. Let me out." The pain was intense. There was no room for this. "Stop the truck." Sal reached over and yanked the wheel toward him, sending the vehicle careening toward the brush that grew sporadically alongside the road.

The driver let out a stream of curses and slammed on the brakes.

Sal was already opening the door and rearranging the bags he'd had on his lap. "Here," he thrust a sizable bill at the driver. "He prayed it was enough to buy his loyalty. "Go. Take these to my house." He pulled out another bill. "When you get to the next village, ask for the big house. They'll direct you. It's not very far from here. Nothing I have would be valuable to you. But if anything happens, I will find you. That I promise. Go!"

His voice shattered. His hands shook. *Dio*, he had to get out of here before this stranger witnessed something he'd never believe.

Sal slammed the door and let the dust fly up over him. There was no time to run, and nowhere to go. At least the driver had the presence to take off. The haunted look of fear in the man's wide eyes was the last thing Sal's human eyes acknowledged.

Dust clogged his nostrils and burned his eyes. For once, he was glad the change was quick, despite the tearing pain that accompanied it. He needed to follow the truck. He couldn't take the chance the driver might feel tempted to stop and investigate his cargo. Or see if he couldn't make a little more cash peddling it off to the locals.

Meeting up with a persuasive leopard would force him to reconsider. Or...

Sal wondered if he could actually kill someone. He didn't think so. Biting into Julia's shoulder had been a difficult decision. In the end necessity had won out.

He loped behind the slow moving truck, careful to stay behind the cloud of dust, and remembered that moment. He'd driven out to the wreckage site the moment he'd heard the crash. But halfway there, the change had hit him.

When he'd found her, her arm was badly broken. Several hyena were tracking her, as well as a she-leopard with cubs to feed. There was no way he'd leave her to die that way.

But getting the healing formula into her arm would be more challenging than he thought. It was starting to get dark and the hypodermic too difficult for his paws to negotiate.

In the end he'd stood over her and claimed her as his. Those eyes, tear filled and wide with shock, would haunt him forever. He couldn't hurt her again if he tried.

He'd bitten the hypo then and let the serum drip from his mouth into the wounds he'd made. He'd prayed it'd been enough.

Ahead of him, the driver slowed. He could hear the reason—an oncoming vehicle.

He was left out in the open. Easy prey. These were the chances he didn't want to take. Why couldn't things go as planned? Everything he needed to cure himself, and Paolo, was right there in that truck cab. The healing serum was nothing in comparison to the anti-transformation serum he needed to perfect. Time was running out.

Sal sprinted forward.

Too late.

Someone yelled out the window of the passing car. Tires dug into the dirt and coughed up an opaque cloud. They were coming after him. The white leopard was a legend, and capturing it would make a man a hero.

Sal computed what it would take to leap to the top of the covered bed of the truck. Muscles were fatiguing fast. He wasn't made for long distance running.

The telltale *chunk* of a shotgun being loaded made the decision a final one for him. He launched himself upward.

A shot whizzed through the air much too close to his head. He dropped to the roof of the truck and flattened himself to the white cap. Two boxes had been tied aboard. They offered a slight amount of cover.

All he could do then was pray.

* * * * *

Julia opened the door once she confirmed it was Sokhra.

The housekeeper had saved her from unspeakable things the two days before. Sokhra had responded to Julia's screams by bursting into the lab carrying a strange looking gun.

Paolo had taken a step back and made some hissy-growling noise at her, then let loose in a gasping of Italian that could only have been pure filth. Julia stood frozen in place while Sokhra had leveled the gun at the boy and pulled the trigger.

Since then, Julia had listened to Sal's instructions and remained locked in his bedroom.

"Paolo," Sokhra said, making a shooing type motion with her hands.

Julia nodded. They'd struggled through sign language for the last day, but were finally starting to communicate with some success.

Of course, hearing Sal's warning echo in her head helped. There was something wrong with Paolo. Something seriously wrong. He was dangerous.

The night before, Sokhra had brought supper up to the bedroom and managed to infer that Sal was due home. At least that's what Julia thought sketched out clock and frantic pointing to Sal's picture meant.

She'd laid awake most of the night, listening for him to come in.

To Julia's knowledge, Sal still hadn't shown up. The housekeeper looked worried. Her face held no trace of a smile and her movements lacked their regular efficiency. Had something happened? Did Sokhra know and was unable to tell her?

That would be the worst. She rightly couldn't think of any news that would devastate her more. If something happened to Sal while he was gone...well, she may never make it home.

Julia reached out for Sokhra's hands and sought out eye contact.

She breathed a sigh of relief. It wasn't grief. Not the heart wrenching grief that she would expect to see clouding the woman's black eyes. Julia guessed it was still simply concern.

"Hoo-laa," Sokhra grinned as she tried to pronounce Julia. Her lips shifted as she searched for the next word. Finally she shrugged and pointed to her mouth, then pretended to hold a spoon or fork and feed herself.

"Eat?" Julia prompted.

"Eat." Sokhra repeated. "Hoo-laa eat." Then she pointed to the door and then to the floor.

"Yes. Julia eat." She wasn't necessarily hungry — her stomach was too busy doing nervous somersaults to trigger an appetite. And Sokhra wanted her to go downstairs. At least she still held that gun — tranquilizer, she knew now. At least it was something. And she said Paolo was out. It would be nice to escape these four walls for a little while.

"Boom." Sokhra stopped Julia from following her out of the room.

What? Boom? Julia shook her head at the shorter woman and held her hands up. "Boom?"

Sokhra pointed to the nightstand. "Boom."

Julia walked over and pointed.

Sokhra nodded and flashed her teeth.

Boom. Nightstand. Lamp. Journal. Glass of water. Nope. No boom there.

Sokhra said, "Hoo-la." Then made a fist and pull it toward her.

This was what frustrated her like nothing else. The never ending game of charades that tried both their patience. But she'd gotten it. She opened the drawer and lifted the gun. The clip was in it. No bullets lying on the bottom of the drawer.

"Gun? Boom?"

Sokhra grinned and reached for the outstretched weapon. With the ease of a pro, she checked the chamber, flipped the safety and handed it back to Julia.

"I don't want this." She shook her head and tried to hand it back. She didn't want, or need, the gun. She put it back in the dresser.

"No." Sokhra had that universal word down pat. "Boom."

Why would she need it if Paolo was indeed out? The gun made her nervous. She didn't know enough to handle it properly.

But Paolo scared her. Deeply frightened her. Possibly even more so than when the white leopard had stood over her. At least then she understood. That had been an animal instinctively attacking. Paolo was...not entirely human.

Putting that into words, even mentally, shot a chill through her.

So what was Sal? Maybe it was a good idea if she carried the weapon with her after all.

Sokhra grabbed her arm and pulled her down the hallway. Words were useless. What she wouldn't give for a simple answer to her question, "Why?"

The gun felt foreign in her hand. It was heavy, awkwardly balanced unless she tilted it up to aim. If she had on a pair of jeans, she might have been able to holster it in a pocket or even the small of her back. People did that all the time on TV. But the elastic waist warmup pants she'd grabbed from Sal's drawer weren't made for carrying a weapon.

She thought they were going to eat. But Sokhra led her straight through the kitchen and into the lab. What kind of ploy was this?

She forgot her hunger, however, when she saw what lay behind that door. The lab was a mess.

Paolo.

Now she saw the need for the gun. Her first thought was that she was going to kill that boy for doing this to her, to his uncle. Unbelievable.

She walked over to the station where she'd been taking notes. What she'd written out was safely upstairs. Thank goodness.

Slides were scattered on the counter and the floor. She picked them up, put them in order as best she could. Only two were broken. Notes were all there too. All mixed up and crumpled, but intact.

It was only then Julia let out her pent-up breath. Maybe she'd done it. Lord knows she'd practically climbed up on the counter to get away from the boy—monster—whatever he was. She could have pushed the papers together or tipped the box over.

Sokhra tapped her on the shoulder. Julia nearly jumped out of her skin.

The smile that normally split the woman's face into a series of wrinkles was gone. Julia followed her pointing finger to realize why. Just inside the door were three suitcases. Expensive leather suitcases. They could only be Sal's.

What she wouldn't give to speak Sokhra's language right now. "Sal?" she asked. Was he here? Was he home? No, if he was, she wouldn't be looking so...worried. Like a mother when her son was late for curfew. Sal didn't seem the type to worry her. He was organized, orderly.

Sokhra shook her head.

What did that mean? She had a million questions and answers were going be impossible to get. "No Sal?" That was simple enough, right?

Of course, Sokhra's responding shake of the head could mean she was saying "No, no Sal," or "I have no clue what you're asking me."

Her chest rose with a heavy breath.

Sokhra didn't stop her when she walked over and hoisted one of the bags up onto the nearest table. Had he any idea what he was doing to his housekeeper? Or her? Damn it. She jerked the zipper on the side pocket open and reached inside. How dare he worry them like this?

He could have called. He'd called before. How hard was it really, to pick up the phone and say, "Hey, I'm taking a side jaunt to wherever but I'm sending the suitcases I don't need home ahead of me". He'd pay for this. She already had plans to take a stand, and boy, oh boy was he going to hear about it when he finally strolled in.

Julia tucked the ticket stubs back into the pocket. He'd flown back to Khartoum from Cairo. Last night.

So where had he been for the last—she consulted her watch—sixteen hours?

The main compartment of the luggage held exactly what she'd expected to find. Clothes. His standard fair—casual cotton trousers and short sleeve shirts.

Strange. She picked up a navy polo shirt. It looked to be covered with white fur.

"Whatever," she said, tucking it back in and zipping it back up. All that meant was at some point, someplace he went there was a white cat. Or dog. Or hamster. Maybe he was checking out white mice or rats for lab experiments.

She was making way too much out of this.

And Sokhra just stood there, arms limp, watching.

What the hell was going on?

* * * * *

Sal limped up to the house.

The grand chase for the white leopard ended when the truck he'd hired veered off the road and tipped onto its side. He'd been thrown and managed to crawl, bruised, into a thicker bit of brush.

There he'd lain until someone had provided help getting the truck righted again. It was all he could do to stand down when the driver paid the good Samaritan with the box that he'd protected all the way back home. The gift he'd intended for Sokhra, a porcelain angel, had likely cracked when the truck tipped. But Julia's piece, a solitaire sapphire necklace was more payment than either of those two men out there deserved.

At least the rest of the items, all stacked and hopefully well packed in his suitcases, were delivered to his house without a hitch. Still unable to shake the leopard form, Sal had watched as Sokhra accepted the bags with a long face. She'd stood at the door for nearly ten minutes after the truck rolled away and stared into the horizon.

He should have gone to her. But he couldn't take the chance Julia was there, with her. This was not the homecoming he'd planned.

His reserves had long run out. All he wanted to do was sleep. But reassuring Sokhra — and seeing Julia — drove him forward.

It'd been hell climbing the stairs to his bedroom. He'd run too far today, and then changed back when he was miles from the house. And then he'd found his bedroom empty. Paolo's room too.

And Julia's room.

Adrenaline offering a temporary boost, his pace picked up as he aimed for the kitchen. Empty.

His lab? Were they all in his lab? Or...no, no, he'd seen Sokhra earlier. She had to be here somewhere.

He pressed his ear to the door. Not that he'd hear much, unless Paolo roared or one of them yelled or screamed. They could be somewhere else, too. Maybe she'd tucked Julia away in the basement to keep her safe. Or maybe she'd put Paolo down there, to keep him away from Julia.

Still, he opened the door quietly. Relief coursed through his ragged veins. She was here. Alive. His Julia. He paused for a moment and just took her in. His main concern was unfounded. Nothing in the fluid way she moved indicated she was injured in anyway.

Then she reached up to push a loose strand of hair behind her ear. That was his job. He wanted to feel the softness of her cheek against his fingers and smell the sweetness of her hair. She hadn't seen him yet. Hadn't shocked him senseless with the vividness of her eyes.

Damn, he loved her. Any doubt of that had disappeared in Cairo when he'd talked to her on the phone. He'd felt like he'd left half of himself behind. And now the slam of emotions into his chest at seeing her — just confirmed he'd found where that half was. It was her.

Their relationship was starting to take baby steps in the right direction. It had been a terrible time to leave. Chances were, he'd undone every inch of progress he'd made by leaving the country without her. So getting what he wanted — a warm welcome home — was not going to happen.

In fact...he blinked again at her. Damn his heart for blinding him. He'd looked right past what she was doing to concentrate on his own wimpy emotions. Maybe he could make an anti-love serum next. Something that would force his brain to concentrate only on work.

"What the hell are you doing?" he roared, pissed more at himself than her, but panicking when he saw her unzipping the lid on the final suitcase.

"Sal!" she ran toward him. He almost believed she looked happy to see him. But then she stopped. Probably because she saw the look on his face.

"What are you doing?" he demanded.

"Where have you been? Do you have any idea how worried we

were? You have no idea what was going through my mind. I was trying to figure out why the luggage got here before you. See if you'd sent it on with some sort of message inside."

"I didn't." He lifted an eyebrow. What kind of excuse for snooping was that?

"No kidding."

"There are—"

"The vials that were packed in dry ice are already in the fridge. The others are stacked right there, waiting for you to come home and do what you will with them. Blood—was that blood? Anyway, two of the bags had broken. Looks like the weight of something smashed them. And I'm not sure they've been kept as cool as they should have. But I put them in the fridge as well." She recited it all as efficiently as a secretary to her boss. He studied her eyes. Any emotions there were hidden. Why, Julia, why?

Sal nodded, then leaned over and lifted the lid of the final suitcase. "Here." Hopefully he could get her to react this way.

Julia gasped. "What?"

"These are for you. Not that you don't look incredible in my pants, but I thought you'd like something in your size." Carlotta had crammed everything he could have imagined plus more into that suitcase. Julia's eyes nearly bugged out as she lifted a short, sexy cotton nightshirt. Then a sun dress. Sandals, pants, shirts. And he knew she'd be thrilled to find makeup and lotions and all that stuff women love wrapped beneath the clothes.

Julia looked down at herself. It wasn't for him. She looked beautiful no matter what she wore. But she was surprised. "For me?" she squeaked.

He wanted to smile. Just had no strength left to pull his face muscles into one. At least he'd evoked some emotion. He reached out and pushed the hair off her cheek. "For you, *amore*."

She surprised him by tossing her arms around his neck and leaning in on tiptoe. "Oh, thank you, thank you."

His body wasn't too worn out. It responded like a match on dry timber. He was almost afraid to touch her. His hands grazed her rib cage. Christ. He couldn't do this.

"Back up, Julia, unless you want to know how much I missed you."

She sucked in her breath and stepped back.

Before she could respond, negatively, he said, "Thank you for seeing to the supplies."

She nodded. He tried to change the subject but his mind was still stuck on her. The slight pink tinge of embarrassment on her cheeks, the way she stared at him and then looked away when he stared back. And here he'd expected a slap in the face, not a hello hug.

"Hoo-laa?" Sokhra interjected.

Sal looked past Julia for the first time. Great, now he felt bad. He'd totally missed seeing her stand there by the door. With a..."What the hell is going on, Sokhra? Why do you have the tranquilizer?"

He looked around. Sure enough, the handgun from his bedroom was only a few feet to Julia's right. "And why does Julia have my gun?"

Obviously his concerns hadn't been for nothing. But they were alive, and looked well. A lot better than he felt, to be sure. His head screamed with the effort of digesting all this at once.

Julia was still too close. His body felt drawn to her, reacting like metal shavings to a magnet.

"I'll take it from here. Take that bag up to my room and put your things away. My room. Not yours." He started zipping it up for her. "And carry the gun with you."

Sal walked over to Sokhra. Obviously, things weren't in the same state he'd left them in. "Where's Paolo?" he asked.

"Out. As a leopard again."

"Why the guns? Has he tried to attack? What has he done?" He'd had to do something to cause Sokhra to stand at the door like a guard.

She uncocked the gun and handed it back to Sal. "He leaves me alone. It's her he wants."

"Why?" Jealousy was one thing. He just didn't understand the fascination with Julia. No. He did. But if the circumstances were reversed, he could never imagine striking out at her. "Is his intent to harm her or kill her?"

When the woman's eyes grew big, his gut clenched.

"Tell me. What did you see?"

"Half-formed he came in here. She was working. I don't know what he would have done, but he had her cornered. She's locked herself in your room since then. I brought her down here today when your luggage arrived. It was my idea she bring the gun. Just in case."

Per l'amor di Dio, half-formed? Christ. He willed his blood pressure not to cause his head to explode. There was way too much to digest. He'd let his temper go to hell when he finally dealt with Paolo. Not Sokhra. Not Julia.

With teeth clenched, Sal nodded and shoved his hands in his pockets. Julia still stood there, watching them, her eyes narrowed to slits. Probably pissed as hell because they were talking and she couldn't understand. And it had to be obvious they were talking about her. "Julia?"

Her lips were set tight. She pulled the suitcase off the table and towed it behind her as she approached them.

"Get the gun," he ordered.

She looked over her shoulder. For a minute he thought she'd refuse.

"Sokhra said Paolo came in here and tried to attack you?"

Julia stopped and looked up. *Dio.* He had, the dark haunting was there, in her eyes.

"What did he look like when he came after you?"

She swallowed and shook her head. She picked up the gun. Her fingers rolled the gun over and over in her hands. It made him nervous.

"You have to tell me. I need to find him. What did you see?"

He could have sworn he saw moisture in her eyes, but she blinked and tossed her hair back. Then lifted the gun. At him.

"He was deformed. His teeth weren't normal. His eyes weren't normal. He just growled. What have you done? What did you do to your nephew? Who are you?"

"Put the gun down. I'll explain everything. I tried to before, but you wouldn't listen." He watched her eyes. They were dry now, but her lip trembled. He'd driven her to this? "Julia, please. Come with me upstairs and we'll talk it through. I'm here and you have nothing to worry about. He won't attack you while I'm here."

"How can you just say that?"

"Because I know." He lied. Flat out lied to her and it didn't feel good. Paolo was unpredictable and very dangerous. Regardless of Sokhra's pleas to have mercy, his only choice was to use the tranquilizer gun to take him down and then treat him like the wild animal he'd become.

But he had to live long enough to do that, and right now he wasn't sure Julia was going to let him.

"Please. Let me explain. The work we're doing here in the lab is to help Paolo. That's why I had to go. Don't think I didn't want to take you, but I couldn't this time."

"Cut the crap, Sal, I'm not stupid. You've now brought me clothes. I might as well settle in for the long haul, eh?"

"I wanted you to be comfortable."

"You never asked what I wanted." He watched as she shook the gun to prove her point. One fatal squeeze of the trigger would be all it took.

"I know what you want. You want to go home to Albany, New York and be Dr. Haverstock." He thought he'd enjoy revealing what he'd learned from his brother. But the look of shock on her face made him feel like he'd betrayed her even more.

"You bastard." She lifted the gun's aim from his chest to his face. There was nothing humorous about staring down the barrel of his own gun.

"I'm not perfect. But I'm not trying to hurt you. Truth is," he lowered his voice and did his best to speak earnestly. "I need your help."

She laughed. "Help? Sharpening your pencils? Typing in your research papers? Give me a break."

This was going badly.

"I was hoping to use the clothes as temporary payment for your assistance in the lab. Obviously you've held some details back from me. How am I supposed to trust you after that?"

She shifted her weight from foot to foot and chewed on the side of her mouth. A crack in the facade, he hoped.

"I'll lay it out for you. I'm too tired to play games. I need your help in the lab. Paolo has come in contact with an early batch of the healing serum. Instead of healing the cells, it invades the surrounding cells and changes the genetic make-up."

"To what?"

The gun was still up, pointed, but her blue eyes sparkled with a hint of curiosity. He needed to keep talking.

"The serum is created from leopard blood cells. Leukocytes."

She nodded.

"To get the healing serum to work, there had to be a catalyst to get it started once it was introduced to damaged cells and tissue.'

Another nod. Good. She was following.

"Obviously this was a trial and error basis. Unfortunately, one of the first experiments had a catalyst that was too strong. As I said, it invaded the cells of the host, turning them into the cells of the donor."

He let her digest that. She blinked at him a few times, her bottom lip caught between her teeth.

This conversation should have taken place in his office, or over dinner. Not with tempers already flaring, patience long disappeared and a gun between them.

"Give me the gun, Julia. Let's talk about this."

She stared at him. He wished he could read her thoughts.

There was no indication she understood. She simply walked up to him, handed over the gun and walked out of the lab.

Sokhra followed her.

Chapter 12

He had to be wrong.

Julia paced the length of the bedroom and tried to remember what Sal had said, exactly. Her stunned senses must have blurred something.

What he was describing was impossible. That was the sort of stuff that happened in cartoons or comic books.

It was only a matter of time before he came upstairs and tried to talk to her. Preposterous. She couldn't believe this any more than she could his previous full blown fantasy style stories.

What it boiled down to was that he may have had the intention of trying to get her home, but when he learned of her credentials, he decided to milk her for her knowledge.

Bullshit.

She sat down with her notes and wrote. From memory, she sketched the way the cells had changed. Cells.

In a fit of anger, she threw the notebook against the wall. How could there be cells like this?

She needed some answers. He'd gotten the upper hand earlier, but she wouldn't walk away again. Now that he knew her title, he'd better respect it.

When she opened the door the next morning, she saw the Sal she had on that first day. He'd dug a lab coat out of somewhere. The collar was twisted and the back in need of a good ironing. Still needing a haircut, he'd obviously pushed it up off his forehead a time or two, causing it to look a little spiked. The shadow at his chin was the thickest she'd ever seen it.

Stop looking at him. She closed her eyes and leaned against the doorframe. This man was her lover, how could she *not* see him like that. What a traitor her body was.

"Julia," he said as he looked up from the notes he was writing. "Were you just stopping to visit or were you interested in lending a hand?"

Don't be nice to me. I don't want to feel guilty. I don't want to be nice back to you. "Uh…" Why was she here?

"I promised some explanations and now's a good time."

That's what she wanted, wasn't it? But he made it sound… *No, what she wanted wasn't what she needed.* "I'm not comfortable about the way things are going."

"And I don't blame you."

Who kidnapped Sal and sent back this imposter? "Huh?"

Sal pulled up a stool and patted it. "I promised before I wouldn't bite. That still holds. I want to hear what you have to say, having seen these and obviously, having reviewed things when I was gone."

No accusation, no disrespect. She had no clue how to respond. "I think you're lying to me again."

He laughed!

"Humor me then. Humor my lies. I'll translate all of this for you if you'll help me."

"I got a better idea. Why don't we talk about this healing serum and forget this other —" she waved her hand. "Charade."

She figured that'd push a button, make the volatile attitude return.

Nope.

"Well, let's make some of that. I did run out. Never know when we might need it around here. I'd have been out of luck if you'd have shot me, earlier, right?"

She found nothing funny in what he said. "No, Sal, because if I would have pulled that trigger, you wouldn't have had a brain left to think about using the serum."

He nodded, grinning.

She wanted to smack the smile off his face. Why had she come down here, anyway? Glutton for punishment, that's what she was.

"Let's work over here then, so I don't have to put that other stuff away."

She hadn't moved from the doorway. How had she managed to agree to help him? "Maybe this isn't such a good idea. I'll hinder you because you'll have to take the time to explain it all to me anyway. Besides, this isn't what you were working on?" She backed up.

"So?" he shrugged. "I'd really enjoy having some company. Stay with me, please?"

Why, why did he have to do the sad puppy-like eye pout?

This is what she wanted to know, anyway. He was telling her he'd straight out talk her through the details she couldn't translate. She'd be more than a fool to pass up this opportunity. Yet... "I don't know..."

"Listen, I'm really sincerely sorry for not telling you I had to go. It was a rush trip. Getting supplies always is, and I couldn't take the chance you'd get held up in Customs. You have no passport, nothing."

"Sal, I—"

"Besides, I only went as far as Cairo. I'll take you all the way home to New York if you want. But I promised Florence. I can get you to Florence soon. Then I know you'll get the rest of the way home safely."

She opened her mouth to speak, but then closed it. Finally she muttered, "Cairo would have been far enough."

"I would have worried. Bad things can happen to single women traveling alone in strange countries. I know people in Italy, we can get you first class, no hassles in Customs, everything. I'd never forgive myself if something would have happened to you in Cairo."

"I'm a grown woman, Sal. Not a teenager."

"Yes."

Didn't matter now, though, did it? He'd gone to Cairo and not taken her. Rehashing it wouldn't change a damn thing.

"Okay, so cut the act and just talk to me about the serum."

Sal lifted an eyebrow. "The healing serum. What do you call it?"

It was a game. That was obvious. He was playing with her.

"Your magic cure-all. Doesn't matter, though, does it? This was a bad, bad idea. I'm going back upstairs." And she meant it too, until his hand wrapped around her wrist and dragged her back into the room. "Stop it."

He whipped her around in a dance type move that left her right up against his chest. It ripped the breath right out of her. "Sal--"

"Don't go. I want you to stay and help me."

She didn't think she could talk, much less logically answer him. "Why?" As soon as the word came out of her mouth, she regretted it. Talk about opening herself up for more lies.

He leaned down. Oh God, he was going to kiss her. Then what

was she going to do? How could she think with him teasing her like that? "I don't have much time. Together we'll work faster and accomplish more than I could alone. Besides, a fresh pair of eyes," he paused to kiss one of them, "might help me figure out what I'm missing."

She swallowed and kept her eyes closed. His breath ruffled the hair on her forehead. His body said one thing, his words another. Which could she believe, trust?

"Let me go," she asked. "This has to be about work, and work only. Neither of us can afford the distractions."

He kissed her forehead. "You're right."

But he refused to let her out of the circle of his arms.

"Sal?"

His mouth dipped dangerously close. Sweet God in heaven, don't let him do this to her.

He did.

She felt the rumble in his throat as his lips brushed hers. The sound was appropriate—something between satisfaction and agony. She opened her mouth to him and molded her body against his. It'd be so easy to just say "yes" and indulge in the pleasure he brought to her body. He'd proven to her so many times that she couldn't fight it. Once he had her this close, with his breath mixing with hers and their bodies pressed in an intimate promise, she was a goner.

Sal's teeth grabbed her bottom lip, then covered her entire mouth, tracing the sensitive inner part of her lips with his tongue. And all she could think of was having his mouth doing that exact same thing between her legs.

He broke away, stealing her breath and her balance.

"We have to get some work done. We can finish that later."

Julia shook her head. "That shouldn't happen." But she wanted it. More than she could tell him.

Sal still didn't let her pull out of his embrace. He leaned into her and brushed his lips over hers, lightly. What a man of contradictions.

She would *not* let him get her riled up. That's what he was doing, she was certain. Pushing buttons. Proving he was in control. Exhibiting his power over her.

And damn her for letting him. Hell, he had her either way. If he pulled away and she let him, he was getting his way. If she fought him, then he was getting what his body said it wanted anyway. Not that she'd be on the losing side of things. But... "I thought you wanted to work," she asked.

"In a minute."

She pulled back. He let go. She'd call this match a draw. They stared at each other for a moment before Sal touched her elbow and guided her over to the microscope.

They sat down. Julia didn't know what to think. Was he trying to make her crazy? He handed over papers the way a co-worker would. Without eye contact, without expression or emotion. How could he have simply thrown a switch and reverted back to Sal the scientist instead of the man who couldn't help but kiss her?

And he kept it up. Several times she stopped to stare at him, open mouthed, because he was so involved in what he was explaining that he didn't realize he'd guided her hand or even leaned over her. When he did that, all she could breathe in was the essence of him. Who could think about cellular rebuilding when he was doing that?

But things were making more sense now. Experiment wise, anyway. While the serum that triggered the body to rebuild itself essentially worked without flaw, there were some definite drawbacks. One couldn't control the pace or the intensity of the reaction. On her, it'd healed a broken arm—how could she not remember that? The whole night of the plane crash was a foggy memory now.

"What triggers the cells? What makes them start duplicating?" she asked, finally. There had to be an answer to that, or was it just an enzyme lying in wait—sort of a tagalong to the white blood cells that are dispatched to the scene of trauma?

His head lifted from the microscope as if she'd said something incredible.

Her smile was inevitable, despite her late attempts to remain poker-faced. He still wasn't giving her credit for her title, was he?

"Bacteria. Technically, it's an infection that heals."

Whoa. She lifted an eyebrow at him. Interesting concept.

"This study is technically done. There's little more I can do here. But before I turn over all my notes, I need to use this to solve another problem."

From the look in his eye, she knew she didn't want to ask. It had to do with those other cells, with…Paolo. She swallowed. It was starting to feel surreal again. "I--"

"Maybe you should wait until you know more about this."

"You intend to tell me more?" She expected serious firewalls to prevent that. Everything had been such a secret before. Had learning of her credentials changed his opinion so drastically?

He leaned forward, elbows on the table. "I need your help. I don't have much time."

"I don't understand this time thing." She got up and walked to the wall and back. "You've been here for what? Years now? Suddenly there's a problem with time?"

Sal dropped his head onto his hands, still propped up by his elbows on the table. His fingers nearly disappeared as they threaded through the long, dark hair. "There's always a problem with time. These chemicals have a shelf life shorter than milk. But there are other issues too." He stared at her. There was hollowness in his gaze. It mirrored inside her. What haunted him? What drove him with such intensity? She blinked and realized how lonely he must be. How terribly lonely to feel he couldn't share his worries, at least not openly. The few details he had provided seem guarded. He dropped his head again and closed his eyes. Hiding. Again. Like a door in her heart slamming shut. If he just look up, reach for her hands and say, Julia, here's what it is. She'd forget that he'd been lying to her about half of this stuff.

She pulled in her bottom lip and chewed on it as she waited, watching. He probably saw the pity in her face. And the pain. Maybe he'd even see the fierce longing to be something other than his lab assistant and lover.

He lifted his head. For a moment, she thought he was going to say something else. But then shook his head and sat up straight and removed the glasses he wore while working in the lab.

"Listen, I need to take a break. I'm going out on a limb and going to let you see what you can find. Don't disappoint me, Julia."

So now she was a little kid being warned. He toyed with her emotions like he would a quarter in his pocket. "Maybe I should go too, then. That way you can really rest without worrying about your lab." She lifted an eyebrow and silently dared him to egg her on.

"I'm sorry I didn't bring you down here before and — "

"Take advantage of me?" She cringed as soon as the words left her mouth. She'd wanted them to sound light, funny. They sounded as accusatory as could be.

"Do you have to put it like that? You act like I care nothing about you or your feelings." His features turned to stone.

She hated to think there might be a grain of truth in it, but it was there on the tip of his tongue. "Do you? I didn't realize feelings had ever been brought into this equation. Don't waste your time worrying about what I think."

Damn, she was harsh. Maybe that had sounded too cruel. His eyes darkened and his lips set in a tight line. But he didn't retort back at her. That was surprising.

That stung. Sal bit his tongue to keep his barely held temper from saying something he shouldn't. He was tired, hungry and stressed to an inch of his sanity. He should be spending the next seventy-two hours straight in that lab to get the answers he needed. But he couldn't. The very ability to rationalize what he needed to do next had escaped him. All he could think about was Julia. Julia's hair as it curled against her cheek. Her wrinkled nose as she compared her notes to his and tried to decipher what he'd written down. Even the little blush on her cheeks when he'd looked up and caught her studying him. He couldn't deny his attraction to her. Never before had a woman working behind a microscope been sexy to him, but she had him hard and ready every time she wrapped her hand around its base to adjust the focus. He wanted her hand around *him*. Anger faded to desire, which then faded to disgust.

That was why he was taking a break. Maybe a good, hot, wet dream would curb his desires and refresh his aching body. Not likely she was going to offer him anything to ease any of his discomforts. Talk about mixed signals. He'd thought she was just as eager as he was earlier, when he'd come home. Now she basically cut his knees from under him.

He hesitated only for a split second at the door. Turning around would give her the satisfaction of knowing she'd hit him. Better to pretend she hadn't gotten the last word. No, he'd let her stew over his reaction, see if she didn't come around eventually.

Sleep was about as evasive as Julia. After tossing and turning for long enough for his temper to fire back up, he got up and started checking out the room. Julia had lived in this room, slept in this bed for the last few days. He'd smelled her on the blankets and pillows, found evidence of her everywhere. She'd gone through all his things in here. But then, he'd have been disappointed if she hadn't.

He was going to miss her. Sal sat on the edge of the bed and surveyed his room. What did he have to offer her? Why should she want to stay? Stay. Ha. She would leave the moment she had a chance and never look back. Hell, she'd probably talk about him only as the goofy scientist who kept her captive.

But he had to try. Two and a half days without seeing her while he was gone to Cairo were murder. Even his brother had teased him mercilessly about it. He expected some sort of email from Carlotta with a million questions. Questions he wasn't ready to answer.

"Ah hell," he went downstairs.

Julia didn't look up when he came back in. Still holding onto the anger like it was her salvation, he thought. That's probably what he'd do in her shoes, so he couldn't blame her. And the kicker was that he'd said what he had to try to get her to understand he wanted to be on equal footing.

"*Socmel!*" He opened the refrigerator and found blood had leaked all over the bottom tray.

That brought Julia running. "What? Oh!"

He pulled the split bag and dropped it into the trash. There were two left. Two. What the fuck was he going to do now? "What happened to the others?" he asked, grinding his teeth to keep from yelling.

"They were leaking when I took them out of your suitcase. I told you that when you got here."

He remembered something about her putting his supplies away. She might have mentioned the blood. That seemed like days, not less than twenty-four hours ago. "All of them? This is all that made the trip?"

She didn't answer.

He whirled on her. "I asked—"

"Well, what do you think, that I turned vampire while you were sleeping and drank them for dinner? Yes that's all that's left. And I'd check those out before you use them. Whatever you packed them in wasn't very tight. They were rather warm when I pulled them out.

He couldn't help it. He let loose with a stream of curses. Fate seemed to enjoy having a laugh at his expense. He needed that blood. No, Paolo needed it. Desperately. "Without this blood, my research is stalled." He was going to explode any minute now. There was no way to create the serum he needed with the blood in the two bags left and still have enough for the final research he needed to create the compound to cure himself and Paolo. A complete lose/lose situation. "What's your blood type?" he sighed. Might as well get the question of the hour out. He'd been planning to ask her all along. Then he'd hoped his trip to Cairo would avoid the need.

"O negative."

He knew that. There'd been enough splattered on him after he'd bit her to test it for type. He'd guessed negative, but couldn't be sure. He hoped she was right. "Care to donate?" He held his breath.

"Do what?"

"Can I get you to give blood? Just a little...fifty milliliters?"

Surely she could hear his heart pounding against his chest. His very existence depended on this answer. Maybe he should have waited. Gotten her in a good mood first. If he played it right, he could have even made it sound like her idea. That was all a moot point, now. The clock ticked in deafening beats while he waited for her to decide his fate.

"Never mind," he choked, trying to blow it off like it was nothing. "I'll make do with this for now."

"How can you use *my* blood?"

He'd turned back into the fridge and was checking the other supplies. But that made him stop. "Your blood?" Son of a bitch. How did he answer that if he wasn't letting her in on the big secret and all. "I don't need it for the experiment you're helping with, but for this other one, I do."

"Oh. I see." Her flat tone meant she definitely didn't see anything but right through him.

"I said never mind. It's okay." As okay as being shot point blank with a 40 caliber handgun. Cold sweat dripped down his sides. What was he going to do now? Call his brother and arrange for more blood? Start testing the locals? There just wasn't enough time for all that. By then, the antibiotics he'd paid dearly for would be useless.

"Why don't you go back to what you're looking at over there and I'll get started making some other serum up I need to continue on my other studies."

She nodded and turned away.

He leaned in against the cool, white box. It was officially the beginning of the end. He just hoped he could get her out of town before Paolo got to her.

While the Bunsen burner heated the serum, Sal took a sample of his own blood. The bacteria would be evident there. Now it was time to see if the antibiotic had any inclination to eradicate it.

"Need anything to drink?" Julia stood next to him and stretched. Then leaned over him, her breasts brushing his arm. "That your blood?"

When he didn't answer, she reached for his hand and turned it palm up. The telltale pinprick on his index finger was marked with a small welling of evidence. "What's that for?" The contact between them didn't seem to even affect her. His mind was scrambled immediately.

He swallowed, then put the first foot in the grave. "I picked up a bacterial infection in Cairo. Just taking a look at which of these antibiotics are going to kick it the best."

"Ah," she said. "Need anything from the kitchen?"

"No. But thanks."

He watched her walk away. He should have said, yes, I need *you* in the kitchen and in here and in the bedroom and… What the hell had he been thinking when he asked and then retracted his request for blood? He had something to live for. She'd just walked out of the room. But now he'd lied to her about the bacteria. Damn if he wasn't sealing his own fate and couldn't find any other way to handle things.

The timer indicated the serum he used to ward off the symptoms was ready to be cooled. But he'd better start working before he needed it. It was inevitable it would happen. He tucked two filled syringes in the drawer. Now he needed healing serum. Then he could see just what antibiotic would work with the serum he used to slow the symptoms to create a cure. Somewhere, somehow, a combination of these ingredients had to provide a cure.

Julia came back in the room as he was making a list of the things he wanted to try.

"Can I help? I'd love to do something other than stare at that same set of slides," she asked. She took a long drink from the glass she held, then licked her lips.

"Uh." Like he could say any more with his mind wrapped around her sweet tongue the way it was.

"I thought you were going to rest. You look worse now than you did before."

Gee, thanks. Guess that meant she wasn't getting the same attraction vibes he was getting from her. "I couldn't sleep. There's way too much to be done here. I'll sleep later." If he could. He had the sinking feeling he'd be sleeping in the high branch of a tree rather than in his bed beside her warm body.

Julia set down her glass and put her hands on her hips. Her breasts pushed against the material of her borrowed shirt. His shirt. He wanted to *be* his shirt right now.

"Sal?" she asked. Arms crossed over her chest. Damn. She must have realized he was staring.

"Just thinking," he said, then rubbed his eyes. "You're not wearing the clothes I bought you."

She swallowed. Not that he was complaining. That was a different subject altogether though. Right now he didn't need to notice her clothes. "You want to help?"

The wide-eyed surprise on her face made him feel like he'd taken a child into a toy store and asked them what she wanted. "You'd just sent me away."

"You distract me."

The look on her face was anything but tolerant. "I think you're afraid to trust me with your experiment."

"You don't trust me," he said, stepping back from her.

She smiled and tilted her head. "That's different. I am a scientist you know."

"How do I know you have any lab experience? You teach it, not practice it."

"So take a gamble."

"Ah hell, why not." Sal pushed his chair back, grabbed her around the waist and pulled her onto his lap.

"Wa —" Julia opened her mouth.

Sweet Jesus, how could he pass up that invitation? Her lips were sweeter than he remembered, her mouth an open cavity of honey. And when she moaned into his mouth he knew he'd never taste anything as

171

fulfilling again in his life. He had to stop himself from crushing her when she shifted in his lap.

Her tongue grazed his lips and he nearly came in his pants. He had to slow down. Way down. The way she responded, with equal pressure and urgency made that nearly impossible. He snagged her bottom lip in his teeth and tugged gently. Her breath hissed through her teeth. This chair was too small and his need too big. His hands circled her waist. He wanted to hold her against him and never let her go.

"Hold on, *amore*, let's go into my office for this."

His heart paused while waiting for her to argue the point. But with mussed hair, swollen lips and half-closed eyes, she looked intensely aroused. Like him. He couldn't wait to get inside her. To prove she agreed with his silent musing, she wrapped her legs around him and rubbed against his hard-on.

This was one woman who showed him he wasn't in control in the bedroom. Or lab. He nearly smiled. When this place was built, he never imagined he should have created a little space for a sexual rendezvous.

As he carried her across the room, she reached up and touched his cheek. He stopped. Her blue eyes were dark, like impending storms. What he wouldn't give to know what this meant to her. Was he nothing more than a hard cock to relieve some tension? Did she care anything about him? It had, and still did occur to him that she might be using sex to convince him to do what she wanted—take her home. Right now his body didn't care. He knew where his emotions were. Didn't like it, but he was well aware that he loved this woman.

He turned his head and captured her finger in his lips and suckled. She gasped. He released the finger and kissed her palm. If she did that to him he'd be over. "Kiss me, Julia."

Sal had to back up against the doorframe to keep from dropping her. She rose up on his hips and threaded her hands into his hair. He took it as a sign that she'd completely taken over. There was nothing closer to heaven than this, but it was torture all the same. Her moist tongue outlined his lips as he tried to capture hers in a kiss. She nipped gently at the corners of his mouth, then pulled back to look into his eyes.

"You're killing me, here," he whispered against her cheek. She was busy dropping butterfly soft kisses along his jaw bone and—Christ! Her teeth caught his ear lobe. That had never been particularly erotic before but now it triggered some serious jolts that went straight to his groin.

Chapter 13

Julia leaned back and studied his face again. She could find flaws, sure, but right now nothing was as beautiful as this. Cheeks rough with unshaven scruff scraped her cheeks. When she kissed him again, his mouth nearly devoured her whole. And it excited her that she had made him this turned on. But this wasn't enough. His hands weren't on her, stroking her heated skin. Her breasts ached at the thought of him suckling her nipples. "Let's go."

She threw her head back and laughed at the speed in which Sal entered the office and kicked the door shut. But then he stopped. "What's wrong?" she wrapped her arms around his neck and pulled her mouth close to his ear. She took the lobe between her lips again and stroked it with her tongue. He growled, she felt it vibrate against her chest. Muscles in her vagina contracted in need. Her panties were soaked and getting wetter by the moment. This postponement, however, was taking it to a higher level.

"Stop that before I take you up against the door."

A thrill raced through her. But she didn't say he could take her any way he wanted as long as he did. Her tongue grazed his cheek and swept over his ear again.

Almost violently he pinned her to the door. Oh yeah. She crossed her ankles behind his back so he could get his hands free. He had to. She needed them on her body. Now. "Touch me, Sal. Touch me."

And he did.

She'd fought this long enough. It was stupid to think that a little physical pleasure was going to affect Sal's decision on what would ultimately happen to her. In fact, she was stupid to make herself miserable while she was waiting for that verdict. In final, complete abandon to the moment, she leaned her head back against the wall, chin up, and sighed.

The pace she expected to be reckless was anything but. There was no ripping of clothes and scoring of teeth. Though that might be nice, someday. Perhaps her ultimate decision had been clear to Sal, so he'd relaxed. She brought her gaze down to his and bit her lip. He probably had been a little nervous about her stopping him.

Now he'd better worry if he tried to stop. "Give me your hand." She looped one of hers around his neck and brought the palm he'd offered up to her mouth. She wanted him to feel the need the way she did. Her tongue traced the lines in the middle of his palm, then ran up and down each of the fingers. He watched her mouth as she watched him. There was no color left in his eyes. They were all smoky.

She reveled in the power as she suckled and nipped. Before the night was over she wanted to feel his hard cock in her mouth and taste it as he shot come all over her face.

He moaned as she slipped his finger out of her mouth, but she felt his erection twitch against her when she placed his hand over her breast. "Touch me," she instructed. She never knew there was added pleasure in instructing her lover. She liked...no, loved being in control like this.

Her eyes fluttered shut as he almost reverently cupped her breast. Even though they'd had sex before, this was really the first time they'd taken time to get to know one another--when passion wasn't forcing them to hurry it up. Not that she didn't want him too. She panted out his name when he squeezed the tip of her breast between his fingers. How could pain be so pleasurable? But what she wanted was to feel his mouth there.

She tugged her shirt up and guided his hand under the material. When he finally touched bare skin, she shuddered in need. "Yes. Oh God, I love it when you touch me."

He muttered something in Italian. His voice was low, throaty. She didn't care that she couldn't understand the words, because she knew the meaning. She busied her hands on his chest, lightly plucking buttons out of their holes. She wanted to smooth over the tight planes of his chest and explore every fiber of him.

Feather-light, his fingers stroked her breast. God, if he did that to her clit she'd scream for the pleasure of it. Rocking against him did little to ease the precious ache.

"Put me down," she instructed, not at all surprised her voice had the same husky tone. "I want your clothes off."

A secret thrill raced down her as he lowered her to a standing position and slid his open shirt off his shoulders. Mutely. Her breath caught as she looked at him under the harsh white overhead light. He was magnificent. More man than she ever expected to see in the flesh, much less touch and know.

His broad shoulders tapered down into a narrow waist. The muscles on his chest and stomach weren't well defined, but hinted at ripples and shadows as he stretched up and pushed the hair off his face with both hands. Like he was posing for her. If his intention was to whet her appetite, he was certainly going to be surprised when she demanded her dessert right away.

"Pants, too," she said after swallowing her awe. Unable to just stand there, she reached up to cup her breast the way Sal had.

He made no move to remove the rest of his clothes. "Sal?" she put a finger to her lip. "Why aren't you undressing?"

In no way was his reaction detrimental to his maleness. But he was definitely submissive to her tonight. She reveled in the power and yanked her own shirt over her head. "Do you like to watch?"

He licked his lips and placed one hand on the waist of his pants.

Propelled on the drug of the moment—desire, she lifted both hands and cupped her breasts. It wasn't the same as Sal's fingers, it wasn't the sensation of herself rubbing over the hardened nipples that was so erotic. It was watching Sal watch her. "Take them off, Sal."

She slipped two fingers between her lips and drew them out all glistening with moisture. Slowly, teasingly, she circled her nipples, first the left, then the right. "I want you to taste me here."

Without further prompting, he closed the gap between them and assaulted her with his eager mouth. The moan broke free of her throat. Fingers grazed her rib cage and over her hips. She entangled her hands in his hair to hold him there. She never wanted him to stop.

Her skin was on fire. When his mouth left one breast to feast on the other, she gasped as the air hit the sensitized bud. Everything, it seemed, heightened the pleasure when she was with Sal.

"My turn," she said. He needed to be brought to the same high tension level. "Take off your pants." Without waiting for him, she reached for the zipper. The heat beneath her fingers excited her. His cock trembled, as if pushing against the material to touch her. Spirals of excitement flooded her groin.

He was rock hard and willing. All she had to do was spring him free and she could have him any way she wanted. The button gave her a bit of trouble, but soon the zipper slid down and released him into her palm.

"Get these down and out of here." Her orders were getting more harsh, more formal. And he still said nothing. The throb against her fingers was a pretty clear indication that it charged him up as much as it did her.

She had to taste it.

"Sit down." With a hand to his chest, she backed him up and pushed him into the chair. The only sound that escaped his lips was the moan he uttered when she knelt between his legs.

Julia leaned forward and kissed his stomach first, watching the muscles tense and jump as her fingers traced where her lips couldn't reach. He was a bundle of nerves, ready to explode. And in her hand was the trigger.

"Watch me suck your cock, Salvatore. I want to pleasure you with my mouth."

As soon as her lips wrapped around the throbbing head of his penis, he fisted his hand in her hair and stuttered her name. Along with a few other words she couldn't understand. It just encouraged her to continue — but not hurry. He'd get release when she did. This was warm up.

Julia slid both hands up and down his hardened shaft as she licked the tip.

Pre-come flooded her tongue. She lapped it up as quickly as he could produce it; all her fingers stroked him. Never had giving been so exciting for her. She slid one hand between her legs to temper the ache. When she finally was able, his cock would make her come so hard the earth would shake. But not yet. Not yet.

Sal lifted his hips upward. They both knew what he wanted. And she was about to give it to him. She sat up higher on her knees and positioned her mouth over the top of his cock. Her lips rubbed against the velvety tip as he pushed for entrance. His eyes were nearly closed, his head back and hands gripping the arms of the chair so hard his knuckles were white.

"Watch me," she said. She wanted to watch him, to see how her actions reflected on his face. With her tongue, she traced down to the base of his cock as she cupped his balls in her hand. Sal's breath hitched. She licked upward as her own hand slid beneath the waistband of her pants.

Her panties were soaked with desire. She didn't stop nipping and kissing his cock as she furiously rubbed her fluid-soaked pussy.

She knew what she wanted. Two fingers poised at her opening as she poised her lips over his cock. She wanted to feel it pumping hot fluid into her mouth as she fucked herself with her fingers.

Sal growled and pulled her head toward his cock. She smiled, letting the tip push against her mouth. She opened slightly, letting him slide into the narrow crevice she allowed. His groan turned into a growl as he thrust upwards. Her own body reacted similarly as she slipped a finger just inside her pussy.

Then she opened up. His cock filled her mouth with hot, throbbing flesh as she thrust her fingers upwards. A moan escaped her as she rocked against her hand and bobbed her head up and down. The urgency was immediate. She closed her lips over him and sucked until he pulled her back. "Not yet," he growled. That shot a spark through her. He was ready to come. Already.

But she did it again, convinced she could bring the earth down around them. She buried two fingers inside herself and pressed against her clit. Sal's fist tightened. "Julia, oh, God, please."

She felt the same way. Waiting was not an option. They'd both reached a point where there was no turning back. Julia removed her mouth but kept her free hand stroking up and down the throbbing shaft. "I want to taste it all. Give it to me, Sal. All of it."

No answer was needed. She was going to come. Her thumb strummed against her clit as she took his cock deep into her mouth. He held her head steady as he lifted his hips to give her every inch of him. And she wanted more.

If she could have shouted his name, she would have. All she could do was swallow her moan as he throbbed against the back of her throat and trembled with the force of impending orgasm. She was so close.

But he erupted first. The hot come filled her mouth. The feel of his spasms sent her over the edge. She'd done that. She'd given him that pleasure. Her body shook as the shockwave of tidal propulsion scorched through her. Her legs trembled, nearly unable to keep her balance between his legs.

She sucked until she felt his entire body go limp in the chair.

"Sal?" she said, unable to keep the smile off her face.

"Mmm?"

"This isn't what we were supposed to do in the lab today."

He reached up and rubbed his face. She continued to lean on his muscular thighs and look up at his face. Flushed and with his eyes still a little out of focus, he had to be the sexiest thing in this hemisphere. "So? It's much more satisfying." He reached down to push hair off her forehead. "The research will be there, *amore*."

So what? Did that imply she wouldn't be? Of course it did, she was going home. But this was the first he'd said anything to reflect how he felt about her leaving. That statement almost made it sound like he'd miss her. Or at least her body.

It wasn't going to sour the moment, regardless. She needed this release as much as he did, even if he didn't have the emotional attachment she feared she was getting. If it had been about sex, she would have fucked him, not made sure he was completely satisfied. The fact she got off was a plus, but she could do that herself. "I thought there was a time issue?" Damn her for saying that. For bringing it up, rather than asking what he meant by that last comment. *Coward.*

Sal sighed and put both hands on his forehead. She knew it was a move that indicated she was right, but she couldn't help taking advantage of reviewing, and locking into memory, the width of his shoulders and the way the muscles all moved around beneath the tight, tanned skin. For an instant, she wondered what it'd be like to stay.

She rose to her feet and brushed off her knees and that wayward thought. Of course she couldn't stay. For one thing, that option hadn't been given to her. Besides, she had to go back. She had a house, a mortgage, a car payment, a job. People relied on her. No way could she walk away from it all.

"Regretting it already?" his voice held a deep note of something that wasn't joking. Her eyes quickly met his.

"No, no, definitely not." She tried to smile. But the hard lines of his face made the experience they shared seem light years ago.

"Let's get something to eat. I'm starved. Then we'll figure out this lab thing." Lab thing? He didn't sound motivated at all.

Maybe he was just tired. He had, after all, been traveling for about three days straight. "Sure." She'd have agreed to anything right now just to keep him from pushing her away.

That was a switch.

* * * * *

The clock read a few minutes after nine, but it felt like the middle of the night. Of course, her sleeping patterns had been way off since she arrived. Sal, she noticed, was dragging as well. Even dinner hadn't perked him up. Back in the lab, she shared his lack of enthusiasm.

"Let's go, Sal. There's nothing more we can do here. We're both dead on our feet."

She didn't like the grimace she saw on his face. "What?"

"Don't say that. I hate that phrase."

"Okay," she said and closed her notebook. Regardless of what he decided, she was calling it a night. "What do you have left to do?"

He had eight vials lined up, all holding a blood colored liquid. She thought it was blood, for a second, until he picked one up. If it was indeed blood, it was diluted.

"I'm checking to see if these antibiotics have any effect on this bacteria."

Julia pulled up a chair and leaned her chin on her palm. "Any luck?"

"No more than expected. This one's a whole new frontier."

She couldn't agree more. "I'm going to bed." Last thing she wanted to do was walk up those steps alone. Without Sal beside her. Paolo could be out there. Funny, she hadn't thought about Paolo's...condition all day. Well, all afternoon. "Um, Sal," she started, staring at her toe as she kicked the floor. "What's going on with Paolo, anyway?" She jerked her gaze up to assess his reaction.

"Paolo?" he repeated.

She nodded. His face had frozen for a minute in what could only be a form of panic. Then he blinked it away and tilted his head. This is what she hated. This secret keeping. Probably best that she go on up before she said something that erased what happened earlier.

"What you're working on has to do with him, doesn't it?"

Eyebrows lifted. He nodded. "*Si.* Yes. Right. You're exactly right."

So he lied again. He didn't offer anything else, just took a sample from one of the vials and smeared it on a slide.

"Good night."

Squinting into the microscope, she doubted he even locked onto what he was saying when he repeated, "Good night."

* * * * *

Sal pushed the microscope back and made a few final notes. Some of the results looked promising. That was about the best news he'd had all day. Almost. Julia's reaction—holy shit, the way she'd taken over and ordered him around had been hotter than anything he'd ever experienced, and he wasn't a slouch in seduction. But there was something about Julia—something more than her intelligence. It burned in his gut the way he'd avoided telling her about Paolo. About him. The way she'd reacted the first time sat on his mind.

If he'd only known who she was and what she did. They might have gotten a lot farther by now. But he couldn't put the inevitable off much longer. He could tell by her reaction that she knew he was hiding something. And that hurt her. The disappointment when she averted her gaze unnerved him. The last thing he wanted to do was lie. But how to say it, other than the way he already had?

"Dammit anyway." Time was running out. He needed her help. Pride wouldn't save him this time, and worse yet, it would take someone   else   down   with   him. He turned off the overhead light and locked the door behind him.

Change hit him when he was halfway up the stairs. It gripped his skull like a dozen hot irons and tore through his skin with a speed that ripped the breath out of his lungs. Temporarily blinded, he reached for the railing as he fell.

"Hello?" he heard her voice. "Anyone out there?"

Don't let her walk down the steps. *Stay in your room. Lock the door!* But human voice was gone. He'd rolled out of her line of vision, at least. Though the sight of him might convince her of what he wanted. He stretched out his hind legs to ensure the muscles had completed their metamorphosis. But before he could stand, the door clicked shut.

Sal slipped through the dining room and nudged open the sliding door. Paolo'd been this way earlier. He picked up the scent of the young male easily with his heightened senses. He didn't smell a fresh trail, however, so Paolo must still be outside, roaming. More worry. There was more leopard now than boy. A blood sample would confirm that, but knowing the time the boy spent in the altered state, and the fact his human state was deformed were enough. Time was running out a lot faster than he'd told Julia. If he didn't do something in the next few days, he'd lose his nephew forever.

As a leopard, Sal had no trouble following Paolo's trail out of the yard and into the wild savannah that lay beyond the walls. He'd heard talk earlier of reports of a golden leopard. Some even suspected it was a she-lion who was aggressively roaming the area. Paolo should know better than that. At least tonight's trail led him away from civilization.

Sal ran. In some respects, he could understand the allure and the freedom of being a wild animal. If the risk wasn't there for total bacterial domination and the inability to maintain the human mind, he'd probably spend more time as Snow himself. The wide open spaces, the knowledge that as a leopard, you weren't quite king of the jungle, but you weren't exactly prey, either. The biggest threat was poachers. Illegal hunters out for hides. He was top of the list right now with his unusual snow white coat. Not even a ghost spot on him. He'd love to preserve some blood and someday locate the gene that dictates coat color and pattern.

But that was for when he was Sal the scientist. Right now he was able to bound under the half moon's light until he chose to stop.

Paolo had returned to the wreckage. The plane was little more than a skeleton of metal and plastic. Anything useful had been stripped by locals and used as barter. Even the remains of those who died here were gone. Stolen, buried, he didn't know--didn't want to know. Eventually he'd expect Julia to ask to return to this spot. It was really surprising she hadn't so far.

He padded past the torn off wing and followed the stream the way she had that night. In memory, her scent burned in his nostrils. The bitter bite of her perfume, the sweet tang of blood and the sharpness of her fear. She had been a target in the darkness.

He growled low and lapped at the water of the stream. Anything to cool the heat he felt when thinking about her. It was his turn to be frightened. Things had changed for him radically as he got to know her. Some days she was completely predictable, others she'd act completely opposite and he'd find himself caught off guard.

He plunged his whole body into the low stream as he thought about her passion. But she wasn't all about bedroom fun. No, it was the stuff out of the bedroom that scared him. This woman had it all—had fight, drive, common sense and above all, courage.

The warm water failed to cool him down. He raced forward again chasing invisible demons.

* * * * *

Julia rolled over. She fought the pull into the waking world and muttered Sal's name as she willed herself back into deep sleep.

The growl snapped her eyes open. She sat up and yanked the covers up to her chin, scooting back toward the headboard as quickly as she could. The gun. Where's the gun? She fumbled for the light. In her haste, she knocked it against the wall. The tell tale sound of breaking glass filled the room. Slowly, her labored breathing replaced it. Nothing else. No sound of anyone else in here. Must have been a dream. A scary, very real dream.

She started to slide back down into a sleeping position when the floor creaked.

"Sal?" she called. Why was he doing this to her? When he finally did turn on the light she'd read him the riot act for scaring her this way. There was no need to sneak around in his own bedroom.

No answer.

She blinked against the blackness of the room. No silhouettes stood above her, no familiar laughter rang through the room.

"Sal, you're scaring me. Turn on the light."

Nothing.

Shit.

She lunged across the bed for the nightstand as the roar deafened her. The gun. The gun. She needed to get to the gun.

The drawer was empty. What the hell?

She screamed then.

Black shadow against the charcoal room, she saw it. A leopard. She closed her eyes tight, praying that when she opened them, it'd simply be darkness. Nothing moving.

He was still there. As he turned, he roared again.

"Saaal!" she shrieked until her lungs hurt. Oh God. What was a leopard doing in her--Sal's bedroom? Was he after Sal? Or her? Even if it was one of Sal's little pets, it was not behaving like an animal that wanted to curl up and sleep at the foot of the bed.

The tears came then, thrust forth by sheer panic. She licked her lips against the metallic taste in her mouth. The taste of fate. Impending doom. She was going to die in her lover's bed after being mauled by a leopard.

"Go away!" This time she aimed her scream at the cat. "Get out of here. Go. Sal's not here. Check the lab."

The bed gave as something heavy landed at the foot.

"No, no, no," she repeated in a monotone chant as she pulled her feet up as high as she could and wrapped her arms around her knees. She rocked against the headboard. *Please, Sal, help me. Save me.*

The cat lunged.

She raised her arms and fell onto her side to ward off the nails and teeth. Her scream mixed with its cry. They both fell from the bed and to the floor. Sharp pain sliced through her forearm. Her head ached from connecting with the nightstand on the way down. Flashes of light filled the darkness of the room. She closed her eyes as she fought the dizziness that accompanied them. No way was she losing consciousness now.

The cat was near.

There would be no escape. Prolonging the inevitable was possible, but in the end, she couldn't defeat the cat. And if it came for her, it was doubtful it would leave before getting what it wanted.

Still, she sidled up against the bed and tried to slide beneath it. Solid.

The cat itself screamed a hideous half howl, half growl. Victory cheer, she thought, and closed her eyes.

There was no pain. Pure silence. Was she dead? She dared not try to take the deep breath her lungs begged for—what if she wasn't dead. What if—oh, she couldn't be stupid like that. The leopard could pinpoint her immediately with their see-in-the-dark eyes and keen sense of smell.

She wasn't dead for a reason.

The pulled down blanket offered little protection but she yanked it over her head when she heard glass breaking. The thumps and thuds above her were distorted by the layers of quilt. What was the leopard doing?

Then she heard it. A second leopard. Rational thought wasn't possible. She tucked her legs up tight and tried her best not to move, not to breathe, anything that would attract either of them. If she could have reached to plug her ears, she would have. It sounded like the cats were trying to kill one another up there.

The floor beside her shook as they leapt from the bed. The growling was so close. Her heart was about to burst from her chest. Didn't matter. Dying was imminent.

A tail, at least she assumed it was, snapped against her legs. Definitely aggressive behavior. At least she wasn't in the midst of it being torn apart as they played tug-of-war. Not that she felt any differently.

The cat fell back. Nails cut into her thigh as it searched for balance. Then it turned around and growled. Through the layers, she could feel the vibration of its warning and the heat of its breath. Things were getting worse, not better.

"Please, please, please," she mouthed and she tried to make herself as still and tight against the bed as she could.

Where was Sal? Couldn't he hear this? The way the floor shook when one tackled the other had to be perceivable in the lab. If not Sal, then Sokhra...where was she?

Suddenly the blanket was torn off her.

Air gushed out of her lungs. Her arms instinctively went up to protect her face, but she opened her eyes. She had to see.

And she could. Light, probably moonlight, now filled the room with a gray glow. And with it shone the exposed white teeth of the golden leopard.

"Sal!" she screamed and tried to back away.

The cat swatted at her, nicking her arm again. This was it. The end.

But not without a fight. She kicked upward and fisted her hands to pummel the snout of the cat as it leaned back in menacingly. Maybe it was the way they almost glowed with a light of their own, maybe it was the way the shadows hid the rest of its face, but his eyes were eerie. Almost...knowing.

Goosebumps broke out as the leopard stood there, staring her down. There was a rational intelligence there.

And that was more frightening than having a dozen guns pointed at her.

Neither of them saw it coming. A ghostly blur hit the golden leopard in the side and knocked him off his feet. Her hand connected with something around the cat's neck as he fell. There was nothing she could do but close her eyes and cringe as the white leopard soared over her.

As soon as she could, Julia gathered the blanket up around her and sat, backed into the corner between the bed and the nightstand.

Almost within reach of the gun. It had to be there. Bottom drawer. Had to be there.

Her eyes were more adjusted now, helped by the light coming in the broken window. The fighting in front of her was ruthless, brutal. They never showed clips like that on National Geographic. This was a fight to the death. It didn't take a scientist to figure that out. Already both of their light colored coats were streaked with stains. Blood. She held her hand to the gash in her arm to stop the flow. Those claws were like razors.

So were the teeth.

The white cat snarled, its muzzle red with blood. The horror she knew she'd carry with her forever slammed back into her chest with amazing clarity.

She'd been dazed. So tired. So scared. But she remembered the way the leopard had hesitated above her, sniffing her arm, her shoulder, her neck. She closed her eyes and prayed for mercy, but only for a second. She'd had to see him coming. And in his eyes she'd found that same intensity she'd seen in the golden cat.

These weren't standard variety wild leopards. The story of the Ghost and the Darkness—two wild lions who killed for sport—came to mind.

But if that were the case, why was she still relatively unharmed? The leopard had ample chance to destroy her. Instead, he toyed with her.

Her breathing, heartbeat and all thought stopped when the door flew open and banged into the wall behind it. The hero she was, Sokhra stood in the door and leveled her gun at the cats. Could she do it? Could she hit both? What if she missed?

Julia ground her palms against her eye sockets. No way could she witness them knocking the housekeeper down and ravaging her body.

Fear found a new level when it dawned on her. The leopards had calmed. *Were* these Sal's experimental animals? Was this nothing more than the supersize version of two kittens playing?

No. She edged forward to find they weren't sitting docile waiting for instruction. They were circling each other, tails whipping, teeth bared.

Sokhra shouted something to them. The white one hesitated a moment.

The golden leopard took advantage. His large front paw connected with Snow's muzzle.

Sokhra lifted the gun to her shoulder and aimed.

Julia returned to covering her eyes. Tranquilizer gun. She's not killing the cat. Half of her screamed, *Why not?*

She didn't hear the gun. Only the leopard's quick yelp in pain.

Oh God. She clapped her hand over her mouth. The cat darted directly toward Sokhra.

"No!" Julia kicked away the covers. But it was too late. Sokhra stepped back into the hall, and the cats followed her.

Damn blankets. They twisted in her ankles and kept her from running after them herself. She'd fight for Sokhra.

When she got to the doorway, she found the white leopard had hung back. It advanced toward her. She screamed and slammed the door. Her chest heaved, her heart pounded. Freight trains thundered past her ears. Any second and the door would come down in a splintering crash. She'd seen intensity in the eyes of that cat. Something so pure it ate through her core and gripped her in its cold fist.

"Sokhra!" she screamed. Tears fell then. How could that woman have survived those blood-thirsty creatures. It had been just like that at the crash scene. She sat down, right there in the middle of the floor and dropped her head into her hands. "Oh God," she cried as she rocked forward and back. Those leopards had ripped apart the men who'd shared the plane with her. And didn't stop there.

Julia rolled onto her knees and crawled back across the floor to her blanket. So much for control. What kind of fool was she? How did she think she'd have the chance to escape?

"Ow." Something on the floor bit into her knee. Did leopards knock each other's teeth out? Then again, things had gone flying off dressers and tables as they crashed around the room.

She felt the floor and found the culprit. Sal's necklace—the talisman. In the faint light, she couldn't tell if it were broken or not.

Sal. God. He was going to have a fit. She stood up immediately and flipped on the overhead light.

The room was trashed. No, it wasn't. It was destroyed. No amount of straightening would make this room look the same.

The window was broken. Drops of blood and shattered glass littered the floor beneath it. The curtains had been ripped down, one side of the rod ripped from the wall and swaying as the light breeze hit it. But that was just the start.

The leopards' nails had shredded the top of the mattress. Springs and stuffing poked through gaping holes. The lamp was off the nightstand. She was surprised the furniture was actually still where it had been before it all started.

The gun. Where she expected. Waiting in the bottom drawer.

Knowledge of the weapon or not, she wasn't going to be without it.

She held it in her grip and looked through the sights. The safety was off, but close enough for her thumb to disengage. Sokhra had loaded it for her, and unless Sal had removed the bullets, she should be good to go.

She picked up the talisman and went to replace it on Sal's shoulder height bureau.

Only his was there, under a broken picture frame and beside the other gold cross.

Sal's had a black leopard. Onyx. She lifted the necklace up to eye level by the two broken ends. The charm swayed, mocking her.

Tiger's eye.

Golden.

Paolo's.

Chapter 14

Everything inside her came to a grinding halt. Was this the missing piece? "Oh God, oh...God." A maelstrom of understanding swirled around her. She looked around the room. Answers, answers everywhere and she didn't want any of them. It couldn't be true.

But it was.

"Paolo," she whispered, fisting the charm. What was Sal doing to him? And her? Son of a bitch.

She stood her ground as she heard footsteps outside the door. Dread teamed up with fear and fanned the burning in her chest. What would she say to him?

"Julia, listen —"

She didn't need to think, the reaction was automatic. She lifted the pistol to Sal's battered face. "You bastard." She hurled the necklace at him.

He knew what it was before he caught it. Her eyes met him over the shaking gun. "Put it down, Julia. We need to talk. I have things to tell you."

"Start talking, Mister. I'm not using my ears to hold this gun up here."

Sweat dripped down Sal's back. Blood too. It stung as it slid into the cuts along his ribcage. "Fine then. Follow me to the bathroom."

He walked past her, trying not to believe she could do it. In truth, he knew that woman could do anything she wanted. She was certainly capable. And had motive. Dozens of people had pulled the trigger for less.

With the injuries he had, he wasn't sure he'd feel the burn of the bullet anyway. If she aimed right, all he'd know was the fading of pain. But since the pain was only getting worse as he walked and breathed and thought...he knew she wouldn't do it.

"I'll start explaining things in a minute here. Just let me clean out my mouth." He spat pure blood into the sink. The inside of his lips were a shredded mess. His jaw throbbed, but didn't feel broken. Paolo had done nothing to his body that he couldn't fix in the lab. The real damage, however, was the trust that lay in ashes between he and Julia.

"Leopard get a hold of you too?" she taunted. "Serves you right for doing him that way."

He paused, handful of water ready to splash on his face. Whoa. "The golden one? He did this in here, didn't he?"

The nose of the gun wavered as she looked behind her. "Two of them. I thought they were going to kill one another."

God, he needed that cold water.

This was going to be much harder than he thought.

"Where did you find the necklace?" His words were tiptoeing through land mines. Live ones.

She flipped the safety.

Fuck.

He turned away from her so she couldn't see the reaction he knew had to be visible on his face. Fear. Never show fear. The towel he used to dry his face gave him a temporary buffer. He looked at her reflection in the mirror. "Well?"

She took a deep breath. Here it comes.

"You lying sack of shit. I can't believe it. I saw those cells in the lab. I don't understand how you've done it but now I know. You've turned your own nephew into a leopard. What a worthless piece of human flesh you are. Too bad he didn't kill you. You deserve it."

When she paused to draw in another breath he reached up and took the gun away. Just like that.

And just as abruptly, she burst into tears. "Shoot me, Sal. I don't want to live like that. Or like this. I can't bear to watch you do this to him. I'd rather die than be one of your lab rats."

Sal put the gun on the bathroom counter and tried to pull her into his arms.

She jerked back. "Get away." Her bottom lip trembled. Despite the swelling of her eyes and the streaks down her face, she was beautiful.

"Please, Julia. Come with me and sit down and we'll talk. I'll tell you all about it." He just needed a chance to explain. She was a scientist herself. She'd understand. Hopefully.

And she did seem to waver. Her answer wasn't an immediate no. Curiosity. It'd led her to the lab on several occasions. Hopefully her quest for knowledge would buy him enough time to stress how much he needed her.

"I need a drink." She pushed passed him, grabbed the gun with one hand and filled a cup of water with the other. As if she did that every day.

His hope crashed and burned.

"The only question I want answered is why. Why would you do this to him?"

Things couldn't progress the way he wanted. "He did it to himself."

"Bullshit."

At least she hadn't pointed the gun at him again. She just held it, finger near the trigger. She lifted the cup to her mouth. Her pale pink lips slid around the plastic. Her throat undulated as she swallowed. He drank *her* in. It was a distinct possibility he'd never be able to again.

"The serum he took was created by accident. Got something mixed up in the healing serum." He wanted her to digest that before going on. The biggest shoe was left to drop. The fact he'd mentioned it before mattered nil. She'd discounted that immediately.

Her fist crumpled the cup and dropped it in the basket beside the sink. "That simple? A mix up like that? Rather dangerous, don't you think?"

He nodded, though. "Definitely. The healing serum *is* made from leopard blood. Actually from enzymes in it. The enzymes duplicate the cells they come in contact with, using DNA as their blueprints. It's all technical, but what started happening is that the particular blood that got mixed with the healing serum contained a bacteria I was also studying. The enzymes started duplicating the leopard blood *and* the bacteria, not the human cells it came in contact with. The bacteria worked more like...cancer I guess is the best way to describe it. It'd infiltrate the cells and alter them so that they too were carbon copies. Eventually all the cells become filled with duplicated leopard DNA instead of human DNA."

He'd said too much. Too fast. The glassy eyes, the far away look, it meant she couldn't absorb all that.

But he was wrong there, too. She lifted her arm. "So if his blood

191

infected me, the bacteria would start infiltrating my cells and I'd change too?"

"No." His heart was somewhere near the center of the earth. What if she was right? Oh God. It made sense. Why wouldn't it jump? Then he realized what he'd found. It wouldn't start unless she took the healing serum. He'd have to make sure she didn't. "No, you're safe. I have antibiotics. I've been searching for a cure. That's what I'm working on. I have to cure Paolo. I have to."

Her eyes searched his face. She was looking for a thread of hope. *It's here, here. Just trust me.* If she'd only believe.

But he had to tell her. About him. Snow.

"There's more." He took a deep breath and leaned against the doorframe. Why did they have to do this standing in the bathroom of all places? Why couldn't he sit her down and take her hands in his.

"Really?" She pursed her lips. Not a good sign.

"About Snow."

She leaned against the counter and crossed her arms, gun still in hand. He eyed it. It'd be so much easier to spit this out if she'd just put that down. It was a show of good faith to trust her.

Sal turned and leaned his forehead and forearm against the door. The wood was cool enough to feel good on his swollen face. Speaking of healing serum. He could use a dose right now.

But first things first. Julia would decide if he'd be capable of walking downstairs to administer it to himself.

"Snow, yes. He was here. Blame him for the damage to your window."

"I'm Snow."

The seconds passed, each twisting his gut in wrenching worry.

Julia stared at him for a moment. Then closed her eyes. At least she didn't bring the gun up between his eyes. "How can you be Snow when you're human?"

More talking. Talking was good. Bricks of trust. "While the bacteria slowly takes over the body, flashes occur. I can't explain them—have obviously never been able to draw blood during the metamorphosis or while in leopard state. These flashes transform the entire body to leopard. I'm thinking it's like short-circuiting the brain to turn all the human cells off and leopard cells on. After awhile, they turn back off."

"You know how incredulous this sounds, don't you?"

He did. Quite well. "Listen, Julia, I tried to tell you before. I'd have loved to have you help me in the lab. The only reason I flew to Cairo like that is because my supplies were low. I need to find a cure."

"This can't be right."

He watched a light go out in her eyes.

"Julia, please. I love you. I was only trying to protect you. I tried to tell you. You laughed at me and called me a liar, surely you can see my side. I'm scared to death of this thing. Please say you'll help me."

Flat-line voice. "Take me home, Sal."

"I can't, I need —"

"I promise I'll never breathe a word of this to anyone. I'll say I was held captive by natives or something. No one will ever hear your name from me."

Her words crushed him. To her, he was a nobody. He'd saved her life twice. Once right here tonight. Didn't she understand that? Pain soared through his feet and up his back. Good. Let her see it. "You can't go back," he forced out as the crippling agony knocked him to all fours. "I told them you were dead."

He was faintly aware of her letting out a cry and backing up within the small space. His vision blurred, the roar in his ears blocked him off from any tangible sensation for the few seconds his body transformed him physically into the white leopard.

His down time — human time — hadn't been enough to regain his strength. There was no fight in him. And he didn't care.

He forced fatigued muscles to carry him over to where Julia sat. She trembled and cried but tried to look so brave, yet there was a look on her face he could only assume was her insatiable curiosity. He was a freak of nature. She was a scientist. Of course, she had to see.

The last thing he wanted was for her to fear him. His voice was gone. He couldn't comfort her to tell her he would never, ever harm her. So he lay down at her feet and rested his head in her lap.

He smelled her. Behind the fear he could detect the scent that was her unique signature. She was actually allowing him to touch her. He wanted to memorize the sensation.

"I'm at complete loss for words," she started out. "This is some nightmare, right? I'll wake up and laugh about this in the morning?"

He wanted to answer her. Tell her that no, it wasn't a nightmare, but it was something they could eventually find reason to laugh about. If she was just willing to work with him. All he could do was blink up at her and inwardly share her tears. They cut like knives. Each one, another part of his heart dying.

Then she adjusted the gun in her hand. The agony on her face was real. He welcomed what she was offering him. Peace. Freedom from the failure that plagued him. He'd lost Paolo. He'd nearly killed him over Julia and now he was losing her too. He'd seen it in her eyes.

All his work in the lab? Failure. The baby steps he'd taken earlier would get them nowhere. The antibiotics were doomed to expire and he had no blood to make the anti-venom.

The death she offered would be merciful. He knew at that moment that living without Julia wouldn't be living at all.

The cool barrel of the gun slid over his cheek and across his brow. He looked her in the eye. He wanted to know if she could do it. *Do it.*

Then she shifted. The gun clattered to the floor. What he wouldn't give to proclaim his love. To tell her that it'd be okay. It was her or nothing. That was his fate. And he'd beg for her if he had to.

He shivered as she reached out and stroked his head. If it were possible for him to cry, he would have. Nothing hurt harder than her kindness, after all he'd done to her. Hope flew up from the depths of hell and waited. He lifted his head and met her eyes.

He saw pity there. Compassion. But the light was out. She unfolded her legs and stood up.

The moment she stood there was the last moment of his life.

Then she walked away.

* * * * *

Any minute now, she'd wake up from this incredible dream and find herself warm in Sal's bed. Worse case scenario, she'd passed out after hitting her head. Hallucinated this stuff.

But as she closed the bedroom door and leaned against it, Julia knew she was just lying to herself. There was a leopard lying by the bathtub that *was* Sal. She didn't want to try to understand that. The pain

194

in her chest was so intense...she ached. Physically and emotionally ached.

She had no clue how to feel. She didn't even know where to go. Paolo had attacked her. Where was he now? And what about Sokhra? Sal—Snow could probably jump back out the window. He didn't scare her. He should, but he didn't. It was the idea that frightened her beyond death.

What struck her the most was the intensity of the pity she felt for him. He had lied to her. Sort of. He'd hit her with truths too preposterous to believe. How could she have known? He could have taken her to the lab and been completely, scientifically upfront with her and she might have trusted him. But he hadn't trusted her. And now, if he was right about the lab work, then he was a dying man.

She squeezed her eyes against the tears that wouldn't stop falling. All she'd wanted to do was go home. That's all. Why? Why did this happen? How did she get involved in this? What did she do to deserve to have her heart wrenched from her very chest?

She loved Sal. She'd fought it tooth and nail—she groaned at her analogy. But it was true. The last thing she wanted was to fall in love with him. Yet he'd said he loved her too.

And that had cut deeper than any leopard tooth or nail.

Despite the urge to curl up somewhere safe and sleep it off, she knew she couldn't. There were things she had to do. And then...she'd leave. She stood up and put her palm against the face of the door and whispered, "Goodbye, Sal."

She dropped her head so that her forehead rested against the door. Nothing was as painful as this heartache.

In the lab she channeled the maelstrom of emotions into quick, efficient work.

One thing gnawed at her. She had to know if she'd been infected. With trembling hands she scraped against the cut on her arm and prepared a slide. For a moment she panicked. Where were the sample slides?

Easy. Julia blew the air out of her lungs and refreshed them with healing oxygen. All the samples were right where Sal had left them. With them laid out beside her, she put the slide of her own blood in the microscope and peered through the eyepiece. Then compared.

Why wasn't there a slide with the bacteria present?

There had to be. She got up and started pulling open drawers. Sweat trickled down between her breasts as she searched. His office.

The file cabinet was locked. Son of a bitch. He was hiding something. He'd better not be lying to her this time. She looked at the ceiling above her head. Or else she just might use that gun.

Her whole body shook in newfound fear. And anger. And impatience.

She spied the drawings beside the computer. It seemed like an eternity ago that she'd been keying in information into his spreadsheet.

Pictures.

Julia darted back to the lab proper and pulled out Sal's notes.

Sure enough, a labeled sketch of the bacteria that caused this whole mess.

She felt so helpless. Every note and reference was in Italian. But this had to be it. Had to.

Nothing on the slide she'd prepared looked like that. Everything appeared normal. Completely normal.

Thank God. She'd take another sample later. Before she left. Until then she needed to devote her time to making notes.

Damn Sal for writing everything in Italian. So what if it was his native language. Hysterical laughter bubbled up inside her. And she thought she was losing it before. Hell, she'd give anything to go back to when her biggest worry was what to do next.

Now she had way too much to do and not enough time. She wanted to be out of the house by daybreak.

She scribbled notes about everything she could. She listed the names of every compound in the lab and the refrigerator. Carefully, she transcribed the Italian details of the test he was currently working on. She dared not take samples with her. Traveling light was a must. The key was to have nothing that would throw up alarm. The notes would be difficult enough to explain.

She was leaving. She really was.

Ideas swarmed in her head. Once she got to Cairo, she'd call someone she could trust and tell them all about it. Let them help Sal. Then her job was done.

It was the getting there that concerned her.

With the notes as complete as they were going to get, Julia looked around the lab one last time. Funny how things appear so differently than when you first see them. Yet she could remember walking in and seeing Sal, bent over his experiment. He'd devastated her heart immediately with his dark good looks. But he seemed unreachable, even then.

Boy, how things change. Unreachable, indeed. Hopefully his colleagues could help him. From there what he did with this place was all his.

During a previous foray through his desk drawer, Julia had found a bank bag with cash. Italian money. She had no clue of its comparative value or what the amount represented. There were twenty bills. She took half. That should get her far enough to make her plea for help. If she could reach her parents, they'd wire her money.

The first step was always the hardest.

One more thing. She held her breath while climbing back up the steps. There still had been no sign of Sokhra or Paolo. Despite her concern for the housekeeper, the lack of communication available would frustrate her even more. Trying would make it worse. She wanted to leave quietly.

Sal's bedroom door stood ajar. She paused in the doorway, listening for anything. Her fingers hesitated on the light switch. What if he was here, but asleep? It was, after all, still pre-dawn.

A chance she'd take.

Empty.

Things were almost going too smoothly. Where was everyone? What if Paolo jumped out at her again? And why did he attack her to begin with?

Not her problem. Didn't keep it from bouncing around in her already aching head. What role did he play in all this? Why would he willingly subject himself to such...horror? And why was he after her? Things there didn't add up.

She pondered over the idea of taking the suitcase with her. Practicality won out. It'd be too much. But she chose a pair of khaki pants and cool short sleeve blouse. Much easier to carry the money in her pocket. And look neat. She'd get more respect that way.

On a whim, she reached onto the dresser and extracted Sal's talisman necklace and tied it around her neck. Her souvenir. It lay against her heart. Just where she needed it.

And then it was time.

Once more she surveyed the room. Despite the damage, she saw it through emotion's eye. It'd all come full circle in here. Fear, horror, and ultimate pleasure. And somewhere in the middle of it all, she'd fallen in love.

Swiping a tear away, she turned back out into the hall and closed the door behind her.

No one asked what she was doing when she took the keys to the Land Rover from the hallway desk. She hesitated at the door. Not a soul tried to stop her.

She got to the vehicle and behind the wheel without seeing another living person. They didn't even know she was leaving. The sun hadn't broken the horizon yet, at least that she could see, but the sky was a pastel yellow and pink. The smear of clouds that darkened them were just for show. No rain would fall here today.

These were the memories she'd hoped to extract from this vacation. Images of nature's beauty. The amazing culture of another group of humans whose way of life was different than she was used to. She learned something all right. The truck roared to life beneath her hand. Something she'd never forget.

In the rearview mirror she watched the house get smaller and disappear. "Goodbye, Sal," she whispered. Another unforgettable set of memories there. When she got home, everyone was going to ask her about the plane crash and the natives and how did she survive. She'd tell them. Some of it. What they wanted to hear. But that stuff wasn't the most profound. Okay, maybe losing Chelly would be. But even more intensely, she'd remember Sal. His accent. The way he'd smile with his messed up hair and unshaven face. The way he called her *amore*. Like he meant it. Her gut wrenched thinking about it.

She tightened her fingers on the wheel. No one would ever touch her the way Sal had—a way that went so much further than just skin deep. Already, she knew that. It was something she was leaving behind. True love would be nothing but a memory.

That's all it could ever be, she tried to convince herself. There was no way to retrieve those flashes of hope, those moments of ultimate happiness. Why couldn't she bottle the bliss of laying in Sal's arms after lovemaking? Why couldn't a kiss last forever?

"Not possible."

She jostled over the bumpy roads and fought the urge to turn around and ignore all she'd learned for the sake of easing the pain in her chest. The village had to be up here somewhere. She kept the nose of the Rover pointed southeast and never gave up.

The railroad tracks soon became visible in the distance. The sky had turned from rose to pale blue and the sun already blinded her as she drove directly into it. Leading her home. She had to believe that. She kept the tracks to her left and pushed the pedal down a little harder.

This was what she wanted. She was on her way home. But there was no flush of excitement, no trembling with anticipation. Just a monotone acceptance. She did it, she got what she wanted.

The train station was empty. Didn't matter though. She'd wait. She sat on a hard wooden bench and looked over her notes. The building was as she remembered it. But boy had she changed. Not that she wasn't afraid and rather insecure. Back then, she was running to something—home. Today the truth was clear, she was running from something.

Every time the door creaked open, she jumped, expecting to see Paolo or even Sal. She could imagine his reaction, "What are you doing here? I told you I'd take you home."

Could she look him in the eye and say goodbye? She didn't want to know.

The uncomfortable seats forced her to shift her position every few minutes. She should have been warm in Sal's bed.

No. She'd have to look forward to being warm in her *own* bed.

Bed. She hadn't pulled an all-nighter like that in…years. If then. She hadn't ever been much of a night owl. The depot wasn't crowded. She could just stretch out here. Yeah. With her feet up and her head cradled by the stack of notes, she might just be able to close her eyes for a moment or two.

The sound of the train woke her.

Dammit.

How had that happened?

Someone opened the door. The sun shone in like a high-powered flashlight and blinded her. Following it was the blast of a furnace. It stole her breath. How long had she slept? Worse, how was she going to get a ticket to get on the train?

She rubbed her eyes and straightened her papers. It was amazing she still had them. And her money. It was there, in her pocket. Obviously no one bothered with the strange looking woman.

But would they help her?

"What do I do, I need to go to Cairo. Help me. I need to be on that train."

The middle-aged man with seventy-year-old wrinkles smiled and shrugged his shoulders.

"Cai-ro," she repeated, patting her chest and pointing to the train. *Oh God, please, someone help*!

He wasn't going to try. He just stared. She had to do something. There was no way she'd come this far just to fail. She ran outside. There were no lines for boarding. This was certainly not Grand Central Station in New York. Or the bus stop in Albany. For a moment, she wasn't even sure it was a passenger train.

But then she spotted a man helping an elderly woman up into a car.

She ran toward them. "Help me, please. I need to go to Cairo."

"Khartoum," the man pointed at the train and then rattled off what sounded like a tongue twister.

"Khartoum?" she pointed again and then moved her hand like a train. At least she hoped. So now what? She pointed to herself and then into the car.

He shook his head.

"No!" she cried, and tried to board.

He pushed her back.

Failure wasn't an option.

One more time, she patted herself on the chest and then pointed to the train. Then she reached into her pocket and disengaged one of the bills. "Cairo. Khartoum. I need to go!"

A man got out of the car in front of her and beckoned her up. Oh, thank heavens. She jogged up toward the other car.

That's when she heard the growl.

Chapter 15

Everything was a blur. She saw something cross her line of vision heard a scream. The man beside her was on the ground, holding his bloody face in his hands.

Leopards. It was deja vu all over again. Complete dread bottomed out like a slab of concrete in the bottom of her stomach. It pulled her to her knees with disbelief and horror.

Her scream mixed with the others that cried out, both in fear and in pain. It was all she could do.

All around her, the leopards were attacking the people.

Her notes scattered as she was knocked to the ground. The dirt she lay on was already stained with blood. Once again she found herself in a fight for her life. There were dozens of the cats, seemingly bloodthirsty crazed animals, all attacking as if for sport.

Had Sal caused this? Oh God, what had he done?

Then she spotted him. Paolo. It took her breath away to see him like that and know. Other than coloring, he looked just like one of them. He *was* one of them.

He circled the group. Was he their leader? Had he orchestrated this?

She hit the deck as shots rang out over her head. The villagers were firing on the cats. Oh God. Paolo. Did Sal know he was out here? Was Sal? She lifted her head and tried to look around.

All she could see were feet on the other side of the train. People picking up the dead and wounded. It sounded like a war zone. The gunfire never let up. Way too often she'd cringe as she heard the yelp of an animal hit by a bullet.

She had to get Sal. To warn him. He might be able to help, or at least understand.

The truck, with the keys in it, wasn't far—just on the other side of the buildings on the edge of town.

Julia took the chance, and ran.

She didn't get far.

From the corner of her eye, she saw Paolo shift direction and start after her. Her body was already running on reserves, yet she pushed harder. She would not let him kill her. She had to make it. Had to.

Tears blinded her. Breathing was impossible. Between the dust kicked up by all the activity, the smoke from the gunfire and the heat of the day, she couldn't catch her breath. She couldn't feel her legs. The bones had melted.

She collapsed.

It was so unfair. She was so close to going home.

She felt the shadow over her. It shielded her eyes from the red hot sun, but she dared not open them and look into his hungry mouth. "Paolo, no," she whispered as he bent his head. Hot breath scored her cheek.

Bullets hit the ground and even buildings around them. Paolo stood on her back. Like a target. She could feel the nails poking into her skin as he shifted balance. Even if she tried, she couldn't see, couldn't lift her head. And she didn't want to.

Get it over with.

Claws cut in as Paolo shifted his balance backward. She moaned and tensed. Waiting. Always waiting to die.

She rolled over as Paolo pushed off of her. Thunder roared in her ears. Oh God. Paolo? Had someone shot him?

She opened her eyes to find Snow standing over her.

"Sal," she breathed, reaching up to touch his neck.

He'd saved her. He'd come for her.

She wanted to wrap her arms around him. He'd risked his life—

Something was wrong.

His weight pinned her to the ground. His eyes—his eyes were what triggered it. They were glassy. Glazed over.

"Sal?" she asked, trying to push him up. "Snow?"

His front limbs buckled.

Oh God.

Oh God.

Where *was* Paolo? She had to get Sal out of here. Now. Immediately.

"Someone help me," she called out to the crowd.

A man with a spear walked over to her with his hand out. "Oh, please no," she pleaded. He held the weapon right over Sal's head. No way could she let him do it. "Please no."

She accepted his hand. He pulled her legs free of the weight of the white leopard. Then she pushed the man away.

Oh God.

Red stained the entire side of Snow's body.

She leaned down and immediately felt for the bullet hole and applied pressure. "Please don't let it have hit your heart. Please. Please. Please be alive. Stay alive, stay with me Sal. Don't you die. You can't, you hear me. Please."

A hand on her shoulder meant to pull her away from the leopard, but she would have none of that.

"No!" she screamed. Lovingly she stroked his head. "Sal, hold on baby. Hold on. *Amore.*" It felt right to use his endearment. No. It couldn't end like this. She wasn't worth it. She'd rejected him and walked away. He wasn't supposed to have saved her. Again. She leaned her head against him. *Please don't die. I'm so sorry, Sal. Please.*

"Hooleea?"

She looked up to see Paolo, dressed in tattered pants, leaning over them. Paolo, who'd caused this mess to begin with. But addressing that would have to wait.

"Help me." She pointed at Sal and to the truck. "Tio. Rover. Go." He had to understand that.

He nodded and sprinted off.

"Hey," she started to yell, but it fell on deaf ears. A tall man, well dressed in comparison to the natives, grabbed her arm and pulled her away from Snow. Julia didn't like the smile on his face one bit. In fact, it was clear what he wanted.

The white leopard.

He lowered his gun and aimed it at Sal's head.

"No!" she screamed and charged him.

The shot hit the dirt at least four feet to the side. No way was she going to let Sal be taken as some trophy animal. Not unless they killed her to do it.

The man didn't shoot her. He back-handed her.

Bright sparks of light appeared on the inside of her eyelids. And she tasted blood. Dammit, where was Paolo? She couldn't hold them off. She was no match.

Fighting dizziness, she crawled over to the limp form of the cat, directly into the path of the man's pointed rifle. If he wanted to shoot Sal, it'd go through her first. She lay over him. "It's okay, *amore*. I won't let him hurt you again. I promise you that. Paolo's helping me. He's gone to get the truck." God, she hoped she wasn't lying. "I'll get you home and get some serum into you. You'll be fixed up in no time."

She sustained a sharp kick to the ribs, but held on. *Hurry up, Paolo. Hurry up!*

Her grip loosened only when she heard the crunch of tires. She nearly cheered when she heard the ka-chunk of a shotgun being loaded. Sal kept one in the back.

Paolo was going to save him with it.

"*Andiamo*," he yelled over all the confusion.

Her translation—it's now or never. She ignored the stranger's gun that remained inches from her head. Let him shoot her. For the most part, the gunfire in the area was starting to die down. There were no leopards in her immediate view, except for those who'd taken a bullet. Sadly, there were more people down than cats. Men still walked around the trains, guns aimed, as they looked for other attackers.

Paolo handed her Sal's rifle and positioned a tarp beside Sal. And how did he expect to get him into the truck? He was by far the largest leopard of any in the vicinity. As a man he had to weigh in at one-eighty, possibly more. She couldn't lift that, and she doubted Paolo could by himself, either.

But she had an option.

Several men stood around them. Most had weapons. Some did not. She approached them first, gun raised, but not pointed. Trying to speak would be foolish. She pointed to Sal, then to the truck, then waved money between them.

Two men helped Paolo roll Sal onto the tarp and lift him into the truck. She closed and locked the back door. Handing over the money was nothing. Even if that was her way home. She'd have gladly paid more if she'd had it. Just to save him. To give him a fighting chance.

Paolo drove back. She didn't complain. But she didn't relax and try to strike up a conversation either. She didn't understand him. At all.

Usually she could learn enough about a person and see what fueled them.

Sal's nephew was a true enigma.

And if he had inflicted the bacterial infection upon himself, willingly transformed himself into a leopard, why did he do it?

She aimed to find this out before she tried to leave again. Once Sal was well. That shouldn't take long. All she had to do was figure out which was healing serum and apply it to the wounded area. He'd sleep it off and wake up as if it hadn't happened.

Sokhra's face visibly paled when they drove up. "Help us," Julia called to her as she rounded the vehicle. They needed to get him in the lab with the least amount of jostling.

She watched as Paolo and Sokhra exchanged looks. Paolo shrugged and fisted his side of the tarp. She and Sokhra took the other side. They carried him to the nearest lab table.

Now. Three people who couldn't understand one another and one injured man-leopard. How were they ever going to work together to get through this?

Sokhra said something to Paolo. He scowled and left, slamming the door behind him.

Make that two people with no chance of communicating and one dying man-leopard.

The options were limited. Julia wasn't a doctor. Or a veterinarian. She had no means to open the wound and search for a bullet. Hope was sitting in the vials on Sal's lab tables and in his fridge.

Okay. Okay. She paced the room and repeated that as she breathed. Where to start?

Sokhra had stretched Snow out on the lowest counter and had started cleaning the wound. Obviously she was aware of the metamorphosis Sal and Paolo went through. What else did the woman know?

Julia lamented the loss of her notes. All of them. Gone.

She had to start from memory, then review. Time was running out.

Hours passed. Sokhra fussed over Sal. She tried to fuss over Julia too, but other than accepting a small meal and glass of water, she kept buried in recreating the research notes.

Helpless. And she kept asking herself why she was trying. Why? Inside her head she imagined Sal's cloudy eyes as he bent to kiss her. Whether she wanted to accept it or not, her ears burned with the words he'd said. *I love you.* Even if she couldn't stay, she couldn't leave. She had to do this. She owed it to him.

She felt utterly incapable. The information all blurred in her head. There were several serums already made. But what were they? Clearly, they weren't all the same.

And Paolo hadn't come back.

"Sokhra," she called to the woman. Julia'd laid out three of the hypodermics that were filled and in the drawer. The writing on the label was in two languages. Hopefully, Sokhra could read one of them.

The woman, who'd aged ten years before noon, picked up the middle needle and walked back to Sal.

"Wait," Julia called. Did she know? What was she giving him? "Sokhra, no."

She tugged gently on the woman's arm and led her back to the table where she worked.

This was like a high stakes game of charades. One of these vials could hold the healing serum, but it could also hold that bacteria filled potion that caused this whole thing. She pointed to the first needle and handed Sokhra the pen. "What does it do?" she asked. Hopefully the cadence of her voice would relay the question.

Sokhra shook her head and handed the pen back.

Julia sighed. Maybe that was an I-don't-know answer. So she pointed to the third one. Sokhra nodded and pointed to Sal. Then she bared her teeth and brought her arms up in a werewolf type pose.

Julia drew a stick man, then a cat. And put an arrow between them. She pointed to the third needle again and to her drawing. Sokhra nodded and smiled.

Progress. Potion number three was the bad stuff.

So what was the needle Sokhra held in her hand?

Julia pointed.

That was simpler. Sokhra pointed to the leopard, then to the man.

Julia drew the arrow going the other way.

Another smile. But hadn't Sal said there was no cure? Wasn't that what he was trying to find? Maybe he had, and was trying to duplicate it. Or was fine-tuning it.

A sample would be good. A before and after. Julia grabbed a needle and withdrew a small amount of blood from the snowy white cat. After Sokhra injected him—God she hoped Sokhra knew what she was doing—she'd wait a few minutes and take another sample. See what was happening in there.

The blood cells scared her.

On Sal's chart of cells, one through six showed the progression he'd tracked. He was probably a nine. And she could finally see the bacteria. Almost like it was swimming around searching for uninfected cells.

What had Sal said? Something about the cells being transformed genetically into leopard cells. Scary thing was, she didn't see anything *but* leopard cells in the sample.

She took the hypo from Sokhra and let a drop fall onto the blood on the slide. The cells that came in contact with the serum almost seemed to change. But then the bacteria moved in.

Julia looked up at Sokhra and shook her head. Whatever Sal had in that vial, it wasn't enough.

She tossed the slide to the side and made a new slide of blood. Then she took the first, unknown hypo and added a drop.

Julia jumped back from the microscope.

What she saw there was a hellacious nightmare.

The bacteria and cells immediately started multiplying. No matter what, she wouldn't inject Sal with that needle.

Where did that leave her?

Back to square one.

Her brain was overloaded.

Time to stop being a scientist and spend some time with Sal. The emotional impact of it weighed heavy on her chest.

"Sal, I'm so sorry. You have to know how hard all this is for me to comprehend. Please know I never wanted anything bad to happen to you. Ever." She sat in the chair Sokhra had pulled up earlier. It would be so easy to forget the person that *was* this cat and just feel awe for the beauty of him. She'd had a few pets growing up. Memories of the way the cat would curl up on her lap or the dog would sleep on her feet sprung to mind. There was a gentle innocence about them. She found that in Snow. There was an incredible urge to pull his head onto her lap and wrap her arms around him. Her fingers traced over his eyes and between his ears. She wondered what that felt like. If he could even feel it.

So far his chest rose and fell—shallow, but with a good, even rhythm. That alone gave her hope.

"Sal, I wish you could help me. Tell me what to do. What needs to be done to make the healing serum? What had you found before yesterday?" She leaned down and rested her head against his shoulder. "I want to help you. I just don't know if I can."

Over and over she whispered words of hope to him, even long after her arm tired from stroking his head and back.

She needed sleep.

But no way was she leaving him like this. No way was she going to wake up in the morning and learn his condition had changed overnight and she wasn't there to help.

"I'll be right back. I promise. I just need to get a pillow and blanket." Sokhra had pulled out a rough woolen throw blanket to cover him with. But his temperature had seemed so high, she was afraid to put it over him.

She tucked it along his back though, just in case he woke enough to try to roll. Not that it'd help much. "Don't go anywhere," she called out, forcing a laugh.

Sal's bedroom had been put back together. Other than the stains on the light carpeting and the board over the window, evidence of last night's fight had been erased. Sokhra's doing? Sal's? Didn't matter. She wouldn't be occupying this room for a while and she feared Sal wouldn't be either.

If he'd just snap out of the leopard shape she might feel better about it.

Hurrying, she washed her face and tied her hair back. She debated about the time it would take to change clothes, but decided wearing Sal's warm up pants would be more comfortable than sleeping in the snug dress pants. Especially if she was lying on the floor. She needed to get a good night's sleep so she could have all her brain cells working to full potential tomorrow morning. Sal needed her. And he needed her sharp.

Sokhra tried to hand her a plate of food when she passed through the kitchen. The poor woman was at wit's end. When Sokhra's sign language clearly reminded Julia that she needed to stay strong for Sal, she agreed. She picked at the layers of flat bread and roasted meat. It was delicious and she was starving, but thoughts of Sal kept her from enjoying it. Maybe later. She'd have a decent breakfast before getting started.

Guilt forced her to choke half of it down. She'd tried to stand up and hand the plate back, but Sokhra's face—lines drooping in multiple frowns—set her heart on edge. So much of this was her fault. She hadn't turned Sal into a leopard, but he had gotten hurt saving her. Paolo had been after her. She'd caused the rift between nephew and uncle that forced them to fight like wild animals, sparing no mercy.

It should be her on that table. Not Sal.

There was only one way to redeem herself. In her own eyes and probably in theirs as well. Could she save Sal?

* * * * *

Sal faded in and out of the darkness. Each breath was a ragged knife slicing through his side. Occasionally he heard voices. Soft voices. Sokhra. Even Paolo. And Julia.

He'd fought so hard to wake up when he had felt her wrap her arms around him and rest her head on his neck. A lion he wasn't, but at that moment he felt like king of the jungle.

Julia was here. With him.

And he was trapped in this unresponsive body. He couldn't even wiggle a finger, twitch his tail, flick a whisker. Hell, he only knew he was still stuck in leopard form from the reaction of those around him. At least he could feel them. If he didn't, he'd probably give up.

Julia. His reason for living had returned.

He'd watched her early that morning. He'd known she was leaving. But he had no right asking her to stay. What could he offer? His final gift to her was letting her go.

But when Sokhra said that Paolo had left—in a group of leopards, he'd leapt into action. The attack on the train had left him sick to his stomach. He couldn't understand why the animals would do that, even if Paolo incited them. And then to see Julia in the mix of it, with Paolo tracking her every move.

He'd take that bullet again in a heartbeat if it meant saving her.

Chapter 16

Julia woke with a start. For the third time in as many days, she had incredibly erotic dreams. Colorful, vibrant dreams like she'd never experienced before. The touches, the way Sal's mouth moved over hers, the way his fingers stroked her until she was ready to come—her skin still felt it. Her body ached for it.

And then she'd woken up in a cold sweat. She couldn't shake the equally vivid horror that marred such ecstasy.

Why did she keep dreaming Sal's death?

The lab was completely dark. Last night she'd woken up like this to find Paolo sitting at Sal's computer. The faint light of the monitor had illuminated a path into part of the lab. She'd mentally debated getting up and trying to talk to him. But memory of him baring those fangs at her was a giant check mark in the "con" column.

Now she wondered if he'd been able to avert the password. What if research notes were on his computer—notes beyond the basic static details he'd asked her to arrange in spreadsheet form.

She squinted toward the office door. Pure velvet blackness. Had to be early too, because Sokhra was usually puttering around the kitchen by five or six, but no light filtered under that door yet.

"Sal?" she asked. Going to sleep was the worst. When that light went out and she closed her eyes, she knew she would wake up to find the worst had happened overnight. Her blankets were wrapped around her feet as tightly as the fear that squeezed her heart. Before she could go back to sleep, or even try to, she had to know.

She struggled to kneel, and then stand and reached out for him. She couldn't see a thing. Was he man, was he feline? *Was he alive…?*

Her hand connected. Fur. And he hadn't shifted at all. She stroked over the rise of his shoulder and across the bumps and dips of his ribs. Then rested her fingertips over the heart. The test. It wasn't palpable, but she could feel his lungs expand as he breathed.

She let out her own pent-up breath. She still had him.

Time was running out.

The antibiotics in the fridge had been her final options. She'd spent the entire length of two days mixing things in every available combination. And there were no positive reactions when dropped on a slide with Sal's infected blood.

If a cure were here, she hadn't found it. She wasn't used to not figuring things out. The frustration usually spurred her on. This was a challenge that had her ready to cry. Again.

Why hadn't she listened closer when he'd talked about the formulas? Not that he'd offered up a recipe or... Wait. That first night, when she'd read about leopards and humans and... She slapped a hand over her mouth. That had totally slipped her mind. So there *was* something in the database.

She kicked the blankets free of her feet and felt her way to the office. The light disarmed her for a moment. Damn. But she pushed forward. Every second counted here. Failure wasn't an option.

The computer hummed as it kicked on. She shivered. Never had she felt so cold and lonely as this. Things were back to Italian. Probably Paolo's doing. Her fingers were crossed as the little box popped up, so clearly prompting for a password.

She hit enter.

Nothing.

Okay, how about Salvatore.

Nope.

Leopard.

She groaned.

She closed her eyes and tried to think like Sal. Her eyes darted in his general direction. Why hadn't he invented the serum for mind reading? She could really use that about now.

"Why, why, why?"

At least it wasn't a three strikes you're out deal. She put in her name, Sokhra's name, Snow, serum. She fisted her hand and stared, teary-eyed at that mocking little box. What could it be?

"This is ridiculous." She got up and kicked the chair. "If he dies, it's his own damn fault. He's locked us out of the cabinets, the computer—anything we can use to help him he's hidden from us. He did it, not me." Listen to her. She sounded like an ungrateful brat.

Empty words, all of them, and she regretted every last one. Something though, something had to go right. Failure was foreign to her. She always finished the tasks she had before her. Until she arrived in Africa. Hell, she hadn't even made it to her destination. Since then, her life had done nothing but snowball into disaster. But she couldn't fail every time. And certainly not this time. It wasn't an option.

She threw up her hands. It connected with the flowerpot on top of the cabinet. Par for the fucking course. She grabbed the overturned pot and prepared to smash it into the floor. She didn't care. She was so damn tired. So frustrated and nothing, nothing was going right. She couldn't talk to anyone.

She couldn't do it. Couldn't even throw a temper tantrum the right way because she was too conscientious that Sokhra'd be the one to clean it up. Her anger had nothing to do with that sweet woman.

So she put the plant down and muttered that it was its lucky day.

"What the—" A key?

She let loose with a string of curses, all directed at her. Why hadn't she looked? My God, it had probably been there all the time.

Her hand shook as she picked it up and brushed the black dirt off. Her mind raced with the possibilities.

It worked! She gasped as the lock of the filing cabinet popped out. The drawer slid open to expose its contents.

Her stomach sank to middle earth. There had to be fifty files in there. All in Italian.

She'd never have time to review them all.

Think, Julia, think like a scientist.

She was so tired, she didn't want to think at all.

Think of Sal.

Right.

First step. What? "Dammit Sal, wake up!" Maybe she could figure out what she didn't need and go from there. She had to do something.

* * * * *

Sokhra walked in with a steaming mug when Julia was nearly a fourth of the way through the second of three drawers. Judging from the dates, all the files were old—probably when he started his research. Before the healing serum or this bacteria came into his life.

"Thank you," she said as she took the coffee. She sent a silent thanks to Sal as well, for stocking his house with this stuff. Gourmet, probably. Right now she didn't care about taste though. She just needed the energy it'd give her.

So she could figure out her next step, because these files were useless to her.

She fingered through the remainder of them. They all looked the same. The hot coffee did little to remove the coldness that had seeped into her chest.

One more drawer. She had to keep going. But when she pulled it out, she realized it wasn't the same at all.

First off, there were only about three hanging file folders, the rest of the stuff was stacked toward the back. Books, papers, stapled reports. She ignored that—the front folder had her name on it.

Julia froze, then looked back. Sokhra was gone. What the hell was this? She put her coffee on the desk and sat down on the floor beside the drawer.

Nothing could have prepared her for this. Head on collision with a freight train was too mild. She was glad she was sitting down.

"Sal?" she whimpered as she pulled out a passport and opened it up.

Oh my God. It nearly slid from her grasp as she forced her eyes to reread. Her name. Her first name, at least. And her picture.

Julia DeMartiano? The confusion only surfaced for a minute. Who cares? It was valid. She could leave.

She put the passport on her lap and lifted the next envelope out of the file. She shrieked then. A ticket. She lifted the stack of papers to her lips and kissed them. An open date ticket from Cairo to Florence, Italy.

He'd done it. Sal had gotten her a way home. A way home. He hadn't failed her. He hadn't lied. A smothering guilt arched through her, but was almost immediately replaced by genuine warmth. The fuzzy feeling inside her could only be love. She choked and held the papers to her chest. How could she love? How could her love still have a breath left after all she'd learned?

Because of what she had in her hand. What Sal had given her.

More than a ticket home. Sal had never turned on her, never, to her face, ever done anything except try to make her happy. Despite all her mixed up feelings and contradicting reactions, he'd been there. And he'd gotten her what she needed the most.

But why had he hidden it in his drawer? When had he expected to let her go?

"Hoooleea?" Sokhra stood in the doorway, twisting a towel in her hand. She then pointed to her chest and back at Julia.

What she wouldn't give to stand up and tell the woman what a wonderful person Sal was. A way home!

But how could she think of twirling the housekeeper around the room in utter happiness when the man who'd done that, and more, for her, lay there dying?

Julia shook her head to tell Sokhra she didn't need any help—at least that's what she'd hoped Sokhra had asked.

For now, she would put both the passport and the ticket back into the cabinet. They'd be there when she needed them. And she'd keep the key.

In the meantime, she needed to find information on the serum—the real reason she wanted in the cabinet. But the other files held little of any help. Sal's and Paolo's passports, their tickets and stubs from other flights. Receipts, faxes, printed and bound reports, letters from the university. What she wouldn't give to read those.

She took the top one and put it in her file. She'd take it with when she did go. If only for the information on the letterhead. Wouldn't hurt to get in touch with someone from the university some day to check on Sal.

If he survived this, that is.

The hair on the back of her neck stood up when she heard the footsteps. It was *not* Sokhra that had walked back into the room. Which meant...Paolo.

She gripped the handle of that third drawer and watched her knuckles turn white. She was afraid to look. What if...

Sal. Think Sal. "Paolo?" she queried.

He stood over her, his hand outstretched. His eyes were clear. Normal and brown. His half-smile seemed genuine. Based on that alone, she accepted his help and rose to her feet.

Now what? She looked back at the computer, then past Paolo to the now brightly lit lab. She could see Sal there, on the table. Sokhra stood over him.

"I need help," she said, pointing to the computer. "Formula. Serum. Ingredients." She had to gamble he could at least get a hint of what she was asking. She never wanted anything so bad as this. And it was a simple request. The cure for Sal.

Paolo's fingers flew over the keys and before she could compute what keystrokes he made, the pesky password box disappeared and the main menu appeared.

"What is it? What's the password?" Shoving a pencil at Paolo she searched his face for recognition. He'd spoken a little. Her best chance was to continue to try this communication. At least some of their words sounded similar. She tapped the note paper and pushed the pencil in his hand. Then traced the screen in the shape that box had been.

Paolo narrowed his eyes and shook his head. *Oh please no. Don't do this to me. To Sal.* She needed him to understand the dire emergency they faced. But maybe he knew. Hands pressed together in a praying formation, she lifted her eyebrows and tried to plead. He threw the pencil down.

Dejected, her hands fell to her sides. Paolo zipped through screens so quickly she couldn't even try to understand any of the titles or menus.

She had to walk away. Too much to digest. The hot coffee did help to wash her frustration down some. And she needed to convince Paolo that she needed help, specific help, before he tore off to whereever it was he went during most days.

The printer hummed and then clicked as the cartridges moved into place. Julia nearly jumped out of her skin. Clear proof of how uneasy she was around the boy, despite her attempts to trust him. She watched him without looking at the monitor. The lights and colors of the menus he scrolled through so quickly reflected against his dark, darting eyes.

He hit the keys a few more times, almost the way a pianist pounds out his finale. Then he leaned back and crossed his arms over his chest.

Paolo didn't look up at her. Nor did he speak. He just sat back and waited while Julia held her breath. What was he doing? For all she knew, he was printing an email from one of his buddies and was off again. He could care less about all this.

Dammit, why did she have to get all teary-eyed again? She threw up her hands in defeat and walked out of the room. Her energy needed to be used to find this elusive bacteria killer, not feel sorry for herself and her hurt feelings and guilt. Or worry about Paolo.

Sokhra sat beside Sal and rubbed her hand over his paw, crooning a gentle song. Probably a native lullaby.

Don't sleep forever, Sal. Heal, then wake up. Come back to me. Her mind said it, her heart felt it. She'd give up everything to have Sal wake up and be whole. She owed it to him to try to make it happen.

The microscope was her ball and chain for the next few hours. If they hadn't already, the antibiotics would already start losing their potency. And then what? Then the white flag would be raised and she could go home, free as a bird.

So why didn't that have the same appeal as it would have a week ago?

Time to take another blood sample from Sal and get started. Each time she did so, she'd pray she'd see the results of some miracle. That his body had finally said, wait a minute here, and kicked in the white blood cells that should be...

Holy shit.

Blood. Sal had brought back blood with him. Of course, most of it had been damaged and the rest he'd used. Maybe that's how he'd found the cure. But where to get blood?

Her hair fell into her face to disguise the wide-eyed realization. Her blood. His voice echoed in her head. "Care to donate?" he had asked. And he hadn't asked for much. If she had offered up a vein, would Sal be cured right now? Would any of this have happened?

Hang another fifty-pound weight from her heart.

Paolo was going to have to help her with this one. She rushed back to the lab and ran square into the teenage boy. He was a few inches taller and at least forty pounds heavier. Which sent her backwards onto the floor.

Normally she would have quickly gotten up, brushed herself off and apologized profusely. But that something in Paolo's eyes stopped her cold.

They were empty again. Julia's mouth went dry.

He reached down and hauled her to her feet. Fingers dug into her upper arms as he held her in front of him.

"Tio. You...better tio." He let go. She nearly fell. His teeth were changing again. She'd spent too much of her time facing what she'd call looking-death-in-the-eye moments to think standing here this very moment was any different.

But then he shoved the papers in her hand and raced out the door.

Better Tio?

Heal his uncle? Was that what he was trying to say? God bless him for trying to communicate. And for these. Still in Italian. Julia folded the paper in half. Obviously something Paolo felt was important. Useless to her. God, she hated that. Hated that the cure was right there, in her hands and in her veins and she couldn't do it.

She had to try. If she were lucky, Paolo would come back and help. Something about that boy...He'd had ample chances to hurt her, and hadn't. She had to believe it was because of Sal, they were uniting to save him. But she couldn't let down her guard. Not without being sure.

Right. So now what? She sat down the paperwork and closed her eyes.

Blood.

She needed to draw blood. How much would she need? She bypassed her microscope and went straight to Sal. Sokhra remained with him. Her dedication was unparalleled. She just wished she could tell the woman how much strength she passed on, just watching her tirelessly care for the man she worked for.

"Sal," she started.

Sokhra stood and started to leave.

Julia touched her arm. "No, wait." She held up a finger, then turned back to the form stretched out before her. His ribs were much more pronounced now. The luster was gone from his fur. The corkscrew in her chest twisted again. Three days since he'd been shot. Sokhra and she had both wrung out rags of water into his mouth, but he'd taken in no fluids. No food. He needed an IV and monitors. But there was nothing like that here.

"Sal, I think I'm on to something. I need to know. Do something. Blink, wiggle, move your tail, something. Tell me am I right. I need to combine my blood—untainted blood with the healing serum. And I'm thinking an antibiotic. Right?"

That was her best guess. It made sense. She was betting everything on it. Unfortunately, she still didn't have the formula for the healing serum. Sal's miracle discovery. It just might die with him.

Nothing. Not a whisker moved.

Julia sucked in her breath, patted Sokhra on the shoulder and opened the drawer that held the supply of needles. She'd never drawn blood before. Guess this was as good a time as any to learn how.

Sal had sampled his own blood. She knew that, now. He'd monitored how his blood had altered while the bacteria had continued to work on. All the equipment was there, in the drawer. Of course, her unpracticed hands fumbled with the elastic tie. Her patience had been shot a long time ago. Why couldn't something go right? Why?

She closed her eyes when the elastic shot across the counter. Count to ten. Deep breath.

A gentle touch on her wrist forced her eyes open.

She'd expected Sokhra.

Instead it was Paolo. He'd come back. Why hadn't she heard him? Where had he gone? She'd suspected he'd turned leopard and was out roaming.

She looked over at Sokhra. Dear God, were those tears in the woman's eyes? She almost panicked. Almost. Then the woman smiled warmly at Paolo and patted Sal on the shoulder.

Paolo retrieved the elastic and proficiently withdrew a needle full of blood. Instead of handing it over, placed it beside the microscope and pulled out a second needle. She searched his eyes. Did they need it? She nodded. He repeated that one more time. Would that be enough to heal Sal?

Paolo placed Julia's fingers over the gauze on her arm, and capped the needles. Some of the weight shifted from her shoulders. Even if he just stayed there with her, she felt better, she realized. It wasn't that she felt incapable. Well, she did, in a frustrating sort of way, but she hadn't accepted true defeat yet, not when this option was available. It was her final hope.

And now Paolo, who obviously knew quite a bit about the workings in the lab, was going to help. She closed her eyes and sent up a prayer of thanks.

Paolo ran his finger down the notes he'd printed and collected what he'd need. Julia tried to offer assistance, but he ignored her.

"Ahh!" Sokhra screamed.

Julia ran, but she couldn't beat Paolo to Sal's side. A small drop of blood had rolled from Sal's nostril. His breathing had become very raspy. "Oh God. Oh God. We've got to do something. He's dying."

There was no translation needed for them all to understand that.

Doubt was nowhere to be found. Julia didn't need a medical degree to surmise that fluid was filling Sal's lungs. What to do? Her stomach flipped over in final dread. Time was running out. Her mission was failing. The ultimate failure. *Think, Julia, dammit, think!*

"We need to flip him over, or better yet, get him upright for just a little while." But what would hold him? And how to explain what she was thinking to Sokhra and Paolo? She gestured with her arms. Then tried to lift him up. Paolo laughed at that and shook his head.

It'd take a miracle to achieve that before Sal drowned from the fluid and blood in his lungs.

She wished she had an ounce of the boy's cool attitude. Not that she didn't want to smack it off his face and jump up and down screaming, "Your uncle is dying, you little shit. Can't you at least act as if you care?" But there was no time for this. And he was putting in an effort to help. *Didn't mean it. Shouldn't think like that.* But she knew what it felt like to lose someone close to her. Paolo didn't need to go through that.

And she didn't want to again. Under any conditions.

"Stay with him," she ordered Sokhra. Then grabbed Paolo's arm and hauled him back over to the lab. "Let's get this going. He's dying."

She was dying too. Every gasp from behind her, every groan from Paolo as he carefully measured out antibiotic, it all tore off another piece of her soul. She ached to help. Suddenly control of Sal's fate had been ripped from her grasp. She wasn't needed. Wasn't wanted. She could do nothing else. Nothing but watch. And pray.

Paolo stabbed his finger and dripped the blood onto a slide. Oh God, he'd gotten something. Please, please, please let it work. Let it kill the bacteria.

Her brain still fought to remember everything Sal had told her. About cells regenerating. About them searching out the right cells. About a catalyst. Why couldn't she put it together?

She watched him drip a little of the serum he'd created onto the blood and quickly tuck it under the microscope. She could only sit back with awe. The kid knew what he was doing. Obviously Sal had spent some time with him. Only she'd never seen Paolo in the lab, save the time he'd come after her.

That seemed like years, not days, ago.

"What? What did you find?" she crowded close, hoping he'd let her look. He did. And the smile on his face meant more than even looking. "You did it?" Suddenly her heart swelled with all things hopeful. So much that *she* could barely breath. And she looked. The bacteria's walls were disintegrating. Dying.

He could stop the bacteria from invading.

"Yes!" she cried.

She pointed to this and then to Sal. "Hurry up, Paolo. Hurry up and cure him."

Paolo shook his head. No? What did he mean, no? There was enough serum to fill three needles and two vials. Surely that was enough.

"Why? What are you doing?" Someone had popped the balloon of excitement in her chest. Deflated. That was how she felt. Then she noticed the blood sitting beside the serum. Her blood. "What are you doing with that?" She touched the blood filled needle.

Paolo held up a finger and pointed to the drawer.

The drawer that held two more needles. Both filled with serum.

One of which, according to Sokhra, turned Sal from man to leopard. The other she'd witnessed first hand. It was some crazy multiplier.

He muttered something to her and pushed her out of the way to get to the drawer. She saw him lift both needles, then chose one of them.

Oh God no. No.

She tugged on his arm, screamed everything she could. Sokhkra even left Sal's side to pull her off Paolo. "Don't you understand? He's going to kill him. He must want him to die. No, he can't. I can't let him. No. Please!"

Sokhra slapped her then.

Hard enough for her to see stars.

Then darkness.

Chapter 17

"What the hell?" Julia sat up and tossed the covers off her legs. Sal's room. How had she gotten up to Sal's room? It hurt to think. Her head felt like it'd been smashed with a cannon ball. Last thing she remembered was...shit.

She got up and ran downstairs as fast as she could.

"Sal!" she screamed as she threw herself through the lab door. "Sal?"

He was there, same spot. Looking the same.

Limp, dull coat. Raspy breathing. His nose was burning hot. Fever. Christ. And neither Sokhra nor Paolo were in the room. What were they doing, deserting him like this?

Ten hours. It'd been ten hours since she'd been down here. What the hell had Sokhra hit her for anyway? Oh God. The memory of Paolo picking up that needle. What had he done?

The world crashed down around her. But it wasn't merciful enough to take her with. How had this happened? She'd failed him. Completely failed him.

"I'm so sorry, Sal. I wish I could do more, really I do."

She was a fool to believe she could make a difference. Nothing but odds stacked against her. Paolo, the language, the experimental nature of the disease and the cure. She was nothing but an entry-level college science teacher. She taught the kids who took the course because they needed science credits. She didn't make a difference. Why should she now?

One thing she knew. She wasn't leaving Africa the same woman. And she wasn't leaving empty handed.

Julia pulled her file and double-checked her passport. Check. Ticket. She closed her eyes and swallowed. Yep, it was all here. She kept the whole file. Methodically she walked around the lab and picked up her notes. Notes she'd painstakingly recreated. She took the papers Paolo had printed as well. It wouldn't hurt.

Eventually she'd find someone she trusted and see if she could better understand what had happened.

Without realizing it, she'd made the absolute decision to leave. She was a coward. But she'd tried and failed. Sal would die, but she couldn't stay to watch it happen. Not when she'd caused it.

The grief would tear her up. And it'd follow her, for guilt wasn't limited by miles and continents. She'd carry the pain of losing him forever.

But she was leaving.

"Sal, I have no idea if you can hear me or not. I know I've told you a dozen times that I'm sorry. And with God as my witness, I am truly sorry." Tears welled up then, and fell uninhibited onto the white coat. She rubbed them away. "Can you feel my tears? Can you ever understand the pain of such utter failure? I c-can't stay. I can't." She looked up, around the room she'd said goodbye to before. But she knew this was the last time. Tears blurred her vision as they welled up and then fell. She felt nothing but pure grief.

"You don't know how badly I wanted to heal you. But even if I did, would things ever be the same? Could they be? I loved you, Sal. I still do. Despite it all, I found a way to love you. There should be hope with love. And I can't find it."

She broke down then, buried her face in Sal's shoulder and cried.

Sal fought against the blackness. For too long he'd waited, praying for Julia to come through. He'd listened to her cry in frustration and kick things in anger. Sokhra told him how hard she tried, how she never left his side. But he knew that.

Then she said that Paolo had turned himself around. At first he didn't believe her and it frustrated him that he couldn't express his concern. Paolo had the means to kill him. The boy was untried in the lab. What if he injected the wrong serum into him?

He almost gave up then.

But now he was feeling stronger. Instead of the claustrophobic nightmare he'd been stuck in, he felt like he was in a long, dark tunnel, swimming his way to the surface.

Hold on, amore, don't leave me.

He had to get there before she left. Had to convince her to stay.

She was leaving. Forever. Going.

Nooo!

Julia screamed.

Something crashed. She mumbled something. Then yelled, "Sokhra, Paolo, hurry!"

What happened? What was wrong? Why couldn't he reach the goddamn surface of this black hole?

The door slammed against the wall as Sokhra burst in, clucking like a mother hen. "Salvatore?" she shrieked and immediately started examining him.

Julia had backed up against the counter. She couldn't break the stare. Had that been her imagination? Or had he really growled. He'd twitched too.

Her heart thudded against her chest like a bass drum. She was too numb to feel anything. It hurt to hope. She wouldn't let herself hope.

Yet Sokhra tossed up her hands in a what-was-that-all-about gesture.

"He growled," she said. Julia grabbed the woman's hand and put it on her throat. Then Julia growled and pointed to Sal. "Sal go grrr."

Sokhra shook her head and pointed to the ribs.

Hope had snuck in after all, despite her attempts to keep it out. And as expected, she felt it die all over again. Of course it was the fluid in his chest, gurgling. She didn't even bother to explain the jerk she felt. Reaction of the nerves. Very possible if Paolo had injected him with something that was trying to alter his cells.

Sokhra averted her eyes and turned back to Sal. Julia backed away. She didn't belong here anymore. She'd just get her paperwork and go. Now. Before she caused any more trouble.

Sokhra leaned down and picked up the fallen folder before Julia could.

She held her hand out for it, but Sokhra opened it first.

Julia swallowed the fear that the housekeeper would deny her the ticket and kept her hand outstretched. Her gaze never wavered from Sokhra's face as the woman reviewed the papers inside.

Then their eyes met. Julia could almost read the expression on her face and in her eyes. Hell, not only was the housekeeper going to give her the tickets back, she'd probably drive her to the airport. She turned away from the indifferent gaze and looked at Sal one more time.

He'd lost so much weight. And fur—it was starting to fall out. Yet he still was larger and more imposing looking than any of the other leopards she'd seen. A legend. That's what he'd forever be. Her eyes traced the aristocratic line from his neck, through his wide powerful shoulders and across his now prominent ribs and hip. She knew his hind legs had to be like tightly coiled powerful springs, but now they lay limp and useless. His tail curled and uncurled—

She screamed again, this time pointing.

He was moving. Sal was moving!

Sokhra opened her mouth as if to try to say something, but then noticed the slight way the tip rhythmically arched and unarched. Like a little wave.

The housekeeper ran out of the room. To get Paolo, undoubtedly.

Julia picked up the folder where it had dropped from Sokhra's grasp and tapped it against her open hand. "Well, Sal, I guess that means you're doing better than I thought. I should go now. Let you celebrate with Paolo. He's the one, you know. He saved you when I couldn't."

Sal strained upward, outward, but his strength was gone. The edges of the tunnel faded into darkness and he didn't know which was up. "No," he cried out mentally to the retreating footsteps. Such a hollow, empty sound. Such a lonely sound...

* * * * *

"Where is she?" Sal's words burst from his mouth as soon as he could force them out. Two days he'd been awake, but stuck in leopard form unable to question Sokhra or Paolo. Two days without hearing Julia's voice. Without seeing her. He had memories. Strange half-dreams of her. He knew she'd cried. But he couldn't believe she left.

"She's gone." Paolo answered and looked down at his shoes. "Found her ticket."

Sal sat down and held his head in his hands. The weakness of his body pissed him off. But Paolo's words knocked the fight right out of him. His memories were correct then. She'd said goodbye.

His love hadn't been enough. He'd suspected all along it hadn't. That's why he'd withheld the passport and ticket from her. He wanted her to love him back enough to choose him.

He let out a laugh that turned into a cough. And now his body betrayed him and anchored him in place. And he wasn't healed yet.

Paolo'd filled him in on the details. The serum he'd created wouldn't heal them. But it slowed the process down much faster than before. He knew Julia worked so hard on that, but still considered herself a failure. What she didn't understand was with a little more tweaking it'd be done.

"Email your father and see if she's made it to Italy yet," Sal said in a monotone. He stretched out his legs, then forced himself to stand. The pain in his muscles was nothing compared to learning he'd lost Julia again. But being pissed off did nothing to ward off the dizziness.

"Tio, you must rest. Listen to Sokhra."

"I have to work. I have to finish the serum."

"I've been working on it. I want to review some things with you."

Sal leaned against the counter and brought his head up to look at his nephew. "You've been working on it?" Sokhra had said as much, and he plainly knew that's who'd injected him with it. But what did this boy know — how could he work on something so complex?

"I took your notes and followed the directions. Julia had made some guesses. I made them work."

"You made them work," he repeated. Paolo, his nephew, the one who'd tried to kill him, to kill Julia, had saved him. "Why?"

The boy shrugged with teenage abandon and picked up a slide. As he twisted it in his hands he answered. "I was mad at you, but I couldn't let you die."

Sal's head roared like the engine of a steam train. "Still mad?"

Paolo lifted his head and displayed a crooked grin. God, the boy looked like his father. "Kind of."

"Go send that email then. I need to rest. Then you can tell me why you're mad at me."

"*Si*, Tio." Paolo turned toward the lab, but then stopped half way. "She loved you, you know."

Sal's heart kick-started back to life. He couldn't speak. Didn't know what to say.

"She left because she loved you."

What the hell did that mean? Paolo didn't stick around long enough for Sal to even ask.

"Son of a bitch," he growled as his knees gave out after two steps toward the table where all the papers were spread out. He wanted to see. What had they done? What formula had been enough to start wiping out the bacteria?

He couldn't give up. He had to save Paolo. He was long past caring about himself. Julia didn't want him. He'd dared to hope when she had come back, but it had been guilt that drove her, not the love he needed. Guilt wasn't enough to live for.

But Paolo? The kid had seemed to turn himself around. Sal hoped that, too, wasn't guilt driven, but by some realization inside. Paolo hadn't darted the moment Sal had woke up. That had to be good for something.

* * * * *

Sal hated traveling during the rainy season. Avoided it at all costs. But he had to get Paolo home, and even more so, he had to get to Florence. He'd gotten a phone call that scared him more than any of Carlotta's threats.

"My mom probably won't let me come back next year," Paolo said, stealing Sal's thoughts.

"You won't want to. You'll be on the beaches of Sicily with the girls. There's nothing here in Africa for you."

"You are, Tio."

Sal reached over and mussed the boy's hair. It'd been a tough month. Sokhra, bless her heart, had taken over dictatorship and ordered him around like a child. He'd had a curfew, working hours, a set meal on schedule. But his strength had returned. And so had Paolo.

Paolo had been a godsend as well. He'd finally pried it out of the boy—Paolo wanted to be like Sal. He'd been so jealous of Julia he'd simply struck out as a reaction. Sal's heart swelled when he thought of how Paolo had pulled himself together and matured when he needed to. How he'd worked side by side with Julia to find what it took to heal him.

A month, and the sharp point of pain was still there whenever he thought of her. And he did. Every day.

"Hold on," Sal warned as he felt the plane buck through the turbulence. Once they got to Cairo, the trip would go much smoother.

* * * * *

Julia smoothed her straight skirt and jacket. Half a dozen times, she caught herself chewing on her bottom lip. Which meant another pit stop to freshen up her lipstick. And check her hair, and convince herself she didn't need to empty the contents of her stomach. Even if the butterflies thought so.

"Well, here I am." She stood in front of the main Science Hall. Florence, Italy. Although the tall, gray stone structure could have been anywhere. She'd visited a number of colleges with these old, formidable structures standing guard over the knowledge inside.

This one, however, was much different, and it had nothing to do with the architecture at all. Sal had run up and down these steps. What had he thought, that first day, when he'd stood here?

Enough. Ever since she'd gotten the request to come to Florence. Ever since she'd left Africa, she'd found some part of every day that reminded her of Sal. Or something she'd love to have shown him, told him. And at night, when she lay alone in her bed and the loneliness set in, she was miserable.

This mission, she hoped, would help her find closure. In some way or another.

She looked down at her watch. But if she waited any longer, the only thing closed would be the door on that meeting room.

She swallowed and started up the stairs. This was her moment. The nobody college professor from New York was going to present something astounding on Sal's behalf. She just hoped she could do his work justice.

"Miss Haverstock?"

Julia turned as a young woman stepped out of the door marked

Office. "Yes?"

"Dr. Fabrogetti is running late with his current meeting and asks that you stop back in an hour. He is very apologetic."

Julia smiled and nodded.

"There's a cafe in the main hall."

Right. Caffeine. Just what she needed to drown the butterflies with. "Thank you. I'll return in an hour."

The girl smiled and opened the door to readmit herself.

Dark eyes from within the room met hers. And then the door closed.

Familiar eyes that sent her heart skating across the marble floor and down the granite steps. "Oh my God."

Numbly she turned away. It couldn't be. Not possible. She'd only caught a glimpse. Most Italians had dark eyes. And this man had a full beard. It wasn't Sal. It wasn't.

What if it had been? What would she have done?

Why am I torturing myself?

Her good friend and fellow science professor, Sonja, had offered to come along. But no, Julia had to do this alone. She rolled her eyes at herself. What had she been thinking? A little moral support would be welcome. And Lord knows right now she needed someone to calm her down.

"You're not going to look for him, are you?" Sonja had asked, lifting her eyebrow.

"Should I?" She remembered how shaky her voice had been then, just toying with the idea of seeing Sal again.

Sonja couldn't name a reason why she should or shouldn't.

Neither could she. Other than it would force Julia to explain to Sal why she'd left. "Hi, Sal," she'd pretended that day, "Nice to see you made it, no thanks to me. I went ahead and took advantage of that passport and ticket you'd hidden away. I suppose it was a small price to pay to get rid of me and all the trouble I caused you."

Sonja had, of course, swung her book bag at her in a childish gesture. And missed. Which had caused them both to laugh.

No laughing now. Julia counted out unfamiliar bills and paid for her cappuccino. There was much more she'd want to say to Sal. The most of which started with 'Thank you.'

She thought of how she'd felt twenty-seven days ago when she'd arrived in Florence via Cairo. Numb. She'd been purely numb. Looking back, it had been amazing how she'd whisked through Customs. And she'd thought nothing of it when she'd been taken to a private room and given a place to rest.

She'd just gotten up, realizing she needed to talk to someone about arrangements back to New York when the door opened.

"I wasn't prepared for you, Julia. Forgive my tardiness." The woman who approached her looked like a princess. Her dark Mediterranean looks were accented with almond eyes and dazzling smile.

Julia had yet to see another woman fill a room the way she had.

"Who are you?" Julia had asked her.

"Carlotta DeMartiano. Salvatore's sister-in-law. I do not understand why he couldn't accompany you on this trip, but perhaps that is not for me to know, no? You are here and that is what matters."

"I don't understand."

Carlotta picked up Julia's suitcase and smiled. "Follow me. I will get you into the hotel and we can talk."

Julia leaned back and smiled as she remembered Carlotta's idea of talking. Julia hadn't been able to speak one word. Not that she'd wanted to talk, especially about Sal. But those twenty-four hours she'd spent in Florence had been a whirlwind.

Her parents hadn't been surprised to hear from her at all. "I'm so glad to finally hear your voice for myself," her mother had gushed. "That man you've been working with is good at sending us regular emails to update us on what's going on. Has your arm healed?" Then the conversation had turned somber as they spoke of Chelly. Mom knew. Julia had been reduced to sobs for several moments before she was able to talk again. Sal had gone out of his way to support her family. Why?

At that moment she hadn't known whether to smack or hug Sal. If he'd have been there. He'd told her that he'd reported her dead. In truth, he'd been feeding reassurances back to her parents all along. It had been no surprise to learn that Sonja also thought she'd been there of her own free will.

It had been that final, unseen token that had convinced her to do something with the notes she'd carried home. She had failed. He hadn't.

He'd found something incredible, and the world had yet to learn of it. So she was going to set things in motion.

Looking back, she realized it'd be a hell of a story to tell. But not yet. Not when she hadn't gotten to the end yet.

Julia stood up, dried her wet palms on her napkin and forced herself to take several cleansing breaths. If she took her time, she could browse through the school bookstore/gift shop and find herself a souvenir. And one for Sonja. Anything but to let her mind drift back to Sal.

She walked through the store, randomly touching or picking up items and setting them down. She toyed with a boot shaped magnet, rubbing her finger over the raised U in the middle of it, then dropped it back into the bin with all the other identical pieces. Her fingers slowed on the gondola shaped pen. Cute, but... Nothing triggered any emotions whatsoever.

Fifteen more minutes. She stood at the entrance of the store and stared at the "Scientists do it..." stationery and note cubes. This might work. Sonja'd get a charge out of it. She reached for the note pads that finished the sentence "in their research."

The voice stopped her.

The notes fell to the floor. She stepped over them and looked down the hall.

Empty. Now she was hearing things.

This wasn't such a good idea, after all.

She walked as fast as her heels would allow. It was all a miserable idea but she was *not* going to fail. She just needed a little focus, that was all.

This time she didn't pause at the bottom of the steps. She marched up to the door marked *office*. It was ajar. Julia took a breath, patted the French twist that was hopefully still sleekly in place and knocked.

"Julia Haverstock," she said while offering her hand to the man who answered the door. He looked her up and down like she was a blind date and not a visiting professor.

"Ah, yes, Miss Haverstock."

Julia blinked. And that meant...?

"Come in. Take a seat."

Julia complied. The office was packed floor to ceiling with books.

Computers hummed at each of four stations, but their duties were masked with swimming fish screen savers. Dr. Fabrogetti rounded his desk and sat.

This, she wasn't prepared for. This seemed rather informal considering she'd flown in from New York.

"Here are my reports." She swallowed and willed her hand to stop shaking as she passed over a binder. "Most of what you'll find in there are hypotheses with notes on the results of field trials. As we've discussed, Dr. DeMartiano will be able to provide you with the exact data. I should expect he'll review what I have learned and update you with additional test information."

"Sit down, Miss Haverstock."

She fumbled her own binder. She dreaded the worst. No one had been willing to confirm that Sal was still alive. She had to present this as if he was. But what if? "Sir?"

"Let's talk less formally here. Dr. DeMartiano has been one of my colleagues for a number of years, and frankly, I find it rather odd that he'd never even hinted at the discovery of something so...earth shattering."

Julia located a chair, but had to lift a stack of textbooks from it. The dean of science merely watched her, a faint smile of amusement on his lips.

As if he was intentionally trying to trip her up. Damn good job he was doing, too.

"I can only surmise he was waiting until he had sufficient data." The chair was wobbly. She sat with her back straight, her hands wrapped tightly around the other reports she'd brought. Hopefully she looked the pillar of control and efficiency.

She watched him tap his fingers together. God, she hated that. "And in the meantime, you've stolen his data, created the report and intend to propose it to the very university that has funded the research. Such arrogance, Miss Haverstock."

Julia jumped to her feet while her heart slipped through the crack in the dusty wood floor. No, it wasn't like that! "Sir, I believe you're mistaken."

"Mistaken?" he likewise stood and shook the bound copy of Sal's research at her. "I've enough information here to recommend your license to teach be revoked."

"Sir, I—"

"Sit down, young lady."

No. She wouldn't fail. Couldn't this time. "Sir, before I listen to you, I'd ask you have the courtesy to hear me out. Open the folder."

She waited until he did. Not that he bothered to look at it.

"If I had sought recognition for this, I'd have simply published it through my local university. I'm sure something of this magnitude would have enlisted interest from Harvard, Yale, Johns Hopkins..."

"Your point, Miss Haverstock?"

She straightened her shoulders. "My point is that if you'll stop believing your ridiculous assumption about me, you'll see that my name isn't anywhere on that research."

"Why isn't it? You helped."

Julia sat down. Dr. Fabrogetti had not said that. The man standing behind him had. She gulped in breaths and stared.

Sal.

Chapter 18

She opened her mouth, but closed it. What could she say?

"What are you doing here, Julia?"

She searched his eyes, hoping to find something softer than the black ice that bore into hers.

"I—I—"

"Stand up and speak. Tell me why you felt it was so important to go above my head and provide this information to Dr. Fabrogetti?"

"Because *you* wouldn't." That much came out easily. It was true. "You lacked the resources to research this find to its fullest potential. All I wanted to do was generate some interest—"

"Interest?"

This wasn't her Sal. This was another man who looked like him. She could deal with him. Until she looked him in the eye again. Her composure slipped a little more. "I feared you would not...be able to present this. When last we spoke, you had...complications with your other research."

He lifted an eyebrow.

Her eyes darted to the dean. She had no clue how much he knew, but she was willing to bet the leopard transformation was still their secret. Feeling a little stronger, she continued, "Perhaps you ought to read the thesis before you question me. I think you'll find it outlined there in the detail you're asking." She looked from man to man and finally said, "I can't imagine why you asked me to fly all the way to Florence for this third degree, but it's your dime. I'm going back to my hotel room."

She turned and walked out.

Closure my ass. She was slamming the door on this chapter of her life.

Julia walked away, shaking with rage and hurt. Why hadn't she factored Sal into this. Never in a million years did she dream she'd see him, much less have him interrupt what she was proposing.

"Wait until Sonja hears about this one," she muttered as she hailed a cab.

Back in the hotel room, her hands shook as she tried several times to dial. When she finally got it right, Sonja's machine picked up. Son of a — well, Sonja would have to wait. "I'll call you later. You're not gonna believe what happened today," was Julia's message. Then she kicked her shoes off and threw herself backwards onto the bed.

Someone just come and stick a big red "Reject" sticker on her forehead and be done with it. Her only consolation was she and Sonja had done this on their own time. She wouldn't have to face her colleagues as a failure. No, that's wrong. She didn't fail. They did. They failed to see beyond their own pompous attitudes and see what she was handing them. She asked for nothing in return.

Julia groaned and rolled over. When did her plane leave again? Tomorrow, late afternoon, if she remembered correctly. Not soon enough. But when she'd booked it, she'd figured the university would speak to her again in the morning before she left.

Four o'clock was close enough to dinnertime, right? She'd give Sonja an hour to get home. She dialed room service and ran herself a bath.

Sal left Dr. Fabrogetti's office with a dog-eared copy of Julia's notes in his hand. Okay, so he had underestimated her. He had been prepared to shoot down all her proposals with the drawbacks he'd discovered, but she'd clearly stated over and over that the information was simply propaganda and hypothesis. She never promised anything.

And she was right. Her name was not anywhere on this thing. His name, on the other hand, was plastered all over it.

This wasn't for glory. But he didn't understand why.

That's what he was going to find out.

He flashed his smile at the desk clerk, and was rewarded with Julia's room card. Too easy. The knowledge she'd just called down a room service order was much better. He had a plan. And it was so cliché she wouldn't dream of it happening.

He paused in the restaurant and changed the order, then flashed Julia's card. "I'll take it up."

The bourbon he nursed as he waited did little to calm his nerves. For a brief second he'd seen something on her face that he still couldn't define. That moment she'd pulled her face up to search his. That second of recognition. Joy? Surprise? Whatever it was, it'd quickly disappeared.

He traced his finger through the ring of condensation his glass left on the heavily lacquered bar top. She'd done a good job. Her spirit was still there, as was the vulnerability. She'd demanded respect, and gotten it. His little kitten could certainly fight when backed into a corner. And while momentarily off balance, she'd stayed in stride and concluded her thought.

"That's my girl," he murmured and slung back the remains of the liquor.

Bad thing was, he was going to have to tell her the project was dead in the water. That all her hard work. His hard work. Paolo's hard work. Gone.

He'd sat with Dr. Fabrogetti and explained what he'd learned. In a perfect world, the serum he found and created would be the perfect drug. There was one hope. And he wanted to talk to her about it. If she'd listen.

"Sir, your meal."

He tipped the waiter and lifted the tray.

Julia wrapped the robe tightly around her and cinched it when she heard the knock. "Coming," she called and pushed the wet hair off her face. Her purse, where'd she put it? Damn. She snatched it up as the room service boy knocked again.

"I'm on my way." She slid the deadbolt and popped open the door.

"How much is it?" she sat her purse on the luggage rack and dug out her Italian money. What bill was what? She'd never get the hang of this.

"I took care of it."

All the money fell from her hand as she turned around. "Get out." She pointed. "You...you—"

"Eat with me. Just dinner. Please?" Sal pushed the door shut with his elbow and placed the tray beside her purse.

Julia's heart thundered in her chest at the memory of another plea for dinner. "No." She shook her head. "I can't. Please, Sal. I can't do this."

"You can't, or you won't?"

Her nerve endings fired right up as Sal's hand slid under her chin and lifted her face up to his. "*Mi amore,*" he murmured.

"Sal, no." She tried to turn away. *But isn't this exactly what she'd dreamed of for weeks? Hoped for beyond anything else when the Italy trip was proposed? Everything was about Sal, yet here he was and she was pushing him away.*

"I've missed you," he whispered and dropped his hand. "Even the way you deny yourself my attentions."

"I do not—"

"Sure you do," he said. She stood there, opening and closing her fists as he picked the room service tray back up and carried it to the table. "Now it'd be a sin to let this food go to waste. You ordered it, remember. So you can't tell me you're not hungry."

"You killed my appetite." She lied. But how could she sit there across from him and eat as if… *Say it, think it. Get it out of your system…* As if they hadn't been lovers. It was all she could think about. "Why are you here?"

"Soda? Water? Beer?" Sal had his head stuck in the mini fridge now. "What do you want?"

He wouldn't even let her throw him out on his ass like she wanted to. Damn him for taking the upper hand. Damn him for crawling right back in under her skin.

"Water."

This was nothing to Sal, she sensed. Almost like he was showing off his apathy. And why shouldn't he? She'd bolted the minute she knew how little she was needed. She couldn't save him. All that guilt and pain crowded in her gut.

She sat down and toyed with her food. He watched her. She could feel his eyes touching her. It forced her to think about every move she made. "What?" she finally barked.

"I'm really hurt. You haven't asked."

She blinked. "Asked what?"

"How I'm feeling."

"You look okay," she said. She gulped down cold water to loosen up her throat. She was bursting with questions, but afraid to hear the answers. There were some things she wasn't sure she wanted to hear him say out loud. *Like how incapable she was or how easy it was for Paolo to fix him once she'd left.*

"Do I?"

Damn him for doing that to her. His voice had softened and reached in around the shield of indifference she'd thrown up. Just to make sure she surrendered, the gentle way he reached for her hand worked like a sword into her gut. She bit her bottom lip and nodded.

"Listen, uh, Sal." She pushed her plate away and stood up. "I'm sorry." She turned away. He shouldn't be here, in this room, eating dinner with her and expressing in his every move that he still had feelings for her. She didn't deserve it.

"Noo!" he roared.

She spun around from the force of his hand on her shoulder. "You are not sorry," he said, his face inches from hers. "I don't want you to ever have to tell me you're sorry again."

She cowered. Black ice glistened in his eyes, but this time, she could see behind it. Fire.

His gaze dropped to her lips. She instinctively parted them. This part of the ritual too, was familiar.

"*Amore,*" he breathed.

She let her eyes flutter closed, anticipating that first, tender soft touch of his lips. Her body trembled. How could this not be right?

"Come to me." His voice poured over her skin like a warm, bubbling stream. Teasing, inviting. It wasn't a question. She was going in.

Without hesitation she closed the space between them and lifted her arms to fist her hands in his hair. "Sal." She opened her mouth to his.

The gentle stream became a raging flood in seconds. She held him close as he rained kisses all over her face, and then pulled his mouth back to hers. Even the slightest pressure of his lips rubbing over hers pushed her level of need higher.

Julia pushed her tongue into his mouth and withdrew it. Then did it again. She wanted to feel him like that inside her.

"I was supposed to come in here and have to use all my charms to seduce you."

"You did," she smiled against his mouth. "Now I'm thinking you have too many clothes on."

"So do you."

She reached down and pulled his shirt from his waistband and slid her hands underneath. She wanted to touch, feel every inch of him, to sear these sensations into memory. Without a doubt, tonight would be her last with Sal. She never, ever wanted to look back with regrets.

Playfully, she slapped his hand away when he reached for the belt of her robe. "Soon enough," she teased. "Get these pants off." Her hand tugged at the button, then slid over the zipper and the prize that lay beneath it.

Julia had expected him to tease her a bit, but it seemed that despite their playful banter, he was as eager to get to the main event as she was.

"Kiss me, Sal. Kiss me until there's nothing left but you and me."

He reached up and framed her face in his hands. She loved it when he touched her face. It was...intimate. More than anything else, the soft way he let his fingers glide over her cheeks relayed his love. "Then forget everything else, *amore*. Forget the world outside this room." He kissed her eyes closed and then brushed over them with his thumb. "Feel only me. Know only my touch. My kiss."

The tips of his fingers traced over her top and then bottom lip. Then, as if what happened before didn't count, he reached over and lightly brushed his own lips over hers.

Amazing. He made love to her face that way. And if she'd just ask, he'd make love to every inch of her body. He alone could make her forget everything else. Which is why she could never forget him.

Her breath hitched.

Sal withdrew.

"What?" No, he couldn't do this to her. Wait. Stop. Come back. "What's wrong?"

"You're not giving it all to me. You're holding back."

She sat on the edge of the bed and ignored the screaming nerve endings that ran the length of her body. He was right. This scared her to death. "I'm not trying to."

He sat beside her then. "Why did you leave me?" Not accusing. Questioning. As if it hurt him. His eyes were pools of reflective ink where his emotions were sketched out, plainly.

"I failed you. I-I...I couldn't do anything else. I caused that to happen to you. It was my fault. And before that. You and Paolo fought over me." She swallowed and toyed with the frayed end of the belt of the robe. "I was making problems and doing nothing to solve them. Then Paolo figured out the serum. I wasn't needed."

"Dammit, Julia, that's not true. Not at all."

She pushed up. This wasn't about him feeling sorry for her. How to make him understand this? "I hurt you, Sal. I don't deserve your love and compassion."

"Do I deserve yours?"

She met his eyes. If they were stacking weights on a scale, then no, he didn't. But he had it. "I can't help it. There's not a switch to turn something like that on and off."

"Exactly."

She had to close her eyes to keep from exploding. It was way too easy to read something into that one word. Three syllables. Could he mean that somehow, despite it all, he still loved her?

One last question. "Tell me, Sal. Did you come here tonight for a bout of sex, or was there something else?"

"The sex, it isn't enough?"

He reached through her woven fingers and fingered the robe ties. But he didn't take advantage. He simply laced his fingers through hers. She nearly choked back a sob at the sight of their hands entwined like that. So innocent, so perfect, yet so impossible.

"I can't see you as the sort that is lacking female companionship. Especially for sport. So what did you come to say?"

"Sex wasn't a bad idea, though, you know?"

"Hey, mister, speak for yourself. You stopped it. I hold you fully responsible." She laughed about it, but knew clearly why he'd stopped. What they had between them was something pretty damn special. With nearly a month of absence, the way she felt about him had only gotten stronger, and being with him again solidified that. Sal was a keeper. There'd never be another who came close to filling his shoes.

But tonight all they could have would be sex. There was no tomorrow for them. But to her, tonight would never have been enough.

Sal stood up then and paced between the door and the table. "Okay. Business then. The healing serum won't work. I've already talked to the science team, and they agree, it's not worth the effort."

She started to speak and he held up a finger. "The enzyme that does the miraculous things does it blindly. You and me, we got lucky. The enzyme hit the cells that needed fixed and used the genetic code of the surrounding cells to do it. But what if someone has an infection in his or her body—just a common cold. What if the enzymes copied that bacteria? Boom, we've got out of control flu. That's precisely what happened with the leopard's bacteria. I got my hands on contaminated blood and well, you saw what happened."

"You did find a cure then, right?"

"I wouldn't be here without you."

She turned away then. He lied. She'd failed. Miserably. "I told you, Paolo figured it out, not me. The kid's a whiz in the lab. Tell me you're getting him involved in your studies."

He nodded. But kept pacing. "Paolo didn't work it out by himself. He followed my notes and listened to what you said. And you gave blood. Maybe it wasn't your hand that put the final compound into the test tube, but you did *not* fail me."

She brushed that off. "Right. Paolo doesn't speak English, he couldn't have listened to me."

"There you're wrong. He understands a lot of it. He knew what you did. How you saved me. How you came back and did everything possible to keep me alive."

"Saved you?" she snorted. "Because of me, you got shot in the first place."

"You want the truth? Paolo saved you. Did you wonder why none of those leopards attacked you before he did? Paolo had already claimed you."

"That doesn't make sense." Sorry, she couldn't believe that. "But he attacked me."

"No more than I did that first day when the leopards were attacking your friends. Because I lay claim to you, the others left you alone."

She'd never heard of such a thing as laying claim. "I don't understand why those leopards were there anyway. That wasn't normal behavior, was it?"

Sal picked up her half empty water bottle and drained it. "Let me explain about Paolo real quick. He asked me to apologize to you. Paolo's a mixed up teenager who was dying for attention. That's why he said he injected himself. I should have known then the kid had potential in the lab. He duplicated that messed up serum to perfect specs. When you came along, he got severely jealous. He'd never have hurt you. He adored you. But he wanted me to think he was after you, so I'd send you home. I think things snapped into place for him when I took his bullet. You were safe, regardless."

Julia gasped. She never understood.

"And the leopards? They all went...haywire. They were genetic time bombs. The enzyme that enabled them to literally regrow limbs caused overloads of chemicals in their brains. They acted erratically, a little at first, like traveling and hunting in packs. That wasn't normal. But then the attacks on people started. I was trying to save them. Part of the reason I was down there was to hopefully diagnose and cure them. It didn't happen. I expect the government of Sudan will be planning to destroy them. Paolo said they'd started to turn on their own."

Julia wasn't sure what he was saying. "What's that mean to the miracle cure?"

The phone rang. Julia tried to reach across the bed, but the thick terrycloth robe hindered her. Sal walked around and picked it up.

She made sure he saw her surprise. How dare he?

"Yes it is." He winked at Julia. "It's very nice to finally hear your voice, Sonja. Everything worked out perfectly."

Julia stood up. Incredible. Simply incredible. But she couldn't find anger. Only disbelief. This was no coincidence.

He spoke into the receiver again, "I was just getting to the point where I explained that. I'll have Julia give you a call back when we finish."

There's no way she could believe this. Sonja was in cahoots with Sal? Buying the story about men turning into leopards was more credible than this. "What if I told you to get out? What if I didn't want to hear anything else from you?"

He grinned. "Curiosity would get you. And Sonja would tell you and then you'd feel bad. Besides. I don't intend to let you get away again."

She lifted an eyebrow. Those were the best words she'd heard yet, but she had to understand why they'd sent her to Italy on a doomed mission. If that had even been part of the plot. "So? Spill it."

"What I was going to tell you is that the growth enzyme does have a practical application. One that, in theory, seems to share none of the dangers the live application does."

It was so hard to pretend indifference when he seemed genuinely excited. It probably helped that she hadn't gotten up and screamed at him to get out. She still might. But her mind was stuck on the "I don't intend to let you get away" line. That made her want to call Sonja back and squeal into the receiver.

"Okay, practical application, I'm listening."

He continued, "It's quite simple, really. Skin grafts, for a start. Sonja and I did one of those 'let my people talk to your people' deals, and she'll be heading up the American part of the research."

"But you said the leopards..."

"We can synthesize the enzyme now. There's no risk."

Julia picked up the edge of her robe again. So Sonja was going to be his partner, huh? No wonder she was eager to drop Julia at the airport. Julia, the deal-maker.

"I'm happy for you Sal. I know it's not as big as you were hoping, but at least it all wasn't for naught." Like her work. Like that month she'd spent analyzing her scribbled notes and translating the Italian she'd copied.

"I don't think I'll be heading up the research on this end."

"Oh, really?"

"I'm intending to embark on the toughest project to date. Probably the biggest I'll have the chance to do."

She was happy for him, really, she was. She forced her voice to sound interested as she asked, "What is it?"

"I was hoping to have you naked and begging for me when I proposed, just so you couldn't say no, but you're determined to make an honest man out of me."

All the blood left Julia's body. Did he say propose? As in marriage propose? Sal, no, don't do it.

He did.

She blinked away the tears as he clumsily got down on one knee between the two hotel beds. From his pocket he pulled a ruby and diamond ring that glittered like his eyes.

His hand shook as he held it up to her. "Okay. I can do this. Julia Haverstock, will you marry me?"

She didn't look at the ring. "Oh Sal." Swallowing was impossible. There was no answer for this. How could it work? She was just starting to digest the idea that the love Sal gave her was so true, so forgiving and open that he was able to brush away everything she'd said and done. And, she'd realized as he knelt there, how inconsequential the past could be. Now that they were on the other side of the bridge, did it really matter how they got there? Love looks past the flaws and finds the things that matter.

A tear slipped onto her cheek.

He pressed the ring into her hand and closed her fist over it. "You take this. Think about it. I know this was sudden."

Sudden? She hadn't expected to see him again and now he was proposing?

"You know there's still a lot of negotiations we'll have to get through." She watched his face.

A muscle near his eye twitched. "And I have a ton of questions you'll have to answer first."

"First before you say yes, or before you say I do?"

She handed the ring back. Then immediately felt guilty when his shoulders slumped. Rising to her feet, she held out her left hand. "Don't they teach you anything in grad school? You're supposed to put the ring on my hand, not just give it to me."

The snapshot of glistening joy in his eyes was the memory she wanted to carry with her forever. But it disappeared too quickly. She closed her eyes as his mouth came down to crush hers in a kiss that possessed the soul of her.

Her hands reached up and tangled in his hair. His hands slid down her sides and over the swell of her hips. She leaned into him, knowing she'd find him as hard as she was wet.

Now there was no holding back. No wondering what the other person felt, no secrets, at least none that mattered. She helped him remove his shirt. Her fingers radiated to the scar she expected to find.

Sal stopped her. "Don't say it," he said, holding her hand still just below the mark he carried.

She almost had. Healing her guilt wouldn't happen with words, but with time. But Sal would help her. She stepped out of his embrace and leaned down to press her lips to the scar. His muscles trembled beneath her touch.

He smoothed the hair off her face and thumbed away her tear. "Did I tell you I love you yet?"

"No," she whispered and leaned into his hand.

"I love you, *amore*." Sal tilted her chin so she looked deep into the depths of his eyes when he said it. Never, ever could she deny it was true.

"And I love you."

She silenced his groan by pulling his head down to hers in a desperate kiss.

Lips ground against lips and tongues clashed.

Sal reached down and tugged at the tie to her robe. She opened her mouth and her body to him. When his fingers found her taut nipple, she broke away from his lips and gasped.

It wasn't fair. He still wore half his clothes while her robe was falling off her shoulders. She pushed her palm against the hard lump below his waistband. He pushed back in answer.

"Get these off," she insisted. She lifted her hands to her breasts to ease the ache caused by his fingers leaving her sensitive skin.

Sal unbuttoned his pants, got the zipper half way down before reaching down to lift her up against him. The robe slid to the floor, leaving her breasts at perfect level with Sal's mouth.

He took advantage.

Julia arched as his warm tongue lazily encircled her nipple. She wanted to crush his mouth to her and ease the ache. There'd be time for that later. Time to explore and enjoy.

"Make love to me Sal, now."

He took two steps and lifted her until she was standing on the edge of the bed. "We have to try this later," he said, sneaking a nibbling kiss at the juncture of her thighs. She definitely agreed.

While he removed the rest of his clothing, she crawled up to the head of the bed and pulled her knees up. He was beautiful. Still unbelievable that he wanted her. Her.

"Wipe that frown off your face, *amore*," he said, turning to crawl up toward her on all fours.

With his back low, the way the muscles played over his shoulders reminded her of another Sal she knew. Oddly enough, it didn't scare her.

She squealed as he pulled her down beneath him and forced her knees apart. She was ready for him, eager.

"Even if you are cured, you're still an animal," she accused, lifting her hips toward him. He pushed the head of his cock against her damp opening, teasing.

"You bet I am," he said, and growled as he plunged deep inside of her.

About the author:

Melani Blazer's mom swears she was born reading, and by age six, was writing little rhymes. It was something she did for fun—even through high school where she was a writer and the copy editor for the school newspaper. But then practical thinking took over and her college focus aimed at science.

Now, too-many-years-to-admit later, she's rediscovered her childhood escape and taken it a step further. She's written stories in a diverse number of genres, but found her true love in paranormals.

To keep her feet grounded in real life, she keeps house with her wonderful husband of 14 years, an almost-teenage daughter, and her cats.

Melani welcomes mail from readers. You can write to her c/o Ellora's Cave Publishing at 1337 Commerce Drive, Suite 13, Stow OH 44224

Why an electronic book?

We live in the Information Age — an exciting time in the history of human civilization in which technology rules supreme and continues to progress in leaps and bounds every minute of every hour of every day. For a multitude of reasons, more and more avid literary fans are opting to purchase e-books instead of paperbacks. The question to those not yet initiated to the world of electronic reading is simply: *why?*

1. *Price.* An electronic title at Ellora's Cave Publishing runs anywhere from 40-75% less than the cover price of the <u>exact same title</u> in paperback format. Why? Cold mathematics. It is less expensive to publish an e-book than it is to publish a paperback, so the savings are passed along to the consumer.

2. *Space.* Running out of room to house your paperback books? That is one worry you will never have with electronic novels. For a low one-time cost, you can purchase a handheld computer designed specifically for e-reading purposes. Many e-readers are larger than the average handheld, giving you plenty of screen room. Better yet, hundreds of titles can be stored within your new library — a single

microchip. (Please note that Ellora's Cave does not endorse any specific brands. You can check our website at www.ellorascave.com for customer recommendations we make available to new consumers.)

3. *Mobility.* Because your new library now consists of only a microchip, your entire cache of books can be taken with you wherever you go.

4. *Personal preferences are accounted for.* Are the words you are currently reading too small? Too large? Too...**ANNOYING**? Paperback books cannot be modified according to personal preferences, but e-books can.

5. *Innovation.* The way you read a book is not the only advancement the Information Age has gifted the literary community with. There is also the factor of what you can read. Ellora's Cave Publishing will be introducing a new line of interactive titles that are available in e-book format only.

6. *Instant gratification.* Is it the middle of the night and all the bookstores are closed? Are you tired of waiting days—sometimes weeks—for online and offline bookstores to ship the novels you bought? Ellora's Cave Publishing sells instantaneous downloads 24 hours a day, 7 days a week, 365 days a year. Our e-book delivery system is 100% automated, meaning your order is filled as soon as you pay for it.

Those are a few of the top reasons why electronic novels are displacing paperbacks for many an avid reader. As always, Ellora's Cave Publishing welcomes your questions and comments. We invite you to email us at service@ellorascave.com or write to us directly at: P.O. Box 787, Hudson, Ohio 44236-0787.

Printed in the United States
24661LVS00001B/61-723